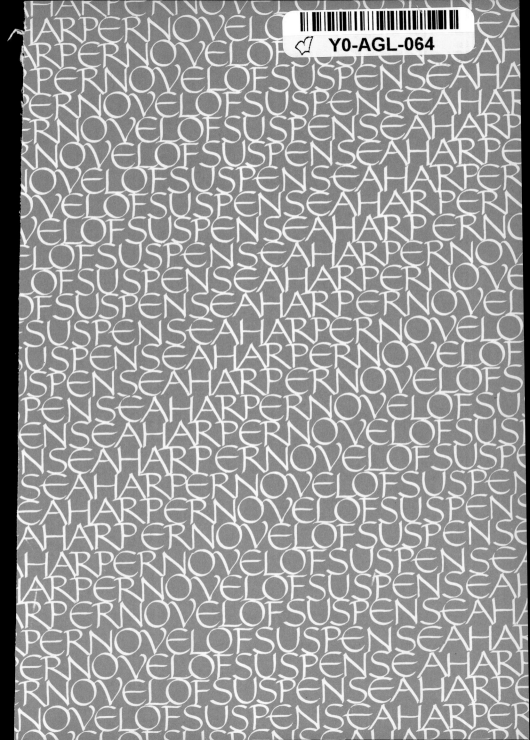

A Dressing of Diamond

A JOAN KAHN BOOK

Books by Nicolas Freeling

Fiction

A DRESSING OF DIAMOND
AUPRÈS DE MA BLONDE
THE LOVELY LADIES
TSING-BOOM!
THIS IS THE CASTLE
STRIKE OUT WHERE NOT APPLICABLE
THE DRESDEN GREEN
KING OF THE RAINY COUNTRY
CRIMINAL CONVERSATION
DOUBLE BARREL
VALPARAISO
QUESTION OF LOYALTY
BECAUSE OF THE CATS
LOVE IN AMSTERDAM

Nonfiction

THE KITCHEN

A Dressing of Diamond

Nicolas Freeling

HARPER & ROW, Publishers

NEW YORK, EVANSTON, SAN FRANCISCO,

LONDON

A HARPER NOVEL OF SUSPENSE

FIRST U.S. EDITION

Library of Congress Cataloging in Publication Data

Freeling, Nicolas.
  A dressing of diamond.

  I. Title.
PZ4.F854Ds3   [PR6056.R4]   823'.9'14   73–18710
ISBN 0–06–011352–9

Peace of mind becomes me
As soft white velvet hands become a man,
As on half-healed wound a dressing—
A dressing of diamond.

La quiétude me va comme
Des mains de velours à un homme,
Sur un bobo cicatrisant
Un pansement de diamant.

—Albertine Sarrazin

ALBERTINE SARRAZIN, a half-Arab illegitimate child, brought up by the Assistance Publique, first adopted and then rejected by a French bourgeois family, was a prostitute at fifteen and engaged in an armed holdup at sixteen. In prison, where she stayed for precisely half her life, she wrote two best-selling novels, which were translated into every European language. Within two years of her release, at the age of thirty, she died under anesthetic upon the operating table. While in prison she married Julien Sarrazin, a criminal, who had rescued and sheltered her following a prison break. At the time of her death, July 10, 1967, she was regarded as one of the most talented and promising of postwar French writers. The scrap of verse above was written in Amiens prison in 1958. She was a friend of the present writer, who never met her. Her memory has been sentimentalized, but she was both a beautiful and a tragic woman.

COLETTE DELAVIGNE was doing her shopping. She looked at carrots, at little green beans, at Moroccan tomatoes; carefully and without interest. It was a prolongation of the working day that was often a heavy drain upon her resources; her boredom with shopping soured easily and turned to dislike, but she was accustomed to unpleasant chores, and she carried this one out like the others, carefully and methodically. The heavy air with its stuffy, slightly sweetish smell, the noise that was like the smell, muffled but metallic with a syrupy note of artificial jollity added by Muzak, gave her a faintly nauseous headache. She had, even after working hours, enough concentration left to pay no attention to this. She walked with small steps, holding herself upright, guiding her wire cart in a series of little pushes and controlling it with her fingertips.

She looked at nylon tights; the colors always that little bit wrong, the cut invariably that bit too mean. She had taken hers off and put them in a large envelope, which was misuse of official stationery. She liked to go bare-legged in summer, but at the office it was felt—strongly—that women should be clothed with dignity, and she agreed. Witnesses would be distracted by her bare knees; she would not allow either over-heated adolescents or bored but lecherous policemen to regale themselves by hoping to catch a glimpse of her underwear.

From behind (to the supermarket shopper more easily led astray from his purpose), she was an appetizing young woman. Calves rather too muscular: it is so with most young women in France. Feet small, with a high instep, in blue leather sandals with cork heels. A plain navy-blue linen frock with a big sailor collar and white piqué edging: no display of sweaty armpit there. French government offices are not air-conditioned. Either the all-too-well-constructed nineteenth-century window is open, with the horrible consequences from the street, or one asphyxiates in academic dust. Colette, being the most junior of the examining magistrates, had the noisiest office; she opened or shut her window forty times a day.

She picked out three oranges after feeling them attentively. She did not regard herself as a skillful housewife, but she was accustomed to weighing evidence. She had, besides, been well brought up. If she again took escalopes of veal, there would be an outcry. On her way back to the fish counter she took three avocados, and once there she took three trout. Annoyingly, she now had to go back for cream. But that was conventional thinking. Avocados took a lot of oil; so no cream. She decided that there were some bacon rashers left, in which trout could be wrapped, that there were some chives still in her window box, that she would take fennel for a vegetable and a pound of apricots for dessert. Colette liked food. That is to say, she liked eating, and didn't mind cooking. (It was nice to be standing, agreeable to be in movement, interesting to concentrate on a physical activity, and valuable to possess a handicraft.) But if not kept in check, Bernard easily became English, with a tendency to gluttony. As things were, it was Bernard's job to buy drinks ("I've quite enough bottles to carry as it is") and cheese ("supermarket cheese!"). Indulged in these areas of male pride, Bernard had learned to accept that he was allowed potatoes only on weekends, in the country.

She waited patiently at the check-out, thinking of nothing at all; noticing that the other lines moved faster than hers, but they always did. Being rueful about that was self-indulgent. The supermarket promoted apathy. One was herded: very well, one was herded. It was enough to try to keep other people's pushful carts from bumping one's heels.

She wrote her check with the speed of a woman who is accustomed to signing her name at the foot of forms a great many times a day. Colette Delavigne was the Children's Judge. It is not a job given invariably or automatically to the most junior of the examining magistrates (though, regrettably, that is still often the case), but she was a woman and, at twenty-seven, one of the youngest judges in France. She wheeled her chariot to the parking lot, content that it did not squeak and that its back wheels seemed willing to follow the front ones. A small thing, but every tiny concession wrung from supermarkets appears as a mighty gift.

Mme. Delavigne's car had been the subject of anxious thought. It must not be showy (Bernard had decided) since ostentation would cause legal lips to lengthen. It had to be small enough to maneuver easily and park handily, but it must not be a ridiculous-looking object. One had to have a pretty car to show off a pretty woman. There was also a large and threatening assortment of "stupid cars" to be avoided.

Impatient with this male servility toward gadgets (who cared, as long as it went?), she had controlled herself while the law got laid down. As though one hadn't enough of that . . . But though she was buying her own car, supported by her own earnings, she allowed Bernard to cast the expert eye. Indeed, she wanted him to. She drove a good deal better than he did, but never said so. Nor did she say she wanted to choose her own car. Bernard, after all, submitted to her judgment in a great many things, even when secretly convinced he knew better. And even now, after a magisterial summing up, and when he had pinned the gold medal to the bosom of the Fiat—so suitable—he was not nasty at her suddenly being "female and emotional."

5

"I would really like the little Alfa very much indeed."

He liked her, of course, to be female and emotional: one cannot make love to a Judge of Instruction, and Bernard enjoyed making love very much. But it was nice of him to swallow his disapproval: he hardly shook his cheeks at all. He didn't walk away and stare out the showroom window, or leave loudly unsaid that he thought it a poor choice. He giggled endearingly, and even lent her the extra money to pay for it. To be sure, he assumed all the credit when it was a vast success. Even the prissiest of magistrates had not made a long disapproving mouth. On the contrary, they enjoyed it. Little Mme. Delavigne and her very fast car. Buttercup yellow! There were jokes about regilding our tarnished blazon. Even M. Zsylotcly, that rather unsympathetic Pole from Béthune, who had been doomladen for six months ("Little Mme. Delavigne will kill herself one of these days"), had come gallantly across with a marvelous imitation chamois leather ("Made in Japan, you see") to wipe dead flies off her windscreen. As for the police, who relish giving parking tickets to magistrates, they revived the charming nineteenth-century verb "to flirt" and conjugated it down to the imperfect subjunctive, a game which little Mme. Delavigne had been known to cheat at.

Colette never left the car outside. Juvenile delinquents were her daily nourishment. The basement garage smelled oddly like a supermarket, of warm metal, synthetically perfumed disinfectant, and fermenting vegetables, and was pleasantly dark after the glare of the June sun. She took the lift. Bernard always took the stairs, because of smoking too much. The top-floor flat in the Résidence Dampierre was the most obvious and, it must be admitted, the most vulgar symbol of achievement. Vera Castang, Colette's one close friend, said it had no taste at all. Colette admitted this. But Vera was Czech, and an artist, and alarmingly exacting. She had suffered a lot in her life. She was married to a policeman—not, surely, the easiest of existences. Colette had never suffered. It was a gap in her armory that frightened her. She was loved by most people, and indulged by all. Vera's finely drawn, almost haggard face disquieted and alarmed her.

She admitted, too, the vulgarity of the flat—and was too honest to blame it all on Bernard. Vulgarity, she argued, was inseparable from luxury. The flat was not really very luxurious. The vulgarity was in consequence moderate, and tolerable. Did not Vera agree? Vera didn't, but did not at all wish to be offensive to a person she was fond of.

It wasn't even a hideous high tower. There were only six floors of a dullish child's architecture with timid little balconies. Nor had anyone demolished any pretty buildings: the site had been that of a Hatters' Castle in the most crenellated and curlicued of Victorian Gothic, and nearly all the trees in the garden had been carefully saved. Vera continued to speak of "Branch Number 6 of the Résidence Monkey-Puzzle," but Colette refused to be ashamed about it. Bernard made lots of money selling yogurt, but he worked very hard. The competition in yogurt is something fierce.

She dumped her parcels in the kitchen, hung her frock in the dressing room, pushed everything else into the laundry basket, and pattered into the bathroom for a shower that would ritually remove the dust of the Palace of Justice. She had not been in court that day: she had been "instructing." A Judge of Instruction, in France, is not allowed to be a member of the tribunal, because of the separation of powers. An exception to this rule is made for the Children's Judge, since it is felt that the trial judge should have the widest possible preliminary knowledge of the circumstances, background, and personality of the child concerned. Colette took her work extremely seriously, was severe about the "secret of instruction," and tried to compartmentalize. A clumsy word, as she was accustomed to say, for an impossible thing.

"But those businessmen who bring home bulging briefcases —so very dull."

While drying herself she noticed that the flat was very still. She opened the bathroom door.

"Rachel? Ra-chel." The child must be out playing somewhere.

They had only one child, produced in student days in a flush of enthusiasm, which had been a great nuisance, but a rather splendid bond with Bernard, who had become a superb diaper-changer and a tremendous expert on baby food, analyzing spinach in the laboratory and in general having a glorious time. He was fond of saying that this had brought him into the yogurt business, and Rachel, now eight, was official taster to all the weird new cocktails, scathing about those Japanese tangerines. Father and daughter had a relationship so close that it caused Colette problems. Were they too wrapped up in each other? Was she, professionally, and in the search for family equilibrium, too detached and even dry? An only child was, in any case, in danger of becoming a nasty brat: the apple of one's eye is a bitter fruit to the taste. Correctives, of a suitably charitable and socially valuable nature, had been sought. Thus, M. and Mme. Delavigne were "godparents" to two orphans who came for frequent weekends and to stay at holidays. Rachel sent toys to, sewed for, and devoted pocket money to Vietnamese babies. She accompanied Colette to crèches and was approved of by various local Reverend Mothers. Mme. Delavigne often had a gnawing feeling that it wasn't enough. But, damn it, it was a troublesome equation to solve.

A Judge of Instruction is named to a post for a period of three years, initially. There are interims and vacations and temporary postings, and situations to be arranged in a flexible spirit, but when one's first real post is that of children's judge in a proper city, when one's husband works in that city in a business administration, and when it is important to soothe and reassure various elderly and chalky male bosoms who can be sniffy about young pretty women using the magistrates' lavatory, one takes pains not to go perambulating a monumental maternal stomach around the Palace in the middle of what is still a probationary period.

"I'll be thirty," said Colette, "and that's quite a reasonable moment to have another baby. And Rachel will be ten. A nice elder sister, and it doesn't matter whether it's a boy or a girl. Out of the jealous stage. And female instincts brought to the fore when they're still climbing trees."

"As long as you have one then," said Vera, who hadn't any, and hated it.

Colette put on a housecoat and flowed tranquilly to the kitchen, stopping to put on a record. But once she was in the kitchen, doubts assailed her. Rachel would have come home and had her "goûter." There were no crumbs on the table. That was one thing, but at this age they are perpetually thirsty and there was no dirty glass. Now, there was one rule which was firm as iron, and that was the instruction that before Rachel went off anywhere she should report it. No note was on the table saying "Gone to Nathalie."

That was downright naughty, and she was angry. She looked in the child's bedroom—no clothes changed. The swimming pool was likeliest, but her bathing suit was hanging on the balcony from yesterday. Colette frowned.

In the living room, surely, there would be a schoolbag flung down, surest sign of all. There wasn't. Colette sat down, picked up the phone, and called Nathalie's mama; Véronique, whose mama had just come home; and Jackie, whose mama was still out. Jackie, a wicked boy with a huge smooth mop of wonderful silky black hair whom Bernard denounced as "a sexy beast," was very suave on the phone; had lovely manners.

"No, Madame. We haven't seen her, Madame; she wasn't playing with us. Oh, yes, Madame, she was at school, but she left a different way. No, I mean we left a different way. Sorry, Madame. Shall we look—round the quarter, I mean—and tell her to go straight home? And I'll phone you, shall I? It's no trouble at all, Madame."

Rachel's bicycle, which she seldom took to school, was neatly parked. Neither the concierge, who had clipped the hedge that afternoon, nor his wife—whose Danielle was a lot older and went to a different school; and who was sagely doing her homework but kept an eye on the little ones—had seen Rachel that afternoon.

This was getting ominous. It was now quarter to seven, and Number 2 inflexible rule was that whatever the circumstances and wherever she might be, Rachel should be home by seven, and do her homework despite shrieks of "I haven't any, truly" before dinner at eight.

Bernard would be home any moment. Irritably, Colette put the trout in the fridge, cleaned the fennel, made vinaigrette for the avocados, and decided to eat the apricots as they were, without bothering to make tart crust.

Seven. No Rachel. No Bernard, either. Colette raced into the dressing room, threw on trousers and a shirt, bursting a button and jerking viciously at her bra, slammed into the lift, reversed the car out with a screech, and drove very fast to the swimming pool, the school, Jackie's house, Nathalie's house—and drew a blank everywhere.

Seven-thirty; home again, tired now, trembling rather, aware that she had driven dangerously. Still no Rachel. Still no Bernard. His phone rang unanswered—he had left and so had everyone else, of course, long ago. Well, he was an adult. Rachel was eight.

"Baba," called Colette jerkily. "Baba," running stupidly into the bedroom.

She put her hand on the telephone to call Police-Secours, mastered herself, for one cannot create a flap just because a child is half an hour late, wiped her hand with a paper tissue, and heard Bernard's familiar Citroën noise on the gravel. She forced herself to wait for him.

Bernard was a stocky man, who in another ten years would have trouble keeping his weight down because his body was slightly too big for his limbs. His neck was too short, as well as his arms, so that his collars always looked too tight and his sleeves too long; buying shirts for him was always a problem. But he had a fine intelligent head, and his short square hands were sensitive and beautifully shaped. His nose sprang straight from between his eyebrows, and he had large, faintly prominent eyes: with the massive jaw and the short neck, this gave something of a strangled expression which, along with a certain open, candid look, led hasty or unwise people to believe that he was a bit of a stupid fellow. A great mistake.

He was singing to himself "Bom-bum-bom-bum" when he opened the door and saw Colette, screwed up and restless, in the middle of the room; very straight, her feet slightly apart.

"Who are you looking for a fight with?" he said pleasantly. "Hey, what's wrong?"

"Rachel hasn't come home."

"Nathalie, doubtless—that odious Jackie, more likely."

"I've been everywhere—all around the quarter."

"Turn that music off. . . . Aren't you getting yourself worked up? It's a fine evening, and it's not even eight yet."

"Her bike's here—her schoolbag isn't. The concierge—nobody's seen her. She hasn't been home at all—that's nearly four hours. Don't say the swimming pool: I looked first thing. She didn't change—she hasn't been here at all. Sorry, I hadn't realized it was still playing. Bernard, I'm worried."

"Yes, I can see. Well—mustn't lose our heads. Look, I'll give us both a drink. Give ourselves time to think."

Docile, she sat down, drank some of the whisky he pushed in her hand, felt sure she had already had time to think—too much. It hadn't really sunk through to him yet. In a little while, she would be telling him to sit down quietly while she brought him a drink. Getting at the truth of a tale, disentangling irrelevance, feeling with her fingertips for tiny twisted golden grains of precision in a sandhill of idleness, laziness, incompetence, malice, gossip, boredom, the wish to be interesting, the hunger

11

for excitement—wasn't that what she did all day? This was just a momentary paralysis: the stunned moment, the invariable disbelief that it should be oneself, not Mrs., Miss, or Mr. A. N. Other, that notable all-round sportsman, tax evader, and victim of criminals.

"My dearest girl," said Bernard. "Now—you've been to the school. To all her friends . . . in the little park? Round the back of the tennis courts? . . . I'd better ring Jackie's father. . . . Now, she may have found a new friend. Someone who lives further away. She may have mistaken the way home, or not even know it. And be too timid to ask. Come, we don't know everyone in her age group—even in her own class. Some people are very irresponsible—let the children play outside till all hours."

"It's almost eight. Everybody's eating by now."

"But you know how she is—obstinate little thing. 'Will I bring you home, dear—do you know your own way? Oh, that's good, because I haven't the car. All right, dear, trot off'—and if she was the other side of the boulevard—where those streets look the same. Take a wrong turning and she's heading back toward the town without realizing. Nobody pays any heed, and she's too shy to speak to a stranger."

"You're creating a whole fantasy," said Colette irritably. "No mother would allow a little girl of eight to go home across the boulevard with all that traffic. She'd either bring the child back or ring up—at the least, if she'd no car and no phone she'd see that the child crossed the road safely. Rachel's not a perfect fool. Shy, yes—but she knows her name, her address, her phone number; she can tell the time, she knows how to come in out of the rain. You're describing a child of five; Rachel's not a baby."

The phone rang; Bernard threw himself sidewise on the sofa.

"Yes? Oh, M. Sillières—good evening. . . . Ah, Jackie told you. You haven't seen her? . . . No, no, not real anxiety, of course, but it *is* eight. A shadow of disquiet, don't you know? . . . Yes, of course. Of course. . . . That's very kind and friendly of you.

Bye. . . ." Bernard hung up. "Why does one pretend that one isn't worried? Sillières says he's been up and down both streets and talked to Véronique's father, and he knows Jackie is a pest and capable of locking her in the garden shed or whatnot, but that in the pinch, when it gets serious, Jackie would admit anything wicked, and anyway he can tell when Jackie's lying, and he realizes now that it's serious. Jackie, I mean. . . . Sorry, I'm rambling."

"No, I understood."

"Well," unhappily, "better face it, I suppose. I'd better ring the hospitals."

Colette, very slowly, got up and poured herself another drink, and fussed a long time over taking a cigarette, patting softly at Bernard's jacket pockets, while a quiet voice, carefully reined in, said "Casualty department, please" three times: to the University Hospital, the Surgical Polyclinic, and the Sainte-Barbara Center. She did not stop him when he left his hand a moment on the receiver-rest and then dialed Police-Secours.

"Give me the chief, please. . . . Bernard Delavigne . . . Mme. Delavigne, the judge. . . . A little girl . . . height . . . color hair . . . eyes . . . frock . . . shoes . . . red schoolbag. . . . My number is 74–84–94. . . . Yes, please, the center out to the city limits. . . . Yes, of course, I realize it'll take some time. . . ." He hung up again. "I'm going to have another drink."

"Yes. But it will have to do now for both of us."

"I realize that quite adequately, thank you." It was the first sign of tension Bernard had given. "We'd be well advised to eat something."

"I'll go and cook. I'm sorry—you realize that up to now I just wasn't capable."

"Of course I do. But there's nothing we can do for some time. They say they've two radio vans and all the available motorbikes, and they'll alert the district posts, but we must wait two hours. We must eat, of course, and bear in mind that she may just stroll in at any second, having twisted her ankle, or dropped her shoe in the pond, or had her bag snatched away by nasty teasing boys. . . . Children can be so foul to one another."

"Yes," said Colette tiredly, "but why didn't she dump her bag here? It's heavy—what would she be carrying it around for?"

"There's nothing more we can do for the moment."

"Yes, there is. Henri."

"Man? Or policeman?"

"Both."

"Isn't that a bit—sort of premature? P.J., I mean."

Henri Castang, Vera's husband, was an officer in the Police Judiciaire. A borderline friend—but a friend, yes; not just an acquaintance.

Bernard rubbed his face with both hands.

"I don't mind if you don't." Colette looked at him from the doorway. She stood quietly; then her hand fiddled with the doorknob.

"I think it sensible," she said at last. "So does the judge. Put it simply—it's a friend at court. Would you rather I called him?"

"No. Go and do your cooking."

The phone rang a long time.

"Castang," said a neutral voice, professionally cleaned of fatigue or irritability.

Moving aimlessly in the kitchen—try as she might, she could not concentrate; she took the trout out to clean them, got a knife, and then looked for them idiotically all over the place, even in the sink, for a long time before realizing that she had put them back in the fridge—she could hear the pattern of Bernard's voice, knowing the way he stabbed at the air with his cigarette to emphasize, head on one side to keep the phone cradled, absurdly beloved and familiar. She felt too drained and stupefied to cook: knives would jump at her and cut her, pots leap up off the stove to burn her. She hovered vaguely in the doorway.

"He'll be around straight away."

"Oh. Good." How stupid it did sound. As though it were a

plumber for a leaking pipe. "Do you really want to eat?"

"Not in the slightest."

"I don't feel up to it."

"Have we some tomato juice? Henri likes it."

"I suppose so." She made an effort. "Yes, we have. Do us good, you mean. Vitamins, or something."

"Mustn't drink," said Bernard portentously.

"No. I don't believe there are any vitamins in canned tomato juice."

"No, but it's sort of thick. Stabilizes."

These valuable dietetic observations were put a stop to at last by Castang's arrival. Nobody would ever believe that the police had now arrived. He didn't even look the part, not properly, being on the small side for a cop, and wiry rather than stocky. A round Mediterranean head, and coarse black hair—the sort that goes gray early, as his had here and there, though he was not much over thirty. A slightly Slav face, not pronounced, but as though it were a germ, as Colette said, picked up from his wife. Some Roman legionary in the past, from Dacia or Scythia. He was quite a good policeman, though, even if he did look more like an extra in *Ben Hur*. He was an O.P.A., or adjunct officer of police, a clumsy piece of bureaucratic nomenclature, in the S.R.P.J., or Regional Service of Police Judiciaire, which is another. The conservative French, still addicted to ancient francs, mostly called him "Inspector"—much as everyone still talks of the Avenue du Bois.

Castang—coming in, sitting down, drinking tomato juice, being explained to—looked, as usual, like a former steeplechase jockey who has got too thickset for the job. Lined leathery face, tweed jackets with lots of pockets, always full of police rubbish which Vera complained about, sharp mobile birdy eyes, a tendency to waistcoats, tough scarred hands, tight whipcord trousers like breeches that horsehair wouldn't stick to, and beautifully polished shoes. When one visited him, Colette said, he was always cutting his fingernails or polishing his shoes, or both. Oh, yes, said Vera resignedly: a cleanliness fanatic.

He was already making notes, in a quick practiced way, black felt-tip, silent, picking up the disjointed scraps of gabble.

"Okay," he said at last. "Want to let me talk for a bit?" It wasn't meant to be sarcastic—just a professional way of clearing the ground. "Good, right to call me, though I'm not in the act yet officially and can't be till a formal complaint is laid. Just here as a friend, but will react as a cop; that's the way you want it, I think."

Colette and Bernard nodded, both somehow vastly relieved already, both far too scared and amateurish and confused: the businessman happy with another businessman, the judge happy with the familiar, solid, well-polished machinery.

"For a start; we can't yet write off some stupid little muddle or misunderstanding; it's still the likeliest. Children do wander off and do silly things and lose their sense of time, and we've got to let the cops have another hour to get coordinated reports. But let's take into account the worst that can happen: those are our fears; we face them. So we have the P.J. here and the way it argues is this, as Colette knows well. Assuming a crime, the child's alive or the child is dead. I have to say that, as you realize, whatever the effort it costs. But I say immediately that it's by far the most remote, and that we have no reason at all to jump at imagining horrors. And, quite frankly, I'm not going to, because there's no evidence whatever, as well as the strong statistical unlikelihood. But we can start building hypotheses of crime, and nine-tenths of that we can leave aside or take as said, because you both know it all; we've discussed it in this room; it's our daily shop—it's the sudden impact of the personal and the subjective that throws us off. So it's my job to remind you that these things are more often stupidly aggressive than violently psychopathic. Psychopath enough to do it, and stupid enough not to see how quickly it will point to him. I'm not, for a second, trying to tranquillize you. It's exactly what Commissaire Richard or any cop of experience will say—the overwhelming majority are crude and easy, and need no more than a day's work."

"I've never had a kidnapping," Colette muttered vaguely.

"No, dear friend, because they're pretty rare, thank heaven. Tremendously publicized when they do occur—and that's a problem we'll look at in a minute—so the public is saturated and thinks vaguely that they occur all the time, and they don't. But whether you've had one or not, you can both see that the instruction may be difficult but the police work is generally simple, because either you have the classic type of the unbalanced girl with an overwhelming need to possess a baby and the typical psychopathic incapacity to resist gratifying desire, with indifference to the notion of a criminal act or its consequences, or you have the frustrated embittered individual with a grievance, generally of low intelligence, who wishes you to suffer pain, indignity, and deprivation because that's what he feels himself."

"They will have their heart's content, then," said Bernard softly.

Castang disregarded this. He wasn't there as emotional consoler.

"Colette, of course," he went on smoothly, "arouses a good deal of fear in the families of her clients, hence resentment, rancor, even hatred sometimes. And it's an obvious inference, since she's the Children's Judge, that somebody might want to strike back at her that way."

"One doesn't think of it—one can't, of course."

"Conceivable, too, that it could be a child's crime. What— let's just think—have you had in this last year which was grave enough to need instructing?"

"Well—there was the child who made the imaginary confession. The two who threw their playmate in the river. And the one who loosened the wheel bolts of a car. And, of course, the children who set the school on fire at the time when there was a perfect epidemic."

"Caused," Bernard put in dryly, "by the publicity given to the first."

"Good point, and I'm coming back to it. But you do see, Colette, that there are a heap of people who'll have to be looked at."

"The parents scarcely ever show resentment, poor things," she said. "They have great difficulty understanding and actually convincing themselves that their children could have done such things. But it's true that apart from instructions I've judged a lot of violent vandalism and delinquency."

"You see," easily, "the terrifying shadow of the really disturbed person begins already to recede. All those horrible ideas of rape and murder fading into nightmare land."

"You're trying to make us feel better," said Bernard jerkily.

"Isn't that my job?" asked Castang, throwing his hands out. "I'm not trying to bullshit a herd of scared peasants. I'm giving facts to an intelligent and widely educated pair of bourgeois parents."

"Selling," said Bernard. "Bits of facts. Carefully selected."

Castang took his time about answering. "As a businessman, and experienced, and knowing the world, and moreover pretty bright, you don't have a very high opinion of the police, and I don't contribute much to bettering it. There's a goodish share of laziness and incompetence; a lot of bureaucratic inertia and apathy. And sometimes downright bad—stupid brutal oafs with ideas about keeping the 'niggers' down. And corrupt, of course —all those commissaires taking kickbacks from brothels. Favoritism too, naturally: a complaint from you, a prominent local businessman, with moreover a wife in the magistracy, will make them all bend over backward even if you didn't have a friend in the organization, whereas a complaint from the poor gets short shrift. And all that, too, we've talked about in this room. There's one thing, though, you haven't experienced yet, and that is how good they can be."

"Otherwise," said Colette rather sharply, "you could hardly

expect Henri to stay in his job, and you'd be surprised at my doing mine."

"Please disregard what I said and believe I'm ashamed of it."

"You don't have to be—all that much. You're a very worried man and you want to hit out at somebody, and what you said was quite true. I'd like you now to think of something I said a few minutes ago, which is publicity."

"Yes," said Bernard painfully.

"I'm just sitting here talking," said Castang, "because it's still a bit premature to ask the cops for the second phase. If we give that sort of instruction, it means mobilizing, since they'd comb out all the bits of waste ground, all the building sites, uh, so on."

"The river," said Bernard coldly.

"Yes, and a lot of other places. Getting all the police authorities informed and coordinated, alerting all the auxiliaries. And the P.J., too, me and all the others, by a formal complaint against X. Colette is a judge, of course, and can give us orders, but that's not even needed: a phone call to Richard will do it. I mean, too, that that's headlines in tomorrow's paper. Journalists here straight away, a television crew—and all the sightseers."

Bernard had closed his eyes.

"Yes," said Castang, "we pay a lot of lip service to the freedom of the press. There's an aspect of extreme morbidity and cruelty."

"Is there any way of stopping it at all?" Bernard said, between gripped teeth.

"Yes, there is, but it's got to be done at the very start, and what's more it doesn't have to be corrupt, putting in the hush and all that. It can be concluded quite legitimately that this won't serve the interest of justice, and I think," drawling it a bit, "that in your position—yours and Colette's, that is—the Procureur de la République might give the necessary authority. There are three drawbacks, or dangers, or whatever you call them."

"That you cut yourself off from possible help," said Colette.

"One—self-evident. A colossal heap of worthless stuff comes in, but there's always the chance of something genuine, and if it comes down to needles in haystacks one needs all the eyes one can get, including the silly, the loony, and even the morbid and malicious. Two: that it might backlash, because it's not easy to keep this kind of inquiry discreet; it imposes several difficult limitations on procedure, there are inevitably a lot of people in the know, and a leak is at all times possible. And if you try to keep something from the press they're apt to be vengeful."

"You mean Watergating."

"Right, and that's number three as corollary: it's easily concluded that an effort is being made to cover something, for personal or political considerations; I'm not spelling it out."

"Which would mean," said Colette slowly and clearly, "that you, Bernard, would lose your job, that I'd lose my career, that Henri—marked as a friend of ours—would at best get transferred with his promotion broken, and that our lives would be ruined. Including Vera's."

"God," said Bernard.

"Hey," said Castang, "easy. Colette, forgive me, you're dramatizing. Listen, we're friends, you've trusted me. You aren't in anything like that sort of situation. No crime or even misdemeanor can be attributed to you; there's no malpractice or attempt to interfere with justice—it isn't even your decision."

"No?" said Bernard hotly. "Whose, then? Not my child, no?"

"No," bluntly. "Proc's."

"The independence of a magistrate," hastily and angrily. "My wife is a judge. Sworn to interpret without fear or favor. I know this much law. The Public Prosecutor represents the state, we the people, blah-blah. He can't put any pressure on a judge—separation of powers."

"Darling," said Colette softly.

"What?" snappish.

"Easy. I think I see what Henri's getting at."

"Quite right, it's all true," said Castang. "But pity the poor policeman. Ground between millstones. Proc decides whether grounds for a charge exist and lays it: we-the-people. Instructs us to pursue an investigation. He finds a case; that's to say, we do and tell him so. He then passes the case to the examining magistrate, who from that moment is the sole authority over us. I know this is all stale cake, but the point is that here is— assuming the existence of a crime, or just a complaint—a magistrate involved. Proc's going to think about the dignity of the magistracy, and the independence of the judicature, and all the rest of it; and he decides—only *he* decides—how to go about procedure. And I don't need to tell you how that crowd stick together. He can decide whether to pull the curtain down on this affair, and whether he does depends maybe a great deal on what you say to him. And how you say it."

"As a judge," said Colette in a dry factual tone, "I can of course launch a police action myself, and a judicial procedure. I can't," more dryly still, "instruct my own case."

"I, on the other hand," said Bernard with acridity, "am the head of the family. I presume I have some say."

"You're wounding me unnecessarily," remarked Colette gently.

He made a palpable effort. "Look, Henri, I've been waiting, too, for the doorbell to go and the phone to ring. It hasn't. I've let time pass. It is now my job to set every possible human agency to work to find her. The legal argumentation doesn't interest me. I lodge a complaint against X and how do I go about that?"

"You've done it. I register it." Castang the drill sergeant. "I'm an officer of police but not an officer of justice. You need a commissaire for that. So I ring Commissaire Richard. He might be at home. Or alternatively, and I think it'd be wiser, Colette rings the Proc—or you do if you so wish. And ask his advice. Because just ringing the police and telling them to get their tail uncurled from underneath their arse is equivalent to inviting the newshawks; they'll be here in half an hour. I might suggest, too, that first you give the municipal police a chance to tell you whether they've found her, or any trace of her, before you take this grave step."

"You haven't a daughter," said Bernard in a voice soaked in bitterness.

Castang's face stayed controlled, like the White House spokesman at a press conference.

Colette got up, walked across the room, and made a business out of tinkle-tinkle with the ice cubes and getting everyone a clean ashtray. She wanted to give the flicker of unspoken hostility between the two men a moment to subside, as well as a moment to show herself that she was in command of her movements, her voice, her ideas. As well as to gain a minute of time, anyhow, anywhere. Bernard was too reasonable a person—and too nice—ever to persecute her with immature resentments about her being a magistrate while he was only a sort of glorified yogurt salesman. But he wasn't himself just now.

"Henri," she said.

"Yes?"

"Sorry—I was trying to think. We have to try and reflect . . . before we can decide what is best to do. I know—that we've no evidence at all, so you can't postulate. But just on the premise of Rachel's being a sensible child really, on the whole, and not often doing silly things—what does your experience tell you is the likeliest thing to have happened? I don't think either Bernard or I are looking just for reassurance. I think we've both got a good grip of reality. Even with nothing to go on, no fact to situate—can you arrive at any sort of outline?"

"Yes, there are a few general guidelines one could take— even, I think, with some confidence in the lack of anything to disprove them. First consider the quarter in general. It's virtually all clear, modern, open. The children play in full view. There are no heavy groups of old trees, no close shrubberies, hardly any old buildings. Precious little concealment. On a clear summer evening, with people strolling everywhere—it doesn't make a pattern for the kind of thing we'd dread. That type of individual is frightened, furtive—they look for more cover; they look for flight and concealment. Then consider Rachel's nature and training. She might not always come straight home if she was with a group of friends absorbed in a game, but she wouldn't just wander off. Even seeing something fascinating wouldn't hold her up for any length of time. Also she's a prudent, sensible child as well as timid. Falling in the pond or losing a shoe—she'd find ways quickly enough of getting in touch with you. Road accidents we've eliminated—no, I think we have to consider a crime, all right. I think someone has stolen her. It doesn't necessarily mean anything personal, though in your particular circumstances there might perhaps be more likelihood of some distorted notion of vengeance. I'd be inclined to discount that at present. There are, sadly, many people who hunt for easy ways to make money. The ones of lowest intelligence find that pretty hard, by definition. Some think of kidnapping a child, and an only child of wealthy parents is the most obvious. A highly neurotic variation on snatching handbags. It's a difficult thing to do, because if you just seize a child and bundle it into a car and drive off fast, it's virtually certain there'll be several witnesses. What other way is there? Some fairly elaborate intricate trap, baited with something really tempting, and I don't mean just a lollipop. One would be inclined to postulate either a gang of rather dull-witted little bandits or someone pretty bright but likewise highly psychotic —shouldn't be hard to trace."

"And how would one go about it—the tracing?"

"You mean if we had Richard here," smiling a little, "because it's not a job for the private detective. I'm pretty sure he'd start looking along the route back from school right away. Not just for the classic dropped bag or burst button—though that, too, naturally—but for any little deviation from the normal pattern of things: strange car parked in an odd place; anyone seen hanging about with apparently nothing to do; some unfamiliar figure pushing an ice-cream wagon or playing the organ—anything. And a house-to-house: the we-have-some-reason-to-believe routine. And back here I rather think he'd like the telephone tapped. Which is, of course, illegal." It was the first time Castang had risked any sort of joke. "Have to be with your knowledge and consent. Because it's evident enough that whoever it is—be it just a demand to stand and deliver, or a dotty gloat about I know a secret and you'd give a lot to know it, too, wouldn't you, now?—will try and poke you, and pretty quick. At that moment we'd want to be there, on the spot and able to intervene as well as listen. Because of course all these people are very prudish about the police getting to know, and they're apt to think up tricky gags about telling you where to drop money by the milestone on the deserted country road, and so on."

"And are we supposed to go to work normally, behave as though nothing had happened?"

"Oh, then I daresay we'd like to tap the office phones, too."

Colette managed something vaguely like a smile. "I don't somehow think the senior judge would much care for a tap in the Palace of Justice."

"No; I think you'd prefer to take a day off. But the phone will ring—and soon: these people are mostly talkative."

"Does a man have to stay here?"

"It's preferable. One can link the line to anywhere. But apart from being able to advise you or, if need be, instruct you rapidly, there might be people hanging round the house. I realize it's a horrible invasion of privacy. But we can put a chap in the cellar—choose a quiet elderly one with experience."

Colette had been making a deliberate effort to disentangle herself emotionally. This wasn't her; this was some other mother in the same lamentable situation. She didn't know Castang. He was the policeman who had been sent to take down details after her first anxious call to the police. She quite liked the look of him. It was reassuring. Seemed a competent man. No—better. Able; an able man.

Bernard had for the past few minutes been very quiet and still. His business training made him a good listener. He had followed, with what one might call a certain deference, the queries posed by the Judge of Instruction. Now he entered the conversation without elbowing into it.

"How long will all this take?"

"If you'll allow me to phone Richard—half an hour to an hour. He's quite possibly at home, or he mostly leaves word where he can be found. At the worst, in a hurry, I can get Lasalle. The material we'd want isn't complicated. When there's no occasion for furtive concealment"—a thin grin—"it takes no time to install. For the rest, I don't know what Richard would see fit to order—tonight, that is. He'd like perhaps to hear first what the urban police have to say or suggest."

"I don't want that phone occupied," said Bernard tightly. "Not even for five minutes."

"I understand that—I can call on an outside line. There won't be any palaver—not when he hears who it is. Take advantage of that bourgeois favoritism—with Richard there isn't all that much of it. Simply that Mme. Delavigne can give him a direct order."

"Very handy for me," said Colette bitterly. "Bernard, darling, I'm thinking about this—this appalling flood of publicity which would burst over our heads. Truly—before you come to any decision, before we ask Henri to do whatever must be done, and I think we have to agree that one of these outlines cannot be too far away from the reality—I'll have to ask the Procureur for his opinion and advice, and take him into our confidence—and I think his experience may too be valuable."

Bernard looked at her dully for a moment, as though not understanding, before pulling himself together.

"If you wish, I suppose so. It seems like tossing a penny. No —I don't want to sound fatalistic. All the decisions are bad. This must be the best."

Colette put her palms over her eyes, screwed them to and fro. She drew her fingertips over her face, as though to be sure it was still there and unchanged. She stood up.

"I'll just throw something else on. Something a little more— respectable," with an ironic emphasis.

"You're taking the car? Drive carefully. Think of the family."

Colette smiled at him, turned, went out rapidly.

The two men looked at each other, looked—as though by a silly coincidence—together at the telephone, looked away again. There was an embarrassed silence.

"How's Vera?" Bernard asked, making an effort.

"Childless."

"I'm sorry, you know."

"I'm sorrier. I know, I mean, what it's like, because of experience—but I can never really get there, never know. Imagination just won't carry that far."

They looked at each other again, this time with understanding.

"How about a real drink?" suggested Bernard, diffident.

"I won't say no. But let's have something to eat. And put a lot of water with it."

They crunched a packet of peanuts. They felt hungry then, and plundered two boxes of salt biscuits. Then they had a glass of milk.

"How's the house going?" asked Castang.

Colette and Bernard had a piece of land out in the country, and a shack on it, which they were building onto.

"Bloody awful builders," said Bernard, and became animated. Two men can talk about the iniquities of builders for an indeterminate length of time.

26

Colette had stuck the car in hurriedly, nose first, and now had to back up the ramp, which forced her to be careful. On the dark silent street she drove slowly, with exaggerated care at the intersections, dreading the sight of another car. Was anyone there, under the trees? Was she being watched? Was she being followed? Even the sight of a man walking a dog struck terror into her. Another man, turning automatically to wonder at the glimpse of a young pretty woman alone in a sports car and driving so slowly, made her sweat. She rubbed her arm irritably against her side. She turned onto the boulevard. The traffic went faster—much too fast. It was reassuring to be passed by people who did not know her, cared nothing about her, running blithely to their pleasures or tensely to their preoccupations, but unaware of her wound.

The Procureur de la République lived in an old quarter of ugly, solid, bourgeois villas built in the second half of the nineteenth century, lumpy things in large gardens overgrown with laurels and laburnums. The curving streets twisted into one another, all bearing annoyingly similar names of Roman emperors. Diocletian, Gratian, Valerian—this was a maze. On the left here, surely, with an oval brass plate? No—she must be in the wrong street. She had been here half a dozen times, and thought—felt sure—it was the second on the left after turning off the boulevard. But had she taken the wrong turn? The quiet streets were lined with large old chestnut trees, all now in full leaf, hiding the ugly villas. With a hysterical giggle, Colette decided she was Barberina, losing her pin at the beginning of the last act of *Figaro*—under the chestnut trees. *L'ho perduta!* Prelude to a lot of dramas.

Suddenly, and with a horrible, heart-wrenching shock, Colette realized that she was, indeed, being followed. An ordinary dark sedan was creeping down the roadway only two or three yards behind her. Her throat filled as though she were trying to swallow a tennis ball. The car, even at that low speed, lurched dangerously as her front wheel mounted the pavement. Colette grabbed with both hands at her steering wheel and her bag lying on the seat beside her. She braked and came to rest in the gutter, huddled and frozen as a rabbit catching sight of a stoat. The dark car came creeping up into the gutter directly behind her: she watched it in her rear-view mirror, clutching her bag fiercely, paralyzed with fear. A hoarse, soft voice came from the lowered window.

"Petite madame."

In an instant all her frozen muscles unblocked. This was no sinister, horrible kidnapper such as she imagined, creeping up to asphyxiate her with ether or leaping to grab and stun her with a rubber club. This was just one of those horrible, yes, but familiar—odiously familiar to women driving in a city at night —tomcats who prowl in cars.

"Petite madame—lost; lonely! Sweet girl, darling girl—bored! Likes an adventure—loves it!" Colette was no longer rigid: she was scrabbling in her bag. It serves for something at last, that object.

Bernard had wanted her to have it—oily smelly thing, heavy and awkward in a bag. And it had been the Proc—irony—who had authorized it.

"You are a young woman," he had said. "People do not hesitate to attempt putting pressures of all kinds upon a judge if they think they see any opening. A young woman can be in a vulnerable position—you drive about in your little car—there are some who would not hesitate to take advantage if they could. I approve of your husband's initiative." She had never had occasion—till now, outside his house. Her fingers opened the chamois-leather envelope, made for one of those immense, bulky pairs of sunglasses. It was an ordinary police pistol, a 7.65 Saint-Étienne, given her by Commissaire Richard, and it had been Richard himself—tall and silver-haired like a Nobel Prize winner, so difficult to imagine with a gun—who had taken her to the police shooting range to teach her.

"Relax. Feet apart. Much like a bow and arrow. Point the front foot. Back foot square. Solidly balanced. You need not be afraid of it. Nasty thing, yes; snake—but a tame snake. The snake knows you, is not frightened of you; the snake only strikes when frightened. Head up. Now, arm up."

The door behind her was opening. Get out of the car, you fool!

"Champagne in the fridge," came the soft hoarse wheedle. "And a nice record on the player." She stood leaning against the car, her left forearm on the roof. She did not "see" the man at all. She would be incapable of giving a description, of the face, even the height or weight. The tomcat sidled, rubbing itself along the bonnet of its own car. God! Isn't it possible to do things without guns?

"Darling—shall I drive yours?" God—only a few feet away. Instead of advancing her front foot, she dragged back the left leg in an instinctive recoil—but she was in a shooting stance. The streetlamp, on the far side of the road, shed a soft oily glitter on the pistol barrel. In the same second, she realized that she had not armed the gun. There were bullets in the magazine but none in the chamber. But the cat did not know that. It recoiled, seemed to crush itself against the radiator of its own car.

"Hey! Careful with that thing."

Colette's left hand felt the soft tremble of the motor which she had not turned off, vibrating the roof gently. The mechanical heartbeat put courage into her.

"Come nearer me and I'll shoot at you," she said.

It stood still.

"Now go. Go, or I'll shoot the car."

It sidled back, uncertain whether it was being bluffed but frightened enough not to try. Colette took her left hand off the dusty metal, planted her front foot firmly on the pavement, snapped the action of the pistol, pointed it fiercely at the radiator.

"Go. Run." It ran.

Suddenly feeling all-competent, unfumbling, perfectly cool, she pressed the button releasing the magazine and dropped it on the driving seat. She couldn't recall whether or not the horrid thing would now fire. It didn't matter; she snapped the action again. Just as it had done when Richard showed her, the bullet in the chamber ejected: just as he had done, she caught the coppery glitter deftly in her left hand. She got back in the car, put the pistol together, laid it on the seat beside her, and threw the car in gear. The car gave an awkward jerk. She'd put it in third instead of first. She corrected, accelerated.

She recognized the Proc's house at once. It was twenty yards farther along. Under the oval plate was a polished brass bell push. Colette looked back up the road. Nothing to be seen. The outside light clicked on, a comforting flood. The gate latch clicked. She walked up the path, glancing back to see that the light reached her car. The Proc himself suddenly appeared on the porch.

"Why—Mme. Delavigne. Pleasant surprise."

"M. Besson—I'm sorry—but there's one of those disagreeable men who follow one at night. I chased him off, but he's down the street."

"Is there indeed? Well, we'll soon settle him. Come in, my dear: ah, I see—he gave you a fright." He reached for the telephone on the hall table.

"Besson here—Procureur de la République, Rue Gratian. Wake up, man. I want a car patrol, and quickly. There's a loiterer here, and I want him pegged. Come on, man, get your thumb out of your bum."

Colette had never heard the Proc talking to policemen quite like this before. He put the phone down and said, "I'll cook his goose," in a high-treason tone. More familiar, even though instead of his robe he was clothed in a Chinese dressing gown. From the umbrella stand he selected a thick stick.

"Now, Madame, if you'll just show me. No need for fear while I'm with you."

Oh, my God, thought Colette; I left the gun in full view on the car seat. But he was already marching along the pavement. When she reached the car, she grabbed the gun and stuffed it guiltily in her bag, almost getting caught when he turned around accusingly—force of habit—and went "Ha?" with his stick at the tomcat's dark car. He stood guard over it in a gleeful way that she felt rather embarrassed about: wasn't this a bit vengeful in the representative of society? She was almost ready to wish the horrid man would get away, was feeling that this was not quite proper in a judge, when another dark sedan appeared in the light, this one containing two uniforms, which jumped out and made a rather ostentatious business of saluting.

"Loitering and prowling," said M. Besson. "There's his car— I daresay that'll provide a few further offenses. He'll be hanging about in the quarter. Legitimate suspicion, conduct prejudicial —take him down and charge him: I'm preferring the complaints myself, and I want an example made."

"Sir," said one.

"Easy," said the other, already writing down the car number.

"We'll make this gentleman regret his nocturnal lecheries." It sounded rather like an ecclesiastical court in the Middle Ages: Proc already seemed to be weighing the respective deterrent value of the stocks and the ducking stool. "My dear Mme. Delavigne, I am so very sorry. Right, officers, that's all." More salutes, and a wave of the stick.

"Now," he was saying two minutes later, over glasses of port, "to what do I owe this unexpected pleasure?" And Colette was making a great effort to be lucid and simple, bothered by the sensation of unreality. And if Rachel was by now home and in bed, having been taken for a ride in the country or something and got a flat tire, and left a note where it had been blown into a corner by a draft, or told the concierge and it slipped his memory, or tried to call up but the phone was out of order . . .

Proc's dressing gown and slippers added to the unreality. And this ridiculous, humiliating adventure, which somehow had been so much more humiliating to herself than to a probably lonely and certainly unhappy little man—she had overreacted wildly. There was nothing but bitterness for her in the prospect of policemen turning from the obsequious to the bullying, with a sanctimonious telling-off in the police court to follow, with a fine of a few hundred francs and a don't-let-it-happen-again. Far worse things lay in store for herself.

An unreal sense, too, about this room: Proc's study, part of the downstairs suite of rooms where she had been three times—to his annual garden party for the Palace of Justice and the bar, and to a couple of his celebrated dinner parties. . . . Everything then was tidied, and a great deal cleared away, because he wasn't leaving his valuable pieces of Nevers and Rouen faïence around to be used as ashtrays or knocked over! Or even pinched, lawyers being notoriously given to every imaginable vice and frailty.

The garden party had been bad enough, for it had been showery weather, and decidedly chilly in this awful house. The agonies beforehand over what she could possibly wear for a summer party in bad weather had been nothing to the reality: women milling about upstairs looking for the lavatory, which was always occupied, and a fearful squash downstairs where Proc, in front of the big carved mahogany sideboard, dispensed hospitality and little jokes while keeping an eye on the hired waiters and seeing that people circulated properly instead of agglomerating into ghastly little cliques giggling in corners.

Not even those agonies could equal the horror of a winter dinner party, where it was most important that Colette, the junior magistrate present—absolutely foot-of-the-table, down where the fish "got turned over"—should not be better dressed than the other ladies present. One couldn't be worse dressed. . . .

Frightful lurid snips of flashback were punctuating her hapless narrative: Bernard's sarcastic and highly obscene witticisms in their dressing room at home, while she dashed about in her underwear trying on one impossible garment after another; Bernard's hypocritical face when he was introduced to Mme. Proc, a full-blown peony in red taffeta; Bernard at table—rather red, too (legal Burgundy, and a dinner jacket that had got too tight for him)—being polite to a lady in beige tulle, his somewhat globular eyes fixed upon her amazing expanse of bosom. (One of Colette's major problems had been "how much tit to show," but she need not have worried.) And Bernard's partner, a lady in clinging silks much tighter than his jacket, whose stays were dreadfully in evidence. And herself, uncomfortably aware that Mme. Proc was aware that Proc was looking down her dress . . .

He wasn't being in the least like that now. He listened in silence, and at the end said, "Dear me; you *have* been in the wars," in an absolutely neutral voice, and poured her a second glass of port, which she took gratefully: she had a feeling that it would be nice to get just a tiny bit drunk.

The fact was that she had never seen him like this before. This was no stiff, pedantic, elderly magistrate, being pompous at the dinner table or making rather too much of an offensive but not very criminal curb-crawler (though she did realize that he had acted in understandable irritation, some of it toward her for involving him, as well as a feeling that his home and his hospitality had been damaged and smeared). Nor was it the professional, often kindly, sometimes unexpectedly large-minded, but severe and rigid man she knew well enough, both in his room and in court, at the Palace.

This was just a quiet, kindly gentleman in late middle age, of vast experience and secure in the possession of great powers and much responsibility, paternally listening to an unhappy young woman begging desperately for help, and considering how best to give it. She had come to the end of the tale, which, despite herself, she had made too complicated, and was stumbling a good deal over the "publicity" aspect.

"Yes," said M. Besson after listening in perfectly controlled patience and not interrupting once, or posing any question whatever, "that is very clear. And—may I say it?—my appreciation of your character and abilities, already high, is confirmed. Now, Madame, I want you to place yourself in my hands."

"I am, I think."

"Good. Now give me your telephone number. . . ." He dialed the number. "M. Delavigne—good evening; Besson here. My dear friend, my sympathy is superfluous and any words I could add are even quite worthless. I say no more than to remark that nothing—nothing—will be left undone. Now if you would have the extreme kindness to pass me Castang. . . . Castang? Besson here. Nothing so far? . . . Very well; I'll have Richard with you shortly. Meanwhile, you have my mandate to act at discretion: observe the greatest compatible prudence. I'll waste no further time; you'll want the phone free. Let's say I'll reinforce you as soon as may be with a technician, and I'll leave it to you to put Richard into the detailed picture: pray give my compliments to M. Delavigne and explain that my precipitancy is the measure of my activity."

He was already dialing the familiar number of urban police headquarters.

"Procureur—give me the night commissaire. Raynal? Besson. You had a report of a missing child, a little girl named Rachel Delavigne. Just summarize the action reports for me, please. . . . Very well. Now pay close heed, please. I want that action doubled. I'll be ringing Richard myself. I want the fullest and most energetic action taken not only as regards your own spheres but the closest liaison. . . . Yes, yes, all that. I want you to ring me in the morning, and after you've given Commissaire

Fabre a closely reasoned account of the night's work I want him to phone me: I'll be at my desk at eight. By the way, you'll have a man brought in, in all likelihood. A nocturnal prowler here in my own street. Charge him—yes. Keep him for the night."

"No," interrupted Colette too shrilly. "No, please, M. Besson, no. I beg of you."

"One moment, Raynal. Correct that. You need prefer no charge. Unless there's a motoring offense—we'll let that stand as mandatory. But the lady who is the subject of this aggression, which personally I regard as intolerable, would prefer not to insist, and so be it. But I rely upon you to wash this sad individual's head for him—understand? And, Raynal, a final detail, but in my view—and note this well—of maximal weight. I take it you have the usual printer's devil hanging around for his morning edition? No press coverage on this matter. Don't be imbecile, man—the child, of course; the other matter is trivial. Not just the automatic suppression of names where a child is concerned, but the whole thing. . . . Yes, that's right, prejudicial to subsequent judicial inquiry. This is a P.J. matter, and must be absolutely uncompromised. You will take formal note that I will hold you personally responsible for press leakage, and I expect a disciplined body to behave in disciplined fashion—is that clear? . . . You will repeat those instructions to Commissaire Fabre, and he will confirm them in a communication to me as soon as he is at his desk tomorrow morning. Is that clear? Perfectly clear? Now go to it. I want every piece of waste ground swept, and I want every individual whose movements are not accounted for interrogated, and I say this with the utmost gravity and solemnity. That's all, Raynal."

Colette shivered. But she had put herself in his hands.

"Are you chilled, my child? Forgive me—my daughter is your age. I do not wish to sound unduly patronizing. Forgive me again—I act toward you as I would to a child of my own. I have also, you know—perhaps I have never mentioned it—grandchildren. My dear girl—forget, for an instant, hierarchy. Forget that I am the representative of the state and the citizen—what, after all, is more to us than a child? Any child. Try to believe me. Forget that you are a magistrate and part of what I like to believe is in some sense my family. Try to give me credence when I say that as much would not be too much were it the most dispossessed and wretched of immigrant laborers. . . ." He dialed another number.

"Mme. Richard? Dear Madame, Besson here. I crave your forgiveness, may I have your good man? Ah, Richard, sorry to disturb your repose. I'm ringing you from home; Mme. Delavigne is with me. A child has disappeared. Raynal is, of course, carrying out the usual verifications, but there are certain aspects leading us to attach what may be a criminal significance. . . . Yes . . . yes . . . The fact is that it is her own child. . . . That's as may be seen. For the present, I feel strongly that we should act with delicacy, and I have decided after deliberation that any publicity would not—at least until we can see round this more clearly—serve our cause."

Richard's voice was soft, and did not clatter in the amplifier, but Colette noticed wryly that the Procureur had the earpiece cupped in his hand and pressed close to his head. That might be the habit of caution—or was Richard in danger of saying something that might be hurtful? She was, in any case, making no effort to overhear; her mind was far off, examining the faintly preposterous spectacle of a procureur in a dressing gown. His missus had been careful not to put in an appearance, whether from discretion or because she had taken off her stays and wasn't putting them on again for the Queen, Colette could not guess. A ludicrous vision of this magisterial pair of conjoints on their hymeneal couch imposed itself—with lurid details—on her inflamed imagination; she felt slightly ashamed of herself. Mention of her own name jerked her back to reality, none too soon.

"Mme. Delavigne very sensibly called Castang—who, as you

know, is on friendly terms with the family—to add his advice to whatever assistance he could give, and quite rightly he urged her to come straight to me. He's there still, as I gather. His view of the matter is that we'd do well to put in a listening post, which is logical, but naturally he can't move until you've made your dispositions: however, since I am in possession of the facts —sadly meager, alas, so far, unless Raynal turns something up, and I've instructed him to keep me in touch—you have a free hand and we've lost no time. I think myself justified in the circumstances in asking you to see for yourself. Yes, and Castang would seem the right man to take over the conduct of a preliminary inquiry, since M. Delavigne feels very properly that it would be premature to lay formal complaint before the possibilities of simple mischance are exhausted. . . . Quite so, and in that event I will ask M. Savornin to take charge of the dossier, being our senior judge. Pending which, Richard—as unobtrusive as we can; I may count upon you. Till tomorrow, then . . ."

"You are kindness personified," said Colette formally.

"Kindness?" said M. Besson, looking at the word as though it were evidence, turning it over and frowning at it, weighing it. "Kindness is no more than courtesy; an attribute of charity, a virtue we endeavor to practice without always succeeding. You showed it, if I may be forgiven the personal nature of the remark, in asking me not to pursue your aggressor of a few minutes ago. I have unworthier levers—my two small grandchildren, who will inherit, as it sometimes seems to us, a world in which charity is a notion to excite derision. But we must preserve them, and try to arm them. My dear Madame, are you really able to drive your little car? Should I not ask M. Richard to pass by and convey you?"

"I'll manage," she said, considerably embarrassed by these flowery proposals. He was being, perhaps, a little too paternal, bending over her with a scrap too much solicitude and a faint flavor of port. "I am very touched, you know," awkwardly.

"We shall hope to remove your apprehensions with the utmost celerity," sailing magisterially out to the hall. "Did you have gloves?" somehow conveying a hint of disapproval that a lady should go out without gloves, even nowadays. "Good night, my dear. Drive carefully. I shall not be expecting to see you at the Palais—or perhaps I should, confident as I am of a fortunate deliverance. All well? Got your keys? Good. I shall not turn out the light until I see you safely embarked."

Talking to Proc was a bit like eating cream cake: nice, but one quickly had enough.

Tides of energy and excitement had come up in her in a feverish surge, filling her with wild illusions, but leaving her flat and nauseated, and lined with lead like some expensive coffin. The last of these illusions, at its height while she felt so buoyed with help and understanding as to be convinced that she would return to find Rachel drinking cocoa on the hearthrug and telling an excited tale of magic carpets, had gone out with a rush in the chilling realization that the old man, while undoubtedly a kind old man with veins of gentleness in his severity, was also a slightly sexy old beast who got a wee bit excited when young women came to him with pathetic tales. He was much too gentlemanly, as well as too professional, to allow little imps to wink at her, but there had been a flicker in the eye there for a second.

The tide went out so terrifyingly fast that she fumbled with the keys in the ignition, had to grip herself, looked firmly into her rear-view glass—noting bleakly that the dark sedan had vanished—and pulled her gear lever too abruptly back into second. Her right foot seemed incapable of accelerating, and the car slackened and crawled, then wavered uncertainly to a stop before the end of the street. Her face was corpse-cold and clammy; she pushed her door open, leaned out, and was violently sick in one frantic jet into the gutter. Rejection phenomenon, came her silly thought. Someone else's heart has been grafted into me. She leaned her forehead on the rim of the driving wheel, letting her whole body go limp as string, vaguely hoping there was no one in the street—above all, no kind person to come offering sympathy or brandy—but not caring a damn if there was, not even if it was another overexcited little satyr with notions of dragging her out and raping her; she felt vaguely that that would be quite nice, and would be a pleasant distraction. Anyway, it would be happening to someone altogether different, not herself at all, and she would only be floating about somewhere as a halfheartedly interested spectator.

Just let her get rid of the lead first. Lead had a vile taste in the mouth: another crisis wrung her belly into a spasm and she retched miserably, finding nothing to be sick with but a little lead-poisoned saliva. She groped in her bag for a small flat flask of eau de cologne, which ought to be there for when Madame the Judge got a bit grimy, physically and sometimes mentally, on long hot dragging afternoons in the Palais. She kept finding nothing but that beastly gun at her blind fingertips, stupidly unable to find the other compartment in the nasty slithery silk lining of her bag. Found it at last, tried to unscrew it to the right, jammed it tight, nearly could not unscrew it at all, managed it at last, spilled a palmful onto her dirty smelly hand, feeling half of it on the stomach of her cotton blouse, smeared the rest across her face, gulped gratefully at the evaporation of the alcohol. The stain upon her blouse was pleasantly cool to her skin. She rubbed at her stomach in a circular movement to evaporate the moisture and dissipate the stain. This seemed to do her good, vaguely. I'm in shock, she thought: I'm doing all sorts of silly things. She decided she couldn't care less if the whole street was full of gaping silent voyeurs, rested her head on the backrest, pushed her body slackly forward clear of the wheel, unbuttoned the blouse, threw the last drops of eau de cologne on her hand, and rubbed it again in slow circles over the pit of her stomach.

Really, Madame the Judge, such ideas to be getting, and on the street in front of Proc's house.

Her mind zigzagged aimlessly. Bernard had been driving her home from that last absurd winter dinner party. It had been very cold, the car icy, with condensation from their twin breaths forming a mist on the windscreen because the heater had not had time to take effect. She had been huddled up, very yawning and soggy, in her fur jacket, leaning forward to wipe the windscreen with her hanky. Bernard—rather drunk, driving erratically, inflamed by heaven knew what but presumably the brandy on the top of galloping frustration induced by all the beige flesh above beige tulle and lilac lace and petunia satin— had become thoroughly irresponsible and had been driving with his hand shoved persistently between her knees and hitching villainously at her skirt hem.

"Oh, you," half between a yawn and a giggle, "do watch your driving, you're lurching all over the place. You shouldn't be driving at all, you're pie-eyed."

"So're you," slurringly snickering—the cold burst of frosty air had suddenly made him much drunker, for he had really been perfectly behaved all evening; too much so—and breathing again all over the windscreen. "Oh, damn the stupid thing; never mind, I'll warm you, chilly wife. Hell, those old bastards have been leering down your frock all evening: my turn."

"Bernard, keep your eyes on the road. Now, Bernard, stop it, you're busting my poppers." He had driven into the garage far too fast, with a loud squawk from the brakes, heaved her out like a sack, pushed her into the lift, and scrambled her ludicrously along the passage, puffing like a walrus in the mating season.

"How do you know what walruses do in the mating season?" asked Bernard querulously, trying to force the latch key in upside down.

"I seem to be getting shown," she muttered, muffled from being flumped upside down into a lot of sofa cushions.

40

Colette straightened up with a jerk, threw the little empty bottle back in her bag, took a deep breath of the summer night through the open window, turned the ignition key, and accelerated firmly, moving her gears now in her accustomed rapid snap, quite clearheaded and stomach settled, but twitching with a need to get home fast and get this over with. Remnants of control allowed her to put the car away instead of leaving it anyhow outside on the gravel, which would only attract attention. The lift was at the bottom, heaven be thanked. She opened the door as quietly as she could, paid no heed to the voices from the living room, unable to care whether Richard had arrived yet or not, and tore into the bathroom, where she threw her clothes into a heap, made love to herself in a nervous frenzy, and collapsed, with her tension snapped at last, on the floor. She dragged herself under the shower, made it very hot, and then made it rather cold to get her blocked circulation running: even on this warm evening, her feet and hands were icy. She felt a great deal better, and spent ten minutes on artificial aids toward a majestic mistress-of-the-house entrance into the living room, where there were at present gathered three policemen.

The atmosphere was almost that of a party, for Bernard was doing his hospitality act, with a great show of lighthearted indifference to the whistling bullets. This was no Mitty performance: she was familiar with it. All that neurotic gaiety was no more than a pathetic determination that his private life should have nothing to do with strangers. She had seen him in moments of extreme fatigue, kneeling on the floor with his head in her lap so that she could massage the back of his neck, spring up to answer the telephone with an anyone-for-tennis voice that filled her with pity and affection. It would wear off, she decided now: they've only just come.

Commissaire Richard, the chief of the Regional Service of the P.J. and Castang's immediate superior, was a tall handsome man who gave an impression of extreme calm. He had always the healthy look of a man who has slept well: his fine silvery hair never got ruffled and he never raised his voice. Neither Colette nor Bernard knew him at all well; Bernard, in fact, had never met him before, and Colette, who saw a good deal of him and thought she knew him well enough, was surprised now to realize that she really knew nothing about him—nothing of any use. That he was good at his job. That his department was run with a meticulous attention to detail, for he was very conscientious and reliable. That his subordinates liked him and trusted him, because when things went wrong he did not try to shuffle the blame onto underlings but took it himself. Seeing him now for the first time in her own living room, in casual slacks and a cotton shirt with flowers on it, he was an entirely new person and the shock was small but real.

He held his hand out, with the usual small but attractive smile and the usual polite murmur.

"Good evening, Mme. Delavigne." He didn't kiss her hand or anything, or try to be the least gushing. "We were just discussing tapping your telephone." The police technician stood politely in the background, being unobtrusive, accustomed to being unwelcome, ready even to be treated with hostility, and wearing a mask of complete indifference which he would not change whatever happened: a man who has heard everything, and seen most. Even if he had had a listening post in my bathroom, she thought, he would not show any emotion or raise his eyes off the carpet. As Castang had promised, an oldish man with graying hair. She went over to shake hands with him.

"I'm sorry to drag you out at this time of night," she said politely. He smiled slightly but said nothing. Whether he was on or off duty, it mattered so little.

"I was just wondering," said Bernard, bubbling irrepressibly like a glass of champagne poured out that second, "which article of the Penal Code it is that reproves electronic eavesdropping."

"Good heavens, I've no idea," said Colette, momentarily

taken aback, since she knew her code as well as most.

"Article 368," answered Richard, playing up effortlessly. "Invasion of privacy. A felony," with precision, "punishable with two to twelve months' imprisonment and a fine of up to fifty thousand francs."

"Ah," said Castang, shaking his hand loosely from the wrist in the gesture meaning "Direct hit." "Listen to maestro."

"I had it just the other day—the photographers who caught the Princess without her bra. 'The material used shall be confiscated.'"

"So," said Bernard with a gust of laughter, "I'll have you all in jail."

"There's a final paragraph," imperturbably, "stating that if carried out in the sight and knowledge of the parties it shall be deemed to be with their consent."

"I bet the photographer tried that," said Bernard.

"He did," placidly, "but he didn't get away with it."

"So no private showing to regale us with?"

"Alas, I never even got to see them myself. Royal Highness's large private detective sergeant fairly tore them out of my hands."

Colette was touched. Richard understood perfectly that these vulgarities were not characteristic of Bernard. For Henri, who knows us better, it is easier. She admired Richard's patience.

"Today we have a collection of other articles, familiar to Madame."

"Articles 341 and 5, 54 and 5," said Colette, not showing off. They were indeed familiar to her; odiously so.

"Sequestration and child-stealing."

"The withholding of a minor," she said bitterly, "from its properly constituted guardians."

"And it's a felony," said Bernard with sarcastic emphasis.

"No," said Richard flatly, "it's a crime."

"I'm glad to hear it."

"It's one of the gravest crimes in the code, M. Delavigne. The

43

kidnapping of a child under fifteen, where fraud or violence has been used, whether or not a ransom is demanded, carries a sentence of criminal reclusion in perpetuity. And I spare you the small print."

"You really know them by heart."

"This is one of the few that stop me sleeping at night."

"And me," fiercely. "And me."

"I don't want to eat into your reserves of patience, M. Delavigne, because you will need them before tonight is over. But the three of us here—we are going to give our utmost. Not just quote you bits of the code, or show you how much we know by heart. We are not bureaucrats. We are men like you. All right, Johnny," not wanting Bernard to be ashamed and to present excuses, "let's get this little job done."

The gray-haired man opened a shabby suitcase containing an ordinary electrician's tool kit.

"I take it you've a cellar, Madame? If you have a chair for me, I'll be out of your way, and the intrusion on your privacy will be kept to the minimum. I can't hear your movements or your conversation—I can only hear the voices when the phone is lifted." He was fixing a small gadget under the instrument's base plate. "It doesn't show, but you know it's there."

"Ingenious," muttered Bernard, "but listen, if you're down in the cellar—that's six floors, and where are you going to lead the wires?"

"Middle Ages, monsieur—don't be offended. This isn't a microphone, and we don't need any wires. It's a tiny transmitter. It would hear everything you said, but, as I explained, we put in this little interrupter, linked to the phone receiver-rest, so that it will only function when the phone is lifted. There are no wires. Down in the basement I can listen with a headset. I can, if need be, record the conversation simultaneously on tape. I have my own transmitter, too, and I can alert the operator in our office at the P.J., and in a matter of seconds I can, if need be, alert the Commissaire here, or if he wants any other officer in the neighborhood—in a car, say, or wherever the Commissaire wants to place a man—in a radius up to a kilometer."

"We don't have anything as sophisticated as the C.I.A.," murmured Castang, "but we're up to average Watergate standards."

Bernard threw himself down on the sofa and made a helpless gesture with his arms.

"No, you're not impotent," said Richard. "On the contrary, you have a very difficult and delicate task. On the instructions of the Procureur, we are going to work this with a complete absence of publicity. That takes away several of our conventional methods of approach, as for example the copying and distributing of photographs. We do have the advantage that Castang, who is going to take the heaviest load in this inquiry, knows your child and is familiar with her. I don't know her at all, and I want your family album so that I can get to know as much of her as I can. That for a start. But what I meant was that if we are to profit at all by this absence of publicity, we have to be certain that your movements arouse no curiosity. For example, several of your neighbors and the child's friends already know, unless I'm much mistaken, that she's missing. You can cover that; it shouldn't be too hard to construct a tale of a misunderstanding, or perhaps, since she won't be at school, a tale of some slight accident which would mean that her absence was not remarked—a sprained ankle or something. Now if you show anxiety and disquiet to the world—above all, if you shut yourself up here with the phone—you do yourself no good, and you do your cause no good. The moment there's any gossip—and all alterations in familiar patterns cause gossip—the press will smell a rat. Indeed, this is a very risky thing we're trying. It isn't often that it's successful. It's a deception, and that's never a good start to a police inquiry. However, in the circumstances we can control it, but only if you—for example—put in an appearance at your office and put a face on things. If your daughter is only laid up with a sprained ankle, it's normal that

45

Madame and yourself take some time off to stay with her, since it is a child of eight. One of you can always be here at home—I suggest that you spend your afternoon here. The effort will help you, too.

"That leaves us. As Johnny remarked, he can link to a car, which we'll use as a sort of mobile headquarters close by. We want to be able to slip in and out unremarked, so I'll ask to borrow your keys to have them copied, and you can count on me to give you a very close account of everything we do and learn, daily.

"Lastly I'd like you to think, right now, of anything in your own life or work that might give us a lead. Obviously enough, Madame's profession brings her into contact with a wide range of unbalanced persons, and there's a strong likelihood that here is where we will find the author of this attempt. The presumption is clear enough: an individual, possibly a parent or relation of a minor implicated in some affair judged or instructed by Madame, is trying to revenge himself upon society, and chooses to strike back at society, personified by yourselves and your child. It seems plain that the Procureur thinks something of the sort to be likely, because otherwise it is very unlikely that he would authorize this silence; it runs against the generally accepted convention, which is that police inquiries should be conducted in public and the usual liberties of the press unimpeded."

"Come, come," said Bernard, "all sorts of hanky-panky never comes to light, and well you know it."

Richard smiled. "It's not only more difficult than you think to keep things dark, and much more rare than the public supposes, but the reasons are generally good. I've known affairs, yes, where scandals involving high functionaries were hushed up in what has sometimes seemed a corrupt way, but there was nearly always a good deal to be said, too, for handling them discreetly. Here the matter is clearer: not only is a minor involved, which is the classic exception to the rule that justice be

46

done in public, but it is possible that the whole thing has bearing on some matter still under instruction or not yet judged. The serenity and impartiality of justice may be menaced. There may be no ransom demanded in terms of money, but there might be a demand for an exchange of hostages, perhaps—the liberty of some imprisoned person. This is all pure hypothesis, of course, but we'd do well to think about it."

"I have thought about it," said Bernard, "and I have also, being married to a magistrate, some experience of the problems involved."

"All my long lecture," said Richard gently, and not at all pedantically, "was meant as no more than an objective viewpoint. If you can bring yourself to think of this objectively, it will very greatly help you—and us."

"But you started by asking whether anybody had cause for grievance against myself."

"I agree that it sounds unlikely. But I've got to keep an open mind—you'll agree that it would be foolish to conclude anything, since we know nothing. That the attack is directed toward Madame in her capacity as a magistrate is no more than the first field of inquiry, the one presenting itself first—possibly, too, the easiest. A large field?" His eyes went round to Colette, who had been sitting, small and unimportant, in the corner of the sofa.

"I don't know at all," she said sadly. "Nothing obvious; I mean there've been no menaces, beyond the usual collection of abusive, dotty, and anonymous letters. My dossiers are all in order, I think. My clerk knows them all, of course. As for looking at them—I've no idea. I'm completely confused and bewildered. The secret of the instruction . . . you'll have to ask the Procureur —there are ways and means—one has to ask the first president, the senior judge of the Appeals Court—I just can't bring the procedure to mind—he designates another magistrate. . . . Oh, God . . ."

"Easy, darling."

"You're much better at this than I am. No, don't touch me, darling; I just need a moment. I'm sorry, Commissaire, I'm not a magistrate at all this evening, just a shocked and frightened woman. I've never known it in practice, but of course there's a procedure; the Procureur-Général, I think, can designate an officer of judicial police, and that would be you, I suppose, to inquire into the background, or it may not be necessary. If I'm still officially instructing a dossier, I can perhaps ask you to enlarge the scope of inquiry into the backgrounds—oh, I just don't know, I'm sorry. Even a judge has to be allowed an emotional upheaval sometimes."

"Don't trouble yourself. I suggest that you try to come to work tomorrow afternoon, if M. Delavigne can arrange to get away."

"Of course I can."

"And of course I will," said Colette firmly, pulling herself together.

"And we'll have something worked out by then," Bernard said.

"It's a complicated existence," she said, smiling, determined to show her control. "Article 67 of the code—you know, the judging of a minor—has twenty pages of close print to itself just in the little handbook."

"I've never counted them," said Richard, smiling. "After all, the one we know best is Article 224."

"Which is?" glad to have the tension broken.

"You tell them, Castang."

"Outrage or insult to an agent of the public order," happily. "And punishable, I'm delighted to say, with fifteen to sixty days' jug or a fine up to three thousand, or both, if you happen to call a cop a cow's skin in a moment of exasperation after colliding your car."

All four laughed. Even gray-haired Johnny, silent in his corner with a glass of tonic hardly touched, condescended to smile.

The telephone rang.

There was instant silence. Richard motioned to Bernard and picked up the spare earpiece at the same moment.

Bernard swallowed, wet his lips, picked up the phone, and said "Delavigne" in a creditably neutral tone.

"Commissaire Raynal, Urban Police. Nothing to report, sir, I'm afraid."

"I see. Well, I must thank you. I suppose that is bad news, or isn't it?"

"It's neither good nor bad, sir. We haven't found your little girl, so I'm afraid I can't allay your anxiety yet on that point, but on the other hand we've found nothing that points to any criminal matter, and that, if I may say so, is good even if it's a negative good. So I want to ask you to keep your courage up, sir, and to tell you that we aren't abandoning this search. We'll now make slightly different dispositions, and widen the scope of our inquiries, and also look at things in a bit more detail."

"Can you tell me a little more about this detail?"

"Well, sir, we put through a request to the commandant of the gendarmerie for the districts outside the city limits, and we ask for the help of the auxiliary police corps, which gives us considerably more men, and we verify any matter that seems to us at all obscure, and—well, briefly, we cover it all again more thoroughly and a bit more slowly. You'll appreciate, sir, that we haven't had time yet for more than routine checks."

Richard signaled with the spare earpiece, gave it to Bernard, and took the phone.

"Richard here, Raynal. The Proc's been on to you, has he? Yes, we're coordinating, naturally. I've been waiting to hear from you to set a prelim afoot, and I'll be beginning as of now; I've Castang here with me. Yes. Yes. Proc no doubt will be wanting Fabre and myself first thing, so if you'd have it all written up for when he gets in? I've nothing to say yet, of course, apart from the obvious inferences: we'll be going over

49

the ground here at dawn. Right, then, old son. And there's a blanket on this, as of course you're aware. What have you given the press?"

"Well, we can't disguise our activity, of course," came Raynal's voice, thin and dry. "The local people are aware what's going on; fellow's not born yesterday. So I've authorized a bald paragraph, using the Proc's formal interdiction to release any details whatsoever. They'll be on to you, too, no doubt."

"No doubt. I wish them joy."

"Okay, then. You'll say to M. Delavigne I'll ring him in the morning? About seven. Sleep well."

Richard put the phone back carefully. "And now I'll be saying the same to you. Do you want a phone by your bed? Johnny will put one in for you. And if you can find means, Madame, to tuck him up for the night. I'll have you relieved, of course, Johnny, in the morning. We'll be going now, because we can't do you any further good here yet awhile. Johnny, you'll give me your buzzer and I'll put it under my pillow. M. Delavigne—sleep! Go to your office exactly as usual. We'll find means to communicate with you if anything at all happens, and I'll arrange to slip in at lunchtime anyhow. Madame—I'm not going to concern myself in matters affecting the judicature, but I want to reassure you that means can be found which will save you all pain and worry where the legal aspects interlock with your personal affairs. So good night to you both. Come on, Castang."

"Good night, and thank you," said Bernard.

"Good night," said Colette desolately, like a nervous child seeing the night-light blown out.

"Good night," said Castang, being the colorless subordinate, and stopped. "And, Bernard—count on me, huh?"

"That thanks for the nice party?" Bernard said, summoning a grin.

"My turn for hospitality. Vera will want to make it a thanksgiving. We'll get Rachel back, you know, and quick. I won't say anything to Vera yet."

"Yes, do," said Colette. "I want to be able to turn to her."

"It's understood," said Castang. "See you."

The two men sat in Richard's car, which had been parked around the corner.

"Tactics," said Richard mildly, lighting one of his thin, knotty Brazilian cigars.

"Not much doubt in your mind?" offered Castang.

"Not a great deal. Failing Raynal turning something up, we'll assume a snatch, without any speculation on the whos and whys; it'll be the hows that interest us first. The legal end you leave to me, as is evident. She was in a stew, of course, but to get her dossiers over the last year combed out won't be a difficult affair. Safe bet Proc is turning wheels right now and that I'll be answerable to old Jérémie, since he's senior judge, in the morning. And he's too experienced to fuss, thank God."

"The legal end," said Castang disgustedly. "While you're all rollicking about in the small print and the ticklish definitions, I'm being regaled with the gossip of the neighbors. 'Just have a look at her flaunting with her new pram, and how does she afford that on her husband's salary?' Come to think of it, that sort of thing would be easy, because the good women wouldn't have missed a trick, whereas in a quarter like this a good half of the female population is out at work."

"Be out there in time for the children going to school," said Richard. "They tack along in groups, and what puzzles me is how anyone could isolate the child, even for a minute or two. There may be some activity, a building site or whatnot, which interests them so that they stand and stare."

"I can't question the children or it'll all be out in no time."

"Try to find a way of turning that difficulty," said Richard unhelpfully.

"You two gentlemen in some trouble?" inquired a voice, polite but nosy. Neither of them had seen the cruising station wagon.

"Er—no."

"You live around here?"

"We were at a party," said Richard blandly.

"Been drinking a little bit, perhaps? You wouldn't mind showing me your papers?"

Knows his job, thought Castang. Body turned a little to the left, disguising the fact he's got his right hand on his gun. Richard flipped open his little leather folder, holding it to the light.

"Sorry, sir, didn't recognize you. There's a little girl—"

"Correct, and I don't want it advertised. No, no, you were quite right—take a good look at parked cars. Anything on any of your reports?"

"Not so far."

"I'll be having a word with your commissaire in the morning. I don't want any obtrusive controlling by day: this area will be sensitive."

"Understood." The station wagon rolled, quietly.

"We'll have to do a bit better than the sprained ankle," said Richard. "This sort of thing's bound to be noticed."

"Man with wildly rolling eyes who chased a little girl so that she fell and sprained her ankle."

"Something along those lines. That might not be a bad approach, let's say, to a school head. I'll see to tighten that up with Raynal. We've got to account for the buzz of activity."

"And to account for me," said Castang.

"You can have the little van with post-office markings. And young Marcel with overalls."

"Tells everyone with eyes to see that the phones are being tapped."

"There's that. Surveyor—no, too fussy, and ties you down. I dislike these pretenses anyhow. Nothing at all—by far the best and most plausible. You are simply yourself, inquiring into a vague report of children being molested. Which makes a reasonable press release. I give you Marcel and a plain car. Park on the square, which is central. I'll know where to find you, and it's close enough to the house. Outside that, I leave it to you: I'll be along at lunchtime, but with any luck there'll be phone calls by then."

"We hope."

"How well do you know this couple?" suddenly.

"Very little, really. Mme. Delavigne is a friend of my wife's."

"That much I'd gathered."

"I've been in the house three or four times—you know, drinks, supper, and they've been to us maybe a bit more often, since, as you know, Vera doesn't like to go out much. We weren't ever very formal. Since the girls are pally, it doesn't mean much when she suddenly says 'Henri' instead of 'Monsieur'—no more than that when she's at home she likes to lay the 'Madame la Juge' business aside for a while."

"Yes, I see. And him?"

"Well, as you saw, he suffers a bit from a slight wish to compensate—she's a magistrate and he's a yogurt salesman, huh? He knows all about it and doesn't go about with it on his back. But he seeks little ways, naturally. So he reads a lot—novels, poetry, you know—and he buys modern pictures. Vera likes him a lot, says he has a good eye. And it comes out, as you may have noticed, in the slightly exaggerated devotion to the child: he's mad about her, and one understands why."

"He faithful to her?"

"I wouldn't know. He doesn't sleep with Vera," grinning.

"A drama around the child—it might be a trick of his?" gazing off into the distance through the windscreen.

"A tricky mind," said Castang carefully, "and some suppressed jealousy. But if it was a trick—the clever thing was to call me."

"Unless," carefully, "the trick would be to discredit you. Listen, Castang—don't be vexed. You've never caught yourself with your hand on her knee, by any chance?"

Castang laughed.

"You don't know Vera very well. And perhaps, with respect, come to that, you don't know me all that well. I can see, yes, given a certain set of circumstances, it would be thought clever, using the child to bring his wife back into line. Throwing total discredit upon her if he wanted—not to speak of me. Isn't it all, though, a bit too fancy?"

"Since you tell me it is, it is," said Richard mildly. "As long as we have taken the possibility into account. To guard against complacency. Just that kind of tricky fake has been attempted, and has perhaps been attempted by that sort of man. Let's both get some sleep while we can."

Castang rode home through the summer night that was tainted with gasoline fumes lingering under the heavy foliage of the chestnut trees. Belated cars were still whisking along the main road, and when they finally trickled to a stop it would be the turn of the big trucks rolling in all night to bring the town its supplies. Police eyes would be watching the markets and the abattoirs, the loading platforms and railway sidings, the rubbish dumps and scrap-metal yards, the garbage collections—and the cemeteries. Those for cars, as well as humans, and for the quite incredible amount of throwaways our wasteful generation amasses so cheerfully. A city this size: that is a lot of work. Sorting out the discards in a great mound of evil-smelling waste —it formed by far the greatest body of police work. Garbage miners we are, thought Castang cheerfully. And paper miners, naturally, in this delightful country where the written word is sacred and where so much ingenuity is devoted to writing everything down on as many different bits of paper as can be invented. Pauvre France! Salt is surely simpler!

Being "condemned to the salt mine" was a joke so old that one had long ago extracted and refined all the humorous remarks, surely, that could be made upon the subject. The tunnels were worn smooth, discolored and dulled by the extreme familiarity of daily usage. It took a sudden jolt of this sort to make one look again. A crime which was one of the few that still had the power to shock, to galvanize apathetic policemen who have seen too many of the grimy little oddities of human behavior. One slogged drearily away at the rock face with so little idea beyond "another cubic yard to shift before knocking-off time" that one had small concern for the beauty or originality of the crystals. Get them out, shove them on the conveyor belt, cart them up to the surface where they will be pounded and refined and weighed and numbered and packaged. One's dull, mole-like eye saw so little.

Suppose Richard had been right? Not, of course, where he, Castang, was concerned—assuming that a magistrate happening to be a brilliant and attractive young woman was to choose a playmate, she would hardly plump for a dim police official with his shabby respectability, his blunt, brutalized perceptions, his mean little ambitions and still meaner little cautions. Richard might say that stranger things had happened, but not to Castang they hadn't!

Colette—hmm, to be sure. He knew very little about her. But Vera knew a good deal, and Vera was a perceptive person who saw a great deal that his rigid, professionalized narrow tunnel of a mind could not grasp. Himself he had, he supposed, a certain virtue in that he tried to struggle against apathetic indifference, not just to accept the rock face and the pickaxe with brutish passivity. He did try to see things a scrap larger, to see the pattern and the meaning in it all. But Vera went further, for she was a light-bringer who illuminated what she looked at. She had shining, brightly burnished qualities. Virtues, one could call them. She was, for instance, the most utterly unselfish human being he had ever encountered.

They lived in a flat that was beyond their means, in a "good" bourgeois street near the town center, good because it was quiet, with poplar trees along the disused towpath of an abandoned canal whose grassy bank the municipality had been at some pains to tidy and embellish. Here they had a small second-floor residence in a tall, narrow nineteenth-century town house whose solid construction had resisted alteration well enough for it to be an awkward flat, but more soundproof than most. The tall, well-proportioned windows gave a nice view on the weedy old waterway: this had been of great value to Vera, itself alone worth the rent they had to pay.

Castang found her reading in bed. She did not always sit up to await his return—which would anyway have been unreasonable and nearly impossible—but she tried, and sometimes succeeded. She was pleased to see him. She put her book down and smiled brilliantly at the dusty, vaguely grumpy figure sitting heavily down to take its shoes off, unbuckle its gun belt, get rid of all the junk a cop carries around in his pockets. A tired cop taking his gun off is something like a middle-aged woman getting out of her girdle. He heaves a sigh, and scratches the tickle, and rubs his stomach with pleasure.

Patience was her foremost attribute. No, a stronger word was needed, but Castang had not found anything better than a Biblical old word standing for an early-Christian sort of virtue: fortitude. The young woman—she was only twenty-eight—had suffered a lot already in her life, and had been enriched by it instead of being impoverished. There was nothing sour or mean about Vera, and Castang, who saw a good deal of sourness and meanness in his everyday existence, was daily reminded of how lucky he was, and made little acts of thanksgiving.

She was not even really pretty. Exotic, to be sure, with a bell of fair hair over strongly marked Slav features. In certain lights remarkably, even startlingly beautiful. She had, too—or had formerly—a beautiful body with unusual harmony: her carriage was stiff now, her walk hesitant and limping. Up to a few months ago, indeed, she had not been able to walk. As a young girl, she had been a gymnast, full of promise, on the national team. After coming to France, she had helped train the girls of the local club until, one day, a neglect of precautions and an unlucky fall had

56

left her with damaged vertebrae. Traumatic paraplegia: she had been stuck in a wheelchair for two years. She had made herself walk again at last by sheer perseverance: courage allied to strength of character.

True, a gymnast is a disciplined person. She had, too, some talent for graphic art, having several strongly marked Czech characteristics besides her cheekbones. Drawing is also a severe discipline. Briefly, Vera since early childhood had learned more from life than just the satisfaction of animal needs.

It stood her in good stead as a cop's wife. She had no experience of love affairs, for Castang was the only man she had known, let alone run away with, slept with, or married. She was pursued by terrors when he was out at work in a job that she knew—and felt—to be at best harsh and ungrateful, at worst ignoble and treacherous, nearly always laborious and liable to become painful and dangerous without any warning. She was one of those persons—and they are fairly rare—whose vivid imagination magnifies pain and danger but who refuse to be cast down by quaking terrors and who meet their nightmares head-on.

To Castang, the unimaginative policeman, this called for a continual effort. He had perpetually to be on tiptoe to keep hold of Vera. He had learned occasionally to anticipate her, but more often to tag on behind, and to be humble without being humiliated. Some of her fortitude had rubbed off on him.

It had made him a useful tool in the hands of his superiors. He was, on the whole, a pretty fair policeman—scrupulous, observant, and patient. A somewhat bright lad who had had no trouble passing his baccalaureate (though it had taken a good deal of doggedness getting through law examinations), he had passed the police officers' entry examination enough above average to give him a fair start. But marrying a political refugee (who are always a nuisance to the constituted authorities) hadn't done him any good. He wasn't quite accommodating enough. In the salt mine, he shouldered his pickaxe sturdily, he did his work to the satisfaction of most, and he was preparing for his commissaire's examination and would probably pass it. If he wasn't unlucky, and if he watched where he put his feet, he had a good chance, seniority aiding, of finishing his career as a rather big fish in a middling pond. But he knew pretty well that he would never be anything but a centurion. It wasn't likely that he would ever be, like Richard, the chief of a criminal brigade in an important town, because otherwise he would have known enough not to marry Vera. To get out of the salt mine, and have a job on the surface, and walk around with the word "engineer" printed upon the plastic plaque clipped to your breast pocket, on a shirt that has no sweat stains, you need to be a bit of a politician.

But in his generally dismal tunnel he had discovered the branch which Stendhal speaks of in a famous metaphor: the bare branch which, left overnight in the salt mine, covers itself in glittering crystals and becomes an object of delight and amazement. The name of this branch was Vera.

She had slid down in bed, so that her face, framed in a crumpled pillow, was square and heavy, with a double chin over the book propped on her chest. She was studying him, as usual, while he went through the conventional movements of undressing and padding into the bathroom to brush his teeth. Saying nothing, as usual. She never did say anything very much. What on earth did she see? He was an ordinary-looking person.

"Anything you want to talk about?" she asked at last. Anything, that is to say, neither too boring nor too technical. She knew, after all, that he had been to see Bernard Delavigne, having been there when the phone rang: "Give them my love" she had said, the way one does. He got into bed, gave the pillow a whack to make it fluff up, and wound the alarm clock, setting it gloomily for four: pity the poor detective.

"What we hope won't be a horrible story with a bad ending —Rachel is missing."

"Oh, God!"

"Yes, right in the bowels. Nothing to tell you, though; I've got to be up at dawn, which is sort of early. Just the obvious checking-up so far, and the beginnings of a routine inquiry. I have to trot around the quarter at first light—see if there's any cigar ash or something. But we're pretty helpless, so far"—turning out the light—"until they get a phone call, which is what we pray for."

"So Colette lies waiting for a call."

"Bernard, too, poor bugger. Much less well equipped for waiting. You know how centered he is upon that child. It must torment one worse than any other crime. Not just the physical vulnerability of a child, but the breakdown in security and stability that a child needs so desperately."

In fact, Castang said none of this. Telling Vera this horrible tale at midnight—what was the good? She would simply lie awake all night living through it.

"Oh," grunting vaguely, "Bernard was in a flap about something at the office. Handy reference book, the Police Judiciaire, knowing its Penal Code by heart. Pick its brains in return for a drink or two. Hadn't asked you because 'the men had to talk business.' But Colette was asking for you. She's not very well, it seems, and is staying at home tomorrow, and if you could get over to cheer her up, she said, she'd be grateful."

"Um," said Vera vaguely. She could drive a car. An ordinary one was difficult because of the clutch, since her left leg was poor at obeying the orders given it, but an automatic gearbox solved that, and except in vile weather Castang took his bicycle to go to work. The "Um" was only a symbol in an equation involving washing machines, shopping—Vera hated supermarkets—and a half-finished drawing.

"I'd like to," she said. "I haven't seen her in a month."

Castang turned the light out. "Got to be up at the crack of dawn, damn it. A place Richard wants me to look at by early light, before there are a lot of people about."

"Why didn't you get back earlier?"

"You know what a gasbag Bernard is. Lot of fussy hospitality to excuse himself taking up one's time."

Vera was not hurt at not having been invited. She liked Bernard, but with a large dilution of indifference: she thought him a selfish person.

Richard's bright ideas, thought Castang vaguely. . . . Now if Bernard fancied Vera, and if I, thinking myself vastly cunning, chose to be a tiny bit complaisant, seeing that Colette is a Judge of Instruction, and a friend at court is a powerful aid to an ambitious cop . . . Bernard quietly takes the child and hides it out with some obscure granny. He need make no scenario, lay no elaborate false trail. All he has to do is say nothing, produce a convincing show of anguish—oh, yes, it could be done. It would be the work of a thoroughly sociopathic personality, but that was incidental. Having dug a pit into which several magistrates and the whole of the local police apparatus have tumbled, the mine can be exploded: you produce the child, explaining that you had removed it from moral contamination and staged this little comedy in order to demonstrate, beyond all possibility of hushing up the scandal, the iniquity of persons in public life unworthily holding positions of great trust and honor.

And if such a plot existed, thought Castang, pursuing the theory to its logical conclusion, the plotter wouldn't even risk very much. A sociopathic personality might be so far gone as not to count the consequences to himself, or to imagine that none existed. The laying of misleading information, outrage to magistrate, contempt of court. And who knew but that with a clever lawyer and in the enormous blaze of publicity, and the extreme discredit into which you had managed to put both police and judge, you could, he rather thought, expect to get away with a good deal by playing the role of the betrayed husband and devoted father protecting the family honor.

Who said I wasn't imaginative? thought Castang.

"Bernard drives himself too hard," said Vera sleepily. He realized with a start that this monstrous fantasy had taken about ten seconds. "All that business of keeping up with Colette and not being just a banal cheesemonger."

"Uh," said Castang, burrowing into his pillow to get comfortable.

"Sleep well." Vera's book, forgotten, fell on the floor with a crash as she turned over.

He tried to cut his alarm off in a split second so as not to wake her, getting out of bed quietly with no flump or flinging back of covers. But while he was shaving he heard the buzz of the coffee mill.

"I'm going to give you two eggs," said Vera, "or you'll be starving by eight."

"Why did you get up? I could easily pick up a crust of bread in a café."

"What a waste of money," disapprovingly, "and anyway why not get up? This way I can get my housework done and I might get over to see Colette, which I'd like to do. I'm simply profiting from the occasion. Are you likely to be back to lunch?"

"Very unlikely," with a face.

"What's this job you're on?" in a resigned tone.

"Suspected kidnapping."

"There are times," she said sadly, "one could almost wish for a clean homicide. And I stay here, doing the dusting."

Castang bicycled to the office, which took him ten minutes. All was quiet; the duty section was playing cards gloomily in the litter of last night's coffee cups. There had been no telephone calls during the night, no alerts, no fresh instructions. He got on to the municipal police.

"Commissaire Raynal—Castang at P.J. . . . Morning, sir, Castang here. I'm on my way to go over the ground on M. Richard's instructions—anything I ought to know? There's nothing on our teletype, but I thought I'd better check with you."

"We've had a real battering," said the voice, dried and wearied. "I've a coop full of identities to check, I've violent drunks, a boy on LSD, and three concealed weapons; I've also two affrays and an unlawful wounding, but I've nothing for you, I'm afraid—nothing whatever. The gendarmerie reports aren't in yet and there are several verifications to make. I'm summarizing any outstanding queries for the Proc and Richard at eight, and meanwhile—you're taking a radio car? Ask Lasalle to check with me around seven-thirty. But it's all negative as far as you're concerned."

Richard had been as good as his word: young Marcel appeared, yawning. "The garage gave me a 204; I've got it outside the door." The smallest-size Peugeot station wagon, dark green, no aerial, nothing whatever to distinguish it from ten thousand others.

The Avenue Mozart had been a cart track ten years ago. The main road south from the town led through a valley, linking a row of villages two to three kilometers apart; anyone in the district over the age of forty could recall when they really had been villages, little rustic dorps full of farmyards and dunghills, with a rustic bus to the town once every two hours. Now they were suburbs, with a suburban service every twenty minutes. The main road was linked the whole way by the parking lots of industry and the forecourts of filling stations into one continuous ribbon of concrete, and even the hinterland of fields was filling up steadily with housing estates, so that the still obstinately resisting strips of wheat or maize or vegetables were bordered with ungainly little heaps of broken roof tiles and sodden cement bags left by builders, and the dusty cabbages would have a fine full nutty flavor of car exhaust. The Delavigne "quarter" had acquired its standing from being situated on the brow of a hill which even Castang could remember covered with vines. The wine had not been of good quality, but the ground had sold for a good price because it provided fresh air and a view. Here and there, a few ragged patches of vines still stood, hemmed in by walls, in little orchards with some rank grass around the edge and perhaps a cherry or a walnut tree too old to bear fruit, where an obstinate old farmer or two had refused to sell.

The Avenue Mozart, lined with immature plane trees, climbed the hill in a gentle oblique slope, leaving the main road a couple of hundred yards before one reached the old village center, where the original country "mairie" still stood next to the fire station and the old nineteenth-century school. On a wall of the school one could see the faded paint saying, "École des Filles"; the building now contained the overflow of suburban bureaucracy: housing office, labor exchange, and social security bureau. The old village fountain still stood—kept because it was "picturesque"—where horses used to drink under a group of fine lime trees, on a square now asphalted and car-parked and surrounded by stunted-looking acacias that gave no proper shade in fine weather.

Castang and Marcel were early enough for the square to be empty, and Marcel parked close in under a real tree that would give them shade: it was going to be another hot day and the later arrivals would find that by lunchtime their little tin perambulators had become scorching sweatboxes reeking of hot metal and cooked plastic upholstery.

Castang looked around. The working day was about to begin, for even suburbanized "country" is earlier in its habits than the town and most of the men had a trip of nearly half an hour to get to work. The shopkeepers were opening their shutters and sweeping their stoops; smells of coffee and bread were drifting across the square; the tobacconist was taking his pile of morning newspapers inside and children were scuttling to the baker; the grocer flung out a garbage can full of yellowed rot with a crash and prepared to throw buckets of water over his wooden stall before winding out the faded blue awnings. At the corner, the café owner of the Belle Étoile was grinding up his metal shutters to proclaim with a noisy advertisement that the driver of the van now unloading meat in front of the butcher's could come and join the two overalled characters who were intending to have a quiet beer before beginning on the garbage-collection round.

"I've had no breakfast yet," said Marcel meaningly.

Stupid boy, thought Castang, glowing in the possession of an admirable wife.

"Five minutes, then, and no more. And pay for it yourself. Get me a paper first." He looked about him, stretching his shoulders in the pale morning sunshine. Yes, there was the new school, a few-score paces down the road on the valley side: the usual low block of wide windows with an asphalt playground in front and an ambitious tulip tree in the middle. From the hillside, the children would come down that little alleyway onto the square, crossing the road here where the two-way traffic was split and slowed, with a cop controlling the crossing at the four daily rush hours. The alleyway led up the hill, here steep and crowded with the older buildings of the original village. One could not see the roofs of the tall blocks of the Avenue Mozart on the brow of the hill from this sharply foreshortened viewpoint, and there were several paths which turned and twisted across the steep hill face. That, certainly, would be the place for him to start.

Marcel was coming back with a paper; he handed it to Castang and bolted for the Belle Étoile. Castang leaned against the car radiator and unfolded it. The outside of it smelled already of sun and dust: the inner pages clung together in a moist, pleasant smell of newsprint that smudged his fingertips.

There was only a small article:

Police last night were alerted by the news of a child missing in an outlying residential quarter of our town. It was at first uncertain whether the child, described as being under ten years of age, might not have wandered off at play while on the way home from school, or have met with some accident in the street or elsewhere. Later in the evening, however, a report that the child had met with an aggressor was contradicted at police headquarters. "We know of no aggressor," our reporter was told by authorities. "We are making routine verifications of a variety of rumors. These alarms are generally the result of a misunderstanding. We have no reason to suppose the existence of any criminal occurrence. We are, however, looking into an unsubstantiated report of a hit-and-run accident."

The name and address of the child concerned has been withheld, under the rule that publication could only cause additional anguish and disquiet to the relatives and would not be in the child's interest. To our reporter's query whether this ruling did not give rise to belief in a criminal attempt, Commissaire Raynal, in charge of the unusual activity at regional police headquarters, replied that this was at present an unjustifiable assumption. "It is far more probable that as a result of some misunderstanding a momentary confusion exists; I have no more to say about the matter."

At the time of going to press, no further news had been received. We understand, however, that the inquiry has been enlarged to include the districts outside the city boundary.

No mention of those gallant officers of the P.J. . . . .

"I'll last for a bit now," said Marcel, chewing noisily in his ear. "Where do we start?"

"Right here," tapping the radio set.

"Bloody hell. All day?"

"There'll be intervals," dryly. "We don't know much about this operation, but if we can intervene at all it has to be rapid. Richard has to know where we are, and we have to be able to transmit or receive a message with no loss of time. You can raise me on the clicker," pointing to the fountain-pen receiver in his breast pocket, the little gadget that tells a department-store manager, or an engineer on a site, or a patrolling policeman that he is "wanted in the office."

"Richard's carrying one, too," Castang said. He picked up the handset and pressed the transmitter button. "Castang here; getting me all right? . . . Good. I'm on the ground. Message for

Richard: we're parked on the old marketplace, by the fountain. Proceeding. Message ends. Put me through to Johnny. . . . Hallo, old son; sleep well? . . . Yes, but not enough. . . . No messages? Nothing whatever? . . . Nothing here, either. I've checked with Raynal—negative all round. You'll be hearing from him on the landline, no doubt. . . . Yes; yes. I know her enough to know she makes a good cup of coffee. Give her the usual consolations; tell her I'm here. I won't be in there during the course of the morning, unless of course things get hot, but you could say to her that my wife will be along later. She'll understand. Say to Monsieur that nothing prevents him going to work as usual, and of course an approach might be made to him in the office, and to string along, naturally, with any demands made. I'll be in to see him at lunchtime, and so will Richard, no doubt of it. Luigi will be along to relieve you as soon as he gets in.

"That's it; anything to query? Leave it at that, then. Bye."

"Where do the parents live?" asked Marcel.

"Up the hill here."

"Must be pretty rich. There'll be a ransom demand, wouldn't you think?"

"Maybe," said Castang briefly. "But then why hasn't there been one already?"

He walked up the hill. One had no idea of the route of the Avenue Mozart from down here, but the Résidence Dampierre was at the brow of the hill, so he took the steepest line. He supposed it was natural to think in terms of a ransom. Between them, Bernard and Colette made a lot of money, and the exterior signs of this prosperity were not lacking: the Dampierre itself, a snobbish building whose front was faced with dressed stone; Bernard's flashy white Citroën; Colette's equally noticeable yellow Alfa. Suppose one assumed nothing more than a gang—for there were generally two or three bright sparks in this kind of act—of the most ordinary, straightforwardly greedy little bandits. And that was a perfectly reasonable assumption.

No idea whatever of vengeance or hatred, but plain naked extortion.

It made a very simple pattern. They might have no notion whatever that Colette was a judge: what interest would her work hold as long as she brought home the money—handbags full of it? They would have looked for nothing more than a rich young couple with one child. Looking up Bernard in the phone book, perhaps following him to work—but concentrating on no more than a crude snatch followed by an equally crude stand-and-deliver. But—he had just answered this himself—why, in that case, hang about?

The bank, of course. They wouldn't phone the night before, giving everybody time to get organized and make a plan. By leaving an uncertainty, they could perhaps hope that the P. J. were not even in the act, and that nothing had been done beyond the sort of vague search described in the morning paper. So they'd wait till Bernard was at his office, and then make one brief call, giving him as little time as possible to set any countermeasure afoot. "Go straight to the bank"—it would not be difficult to find out which bank in advance. "Go straight from the bank to the Prisunic next door. Carry the money in notes in a paper shopping bag, holding it loosely by your side. Walk slowly past the counters, stopping to look at them. That's all."

It could very easily work, thought Castang grimly. Bandits now—even the crudest, the most amateur, the most juvenile— knew enough not to propose the drop-off on the lonely road, the brown suitcase hidden in the long grass behind the milestone. It was far too easy for the police—first to be staked out waiting for the pickup, and second to have the famous suitcase stuffed with old newspapers. The Prisunic would be how I'd work it, thought Castang. Plenty of entrances—too many to cover at short notice. At, say, nine in the morning, enough people to create uncertainty and confusion, but not enough to block all dodging or to jam the passageways and exits. Three people needed. One to snatch the bag and stuff it quickly into a plastic carrier such as fifty others were carrying at any given moment, then pass it quickly to number two and melt like lightning into the crowd: very little risk if one wore inconspicuous clothes. Number two walks quite slowly, attracting no attention. Meanwhile number three, by some simple maneuver—like suddenly screaming "Pickpocket!" or "Stop thief!" or spilling a lot of small coins on the floor—distracts everyone. And by the time the confusion is sorted out, all three can have easily melted away and joined up at an inconspicuous car in the parking lot opposite.

The child is now nothing but an embarrassment and must be got rid of. It has been kept, probably doped with sleeping pills, in a flat or studio in the town. It is bundled into the car, driven out here to the village, set suddenly on its feet on a corner, and will simply wander dazedly toward home with no thought of raising an alarm. That would not enter its head; to find Mama would be the notion that would crowd out every other. It would not have been harmed or ill-treated (the one bright spot in this whole unpleasant scenario): why should it? These were not sadists, deranged psychopaths. Money was the one thing that interested them.

The child cannot even give an adequate description at that age. It had had a sack put over its head. Later, perhaps, a young woman will be recalled who gave it ice cream and had dark hair and was wearing jeans; and a young man with long curly hair. It got given a cup of cocoa and fell asleep. What more in her bewilderment could a little girl of eight have to tell? It was only in books that kidnappers had a handy stammer or a gold tooth, and a flat with a large colored oleograph of President Kennedy, or the Pope, or Marilyn Monroe on the wall. Or, hell: what would a child of that age be certain of recognizing which did not exist in ten thousand dumps? "There was a lamp with a pink shade, and a television set, and a packet of corn flakes on the table, and the man smoked Marlboro cigarettes, like Uncle Fred."

With a very slight but sudden shock, Castang found himself standing on the Avenue Mozart. And there was the Dampierre fifty yards away across the road. By the simple expedient of following the steepest line, he had retraced the path that Rachel followed every day four times, on her way to and from school. Running downhill, it would not be much over five minutes. Ten if the policeman down on the square held the crossers up to let the traffic get a bit decongested. Going back uphill—ten minimum. Fifteen if one took things easy. A child, dawdling on its way home, maybe twenty. But it was not quite that simple. There was no neat, direct, hollowed-out watercourse. (A child, like water, flows along the line of least resistance.) Rather had the water been split into twenty miserable underground rivulets by the inequality of the terrain and the vagaries of inheritance laws, and trickled downhill now fast, now slow, drop by drop, before collecting again into two or three little brooks on the square below, where the main road flowed along the valley and where still farther a little river, hopelessly abased now and polluted, wandered with uncertain steps down into the town to join the big river, its ancient pastoral loops crossed and recrossed by the railway line. . . .

There had been water flowing down. Probably still was. Rusty pumps stood in the corners of overgrown gardens: outside one or two of the oldest houses stood worn old stone wash tanks with the water siphoned up a pipe and lipping over the slimy greenish edge into a storm drain. But there was no direct path. The child, at three different points, could have taken two or even three ways. At the bottom, where the hill was steepest, lay a thickly caked mass of old village houses from the seventeenth century, encrusted along the edge of the square and up the slope, solidly built upon their deeply dug cellars in heavy blind gray stonework. There were four narrow alleys leading up the hill, more or less parallel, wide enough—just—for a car to pass, so that they were all one-way streets, two up and two down. There was a double—even triple—line of unchanged old houses with high-walled narrow gardens and steep-pitched cobbled yards and outbuildings, with the dark dank little streets going up more or less straight between, three roughly modernized in much-patched irregular macadam with tall weeds growing at the corners, one still the slippery uneven cobbles of the early-nineteenth century.

But a hundred yards up the slope a newer road, cut perhaps fifty years ago, crossed obliquely.

This road, the Rampe Notre-Dame, crowned the steepest part of the slope, and had been discovered back around 1930 by townspeople who wished to invest in a little country air, and in what had been then a pretty countrified view, for "pavilions" —pretentious tiny villas with tiny gardens—clung like leeches on both sides of the stony outcrop which farmers had sold off cheap as too awkward to be of much use.

The slope grew easier above this, for which Castang, a bit puffed, was grateful. But the pathway was still crooked, making three corners in as many minutes to skirt what had been little patches of vines, until it popped out, surprising one, upon the bland concrete modernity of the Avenue Mozart, engineered in a long gentle slant back toward the town.

Having completed his topography, he began to work slowly down again with an eye to the details. From the boulevard down to the top of the ramp was patchwork. The building speculators, since this ground had become so valuable, had had to wait for obstinate old peasants to die before wedging ever more expensive constructions into ever smaller and more awkward scraps of wasteland. Even now, they were having to wait for a few minutely morseled and parceled corners of nettle or thistle where some avaricious old biddy, aware she was sitting on a gold mine, was holding out for a better offer—or wasn't having a high wall run up a bare two yards from her own window. . . . Castang had stopped because he had found a likely-looking spot. A piece of old gray house wall, blinded by peeling old gray shutters, looked up and across to a three-cornered bit between two new constructions—and one only a shell, left apparently half finished and seeming abandoned, as though the builder had run out of finance. The corner was no more than a rubbish tip, with rank grass growing round a pile of drainpipes, littered with torn remnants of cement sacks and old cigarette packets. Cars had stopped and parked here. Recently? It was hard to tell on this uneven ground, dry and baked by a week of sunny June weather. Lovers—or fornicators, rather— he thought distastefully noticing a discarded contraceptive. And children have played here, too.

Had the trap been here? There were few passersby, where it was too awkward for all but the residents' cars, too steep for all but a determined pedestrian. In midafternoon there could easily be a blank of ten or fifteen minutes' silence and solitude. A child, meandering slowly back from school, could—yes, it was certainly possible—be snatched here and perhaps quickly anesthetized behind those drainpipes. A rag soaked in ether, which was simply bought in any "droguerie." An involuntary shudder at the sickly asphyxiation of it; the foul smell—until, of course, one has had to do with a disintegrating, desiccating, very dead human being.

A sharp grating creak made Castang turn his head. A shutter had opened. Sunlight pierced the gray barrier, but all it showed was a gray old woman, framed in faded grayish wallpaper and surrounded by fusty grayed bolsters. A biddy airing her stuffy bedchamber for the permissible ten minutes before shutting out all air and light for another regulation twenty-four hours. The biddy regarded him with suspicion.

"Good morning," said Castang sunnily. "Your ground?"

She cackled, snaggletoothed. "Not for sale, young man. And you ain't the first. There's many would like to get their hand on that." It was exactly as he had thought. An old peasant woman still saving candle ends, although her declining years were nicely featherbedded by the judicious sale of corners that had just been good enough to grow a few artichokes to feed to the pig.

"Police," he said politely. "Have you perhaps seen anyone hanging around who had no business here?"

"Ah. They was there last night, poking around with a torch. I seen un."

"Who?"

"More police. They come up the hill with a car—and how come you don't know that?"

"Plainclothes," flashing his badge. "That was the uniformed branch. We had a complaint," casually.

"Complaint of what?"

"Oh, a lady had her handbag snatched. You've seen no vagabond or something similar hanging about yesterday afternoon?"

"I lives round the other side," regretfully. "I only see here at night. Think nobody sees them. I watches them," with relish.

"Who?"

"Fuckers," she said with even more relish. "The builders parks their cars there. But they're gone. Got no money," enjoyably.

"Yesterday afternoon," he offered loosely. "A lady on foot. Say midafternoon, around the time the children get home."

"The children," spitefully. "Brats! I ain't seen," regretfully.

Castang saw that it was the truth. The biddy lived in the front, facing downhill. Except for her spyglass on the fornicators, she had no interest. She might have yelled at children, who would have catcalled bad names. Unable to chase them, she would have abandoned the fight, secure behind the blind wall.

"Rich women," happily, with a glance of hatred up the hill at the bland white blocks whose roofs showed. "They don't pass here much. Too lazy. Easier to take the car round. Serve her right," with gleeful spite. "Putting the prices up."

"I'm much obliged."

"Wouldn't go taking that trouble if it was me, would you, now? But I'm only a poor old woman living alone," inviting pity —anyone's, even his. "Can't even manage the vegetable garden no more."

"I've no doubt you manage," said Castang blandly. Toothless old rattlesnake! She gave him a glance of vicious joy.

"Cops!" she said with disdain, and closed the shutter. She had seen nothing. If she had, she'd have been all over him. Disappointed, Castang moved away downhill. Before he left, he went over to examine the gray wall. Scratched with a sharp stone, in a child's writing, was the legend "Élise is an old bag." He agreed.

Nothing more, down to the bottom of the ramp; nothing but bare roadway and corners overlooked by windows whose grimy net curtains would twitch at the slightest movement. Plenty more women, old and young, hoping it was the bailiff come to repossess the neighbors' television, but interested even if it was only the South-Western Gas Board.

But where the ramp gave way to a fork of two old alleyways down to the village there was something more interesting, which he hadn't seen on the way up because the entrance had not only been to his back but masked by a retreating angle. The courtyard of an old farm; hadn't been worked for twenty years or more. The valley land had been given over when the farmer's grown children had decided that industry paid more, as well as being easier: the vines on the hill slope had been neglected even before the ground of the Avenue Mozart had been acquired cheap, and a discouraged, embittered farmer had been glad to take his profit and retire to somewhere deeper in the country, where he perhaps had relatives. For this yard and the buildings lining it had long been dead. The wooden shutter of the hayloft yawned drunkenly on one rotted hinge. Some shopkeeper in the plumbing trade used the shed as an entrepôt for materials he had no room for: a bath and a couple of toilet blocks stood under the decaying roof, with their protective tape still adhering. A heavily chained and padlocked stable door showed where copper piping and taps—the stuff easier to pinch —was secured, and on the decrepit yard gate was a notice, half rust and half chipped enamel, saying, "Paul Entreprises Sanitaires. In case of absence apply at shop." No chickens had scratched the grass-grown cobbles of this yard for a long time. The shutters of the farmhouse itself were never opened, as could be seen from cobwebs. But someone still lived there, for the lock of the door was kept oiled and there were fresh scratches on the weathered wood.

There was room to drive a car in and park it unnoticed. People did, because there were patches of oil. That would be the usual beat-up Citroën van belonging to Entreprises Paul, plainly the sort of plumber who, when called on the phone by anguished housewives with a leak, always says he'll come and turns up six weeks later—if at all.

Castang was interested. Nobody overlooked this yard. On one side the Rampe Notre Dame stretched dustily, its protective revetment seven or eight yards high and topped with grimy bushes. On the other was an awkward house, built tall and narrow for bygone days of cheap servants, with a "For Sale" notice that had been there two years, at least, because the owner was greedily holding out for too much money. The yard was nowhere overlooked, except perhaps by some ghost like Miss Havisham in *Great Expectations.*

Examining the ground, Castang found confirmation of an old widow or someone clinging on still in the farmhouse. A fresh rabbit dropping lodged between two cobbles. And two more, under a decidedly shop-soiled bidet dumped barely clear of a leaky drainpipe. No rabbit hutches and no sign of hay. Some antique biddy even more decrepit than Élise, who probably lived in one room, along with the rabbits for company. But it was another likely bit of ground—better, in fact, than the other. Nobody opened a window to ask what he wanted, and when he

knocked on the door nobody answered. Hmm. Castang walked
slowly down the alley and back to the car. Marcel was in his shirt
sleeves doing a crossword. There had been no calls and no
messages. The sun was already hot.

"My turn for a quick visit to the pub," said Castang. But he
did not aim for the big café in the square, its bright star now
attracting a dozen customers, but for a decrepit little pub on the
shady side, between the two alleyways, with a forlorn look of
having given up trying. "The Café de la Liberté," Castang read,
with a faint twitch of the nose. Hands in pockets, looking like
a loitering stableboy, he strolled over to the Liberty Bar.

Just as he thought: a place that had given up trying. Nobody
came here but a few old villagers who gathered to shut out the
twentieth century and wrap themselves in the musty curtains
of the old days. A poky little café with half a dozen worn tables
covered in smelly unchanged cloths, an old zinc counter, the
legally obligatory rack of lemonades and syrups that nobody
touched, and some dusty apéritifs made by firms that had gone
out of business in 1950. The old man who came shuffling out to
serve him was deaf, though a sharp look seemed to say that he
pretended to be deafer than he was.

"A white wine," said Castang.

"Glass or chopine?"

"Chopine." The jug was of a pretty old pattern. Even the
glass was more shapely and fragile than "modern" pubs supply.
There was one customer. Castang carried his supplies over to
this table, because the customer was looking at him with a
remarkably spry eye. The funny thing was that he was no peasant. A bourgeois but one from a bygone age. He wore a Panama
straw hat of peculiar shape, like Monsieur Brun in the Marius
pictures, and a kind of tropical suit whose cream color had

darkened to that of old Camembert cheese. Perhaps he lived alone, because he had been breakfasting: a large coffee cup stood amidst the crumbs of a croissant. A little glass brimming with some colorless alcohol stood untouched before him. He did not look dilapidated or drunken: he was washed and shaven. He could be anything from sixty-five to eighty. He had the perfect immobility of all old men who sit long hours in cafés.

"You don't mind?" asked Castang politely.

"Not at all; like company." The lips hardly moved but the voice was as spry as the eyes. "Passing through?"

"In a sense."

"Not selling anything."

"How do you know?" amused, and pleased, because if this old boy liked playing detective he had come to the right shop.

"Bigger café over the road. More animated. More commerce . . . Cleaner, too," as an afterthought. "Dirty old man, that," with a glance at the bar. "His white wine's more honest, though. No, thanks, I don't smoke—no, I don't drink." Dry cackle. "This here is my kicker. Lasts me till sundown."

"Algiers—or Saigon?"

"Hanoi. You want me to talk, I'll talk. But you aren't interested in Hanoi. You're a cop."

"Right, but where does it show?"

"I've seen more. What are you interested in?"

"This old part of the village, going up the hillside."

"What's happened there?"

"Oh, a woman from up on the boulevard going down to the shops—had her bag snatched."

The old man chuckled. "You'll have to do better than that. You're senior—it shows. Handbag! Not even the boys in blue would stir off their arse for that. Not the child that was attacked, by any chance?"

"Shrewd."

"Not shrewd, and stop trying to flatter. Just experienced. Been a civil servant"—tasting his drink—"a long time."

A shrill yell echoed in the alley. Feet pattered outside the grimy window. The children were going to school.

"You don't notice them, sitting here every morning?"

"Why would I notice them? My son was killed at Cao Bang. My daughter lives in Narbonne, doesn't want to know me. I've no interest in children."

"Who still lives in the farm at the top of the road?"

"Old Léon. Crazy old bastard. Wouldn't attack a child, though; not crazy that way."

"Crazy what way?"

"Got a lawsuit going against the mayor for over twenty years. Bloodthirsty old bastard, too. Sleeps with his shotgun. Lets it off at anything that moves." There was a sudden gush of nostalgia. "When I was a boy here, the hill was full of birds. Nothing now —sterile. Léon shot them all. The boys in blue are terrified of him. Come to deliver a summons, get a charge of number five in the seat of their pants."

"No rabbits left?"

"Here?" with incredulity.

"Tame ones, maybe? The old villagers keep them. Like old Élise."

"Élise? You've been getting around. Poisonous old cow. The rabbit would bite her, and die of it. What's this obsession with rabbits?"

"Just wondered. The old villagers do keep them. I thought I saw one."

"Remarkable. Wouldn't let them out. Too many cars—too many boys."

"Old Léon there all the time?"

"Never there at all. Spends his days at the tribunal, presenting petitions to get the Minister of Justice impeached. Or at lawyers' offices. Or at the notary's, changing his will."

Vera would like that. A French version of Dickens's Miss Flite, a figure from Balzac. But it didn't sound helpful, except that he was "never there."

77

"You know all the old villagers."

"Not many left now. But they come here, yes. You mean I hear all the gossip? Would know if anyone was liable to attack a child or such? No, I wouldn't. I'd know if anybody's seen or heard something, yes, and I have to disappoint you. And I spend time in the other café, too," dryly, "so don't waste yours there. But if there's somebody mental floating about—no, I wouldn't know. Nor would you. Because I've been a civil servant all my life, and I've never seen anything to lead me to believe the human race is worth a snap of the fingers." He drank off his "kicker."

"Let the bomb fall, my boy; let the bomb fall," he said.

"I've given you another confidence to keep to yourself," said Castang, finishing his wine.

"It's safe. But let me tell you—you're in the wrong job. Look at me. What do you think my pension's worth? Where would I be, hey?—if I hadn't taken a hell of a lot of bribes. And those mostly invested in stuff that's worthless now. If I hadn't had the fortune to have a bit in Shell, where would I be now? What's a child more or less? I've seen so many die."

"A man has to have something to hold to. Otherwise he'd never be able to hang on. One has to persevere."

"For the good of the state?"

"No, for oneself. Not to give in. What good is it, otherwise, to be a man?"

"You're a goddy. Say the rosary, ring the Angelus at twelve. Like the white fathers in Hanoi. A salvationist, heaven help you."

"What else is there—once you no longer believe in humans?" Castang banged on the counter, brought the old shuffly man out, got separated from a couple of francs. What did that poor old sod believe in, then? That it "would last his time"? It never has. That's why we cling to the memory of our youth, when the army knew how to fight and even the footballers gave all they had. Now they just think of the press conference they'll give after the fight. But he believes in keeping his wine honest, because that's all he's got. I'm much the same."

"Think forward, my boy," said the old colonial hand, sitting there chuckling over his empty glass and his empty coffee cup. "Think forward to when you're my age."

Castang smiled, but went out angry.

A depression. He stood in the sunlight, and shook it off. He went back up the hill. The bare sunny yard and the abandoned sanitary appliances grinned at him like old discolored bones, or the teeth of a retired civil servant. The blind shutters of Léon's house disquieted him now that he could picture an old red-eyed little man, hopping about like a rabbit, aimlessly, scribbling away by the light of a paraffin lamp—because the electricity had been cut off—at a long memorandum concerning procedural faults during a hearing in the Court of Civil Appeals.

Now, look, put a stop to that.

Weren't there any young women in this God-forgotten neighborhood?

He ran one to earth, finally, in one of the gimcrack modern blocks near the top, her absurd tiny balcony full of children's underclothes on wash lines. Worm's-eye view. But it gave a steer to another worm.

Again a depressing performance, because a young, active, pretty woman with three small children, who kept her "on the trot, I can tell you," was only pleased to have someone to grumble to. "Handbag snatched? They'd be welcome to mine; there's never anything in it. Those bloody shops down there, they'd pinch the salt out of your cabbage. Walk down? Yes, and up, too, dragging the shopping in a basket. I've never seen anything. Oh, yes, I know Élise—complains all the time about the children. Old Léon? No, never laid eyes on him. I know that old farmyard but I've never noticed it particularly. I don't know anyone round here. The villagers—of course not. Interested in nothing but money. The rich women on the boulevard? So stuck-up they wouldn't give you the time of day. I'm from the town. Thought it would be nice out here, healthier for the children. But these flats are far too small. And expensive—one does nothing but run after the payments. The school? It's all right, I suppose. Modern, and that. They think up a lot of stuff to occupy the little ones, but the children do no work; it's not like when we were at school. But at least it's quiet here. The bigger children are all these motorbike maniacs—you'd never believe it, even the girls. They roar up and down the boulevard. Don't come up the alley much. Safe? Where is safe now? But no, I've never known anything bad, not yet—no, no dirty old loonies talking to the children or showing themselves, and if there was I'd soon settle his hash, I can tell you. We don't go out at night; where is there to go to? The television, not that it's any bloody use. I'd like to go out, but the man comes back dead tired from work, and one can't afford it, anyway, and who's to look after the children? God knows why we do it; it's a thankless existence. But oh, well, that's the way of the world. Do your job, hope for something better sometime, even if sometime's never. Next year—there's always a next year. Isn't that what the Jews say? On their big feast, don't they drink to 'next year in Jerusalem'? And never losing faith all those years. What'll we drink to, hey?"

"Thanks, not in working hours," said Castang austerely, making a getaway, since plainly this good woman was convinced that he had just dropped in to cheer her up.

He worked his way back downhill again. None of the variations in the route—leading, for example, to "Jackie's house" a little farther down the avenue—showed any possibility of ambush. Anyway, on all the evidence, Rachel had been alone and had not accompanied Jackie's gang. There were those two nooks he had found. For there must have been a car, and there must have been a good deal of hanging about. Perhaps several days had been needed before a moment came when Rachel, even making four trips a day, had passed alone and out of sight and earshot of another child or a casually passing adult. And in the morning, both early and just before midday, there were workmen passing, housewives shopping, windows open everywhere to air bedclothes and shake out dusters. Whereas on a hot, sleepy midafternoon . . .

Back down in the village, the Enterprises Paul were easily found, and a noisy clattering woman in a shop full of ironmongery handed him over to a vague, grayed man, like an old badger, in his workshop, with a perpetually ragged cigarette burning wispily under a ragged gray mustache and his glasses pushed up on his forehead, giving him a perplexed look, as though he could never quite remember what job it was he was supposed to be doing. Castang felt he now knew all there was to know about Mr. Paul.

"Look, I'm a police officer; I just dropped in. We've had some trouble up the hill over the other side: a woman had a bag snatched, and some vague reports of vagabonds hanging about. Now I notice you've got materials stored there in a pretty casual way. Gate all rotted, no proper lock—you ever had any trouble up there? Clochards sleeping there or anything?"

Mr. Paul, from long practice with his frustrated customers, was vague and evasive about everything. Well, yes, they did have some stuff up there but it was mostly junk. A few baths and such were padlocked in the shed. He didn't go up there much —maybe once a week. At night it was as safe as the bank. Old Léon was opposite: it was well known he never slept, but prowled about with his gun looking for rats or whatnot: the old fool would shoot at anything that moved. And who'd go in by day to pinch an old bidet? People did park vans or cars there sometimes, because there was no room on the road below and no parking allowed on the ramp. Rabbits? Nobody up there had rabbits. He had some himself, but not up there. Down here. Did the police think he kept rabbits in his pocket or something?

After this long speech, Mr. Paul rubbed his scratchy jaw with a greasy hand, degreased himself casually with a handful of plumbers' hemp, deftly relit his cigarette off the blowtorch, refreshed himself with a glass of red wine, and indicated that the interview was at an end and the police would do better to go out and catch a few criminals instead of wasting all this time. Castang retired sullenly.

But before going back to his base he trudged up the alley and went again over the ground carefully. The dry ground and uneven cobbles told him nothing. There was still nobody around. Nobody took the faintest interest when he picked up four or five rabbit droppings and put them in an envelope. He didn't know what the technical squad would have to say, but they could tell him, he thought, whether the droppings were, as he suspected, yesterday's. Which might be interesting. And at least it was a proof that there *had* been a rabbit, and he hadn't just dreamed it.

There was no rabbit now.

He went back to the car and sent Marcel for a cup of coffee and a pee. He had a little talk with the office. Richard had gone to the Palais for a conference with legal and police nignogs. Nothing had happened and there was no news. Luigi had taken over the phone stake-out from Johnny. Luigi reported that he was quite happy, with several paperback thrillers Mme. Delavigne had lent him. Yes, she did make a good cup of coffee. She was very white and peaky and had hardly slept, but she was quite calm and controlled. She hadn't been out at all. When he had gone to the bathroom, he had heard women's voices—a lady had come to call, which was good—stopped Madame roaming nervously around. M. Delavigne had looked like death warmed up, so Johnny said, but had gone to the office at the usual time, saying he would pretend he had a dose of flu, which looked convincing. He had phoned to say that the office was perfectly normal, and—in guarded terms—that the mail was in and contained nothing interesting. No office phone calls, either. He was, Luigi thought, putting on a pretty good show. Yes, it was odd that there'd been no news at all. Because everything was now pointing to a criminal attempt and a ransom demand. Perhaps the bandits were waiting to let everyone work up a real sweat and then put in a snap demand at rush hour, just before the banks closed, when checking cars would be twice as difficult.

"Hold your line; there's a call now," Luigi said.

Castang nearly bit his cigarette in two, but the voice, sounding decidedly like Hamlet's father through several electronic relays, was only Richard's. Everything was in order, there were no problems; he would be over at lunchtime, tell Castang, for a bit of a progress report, and here was the Procureur de la République, who would like to have a word with Mme. Delavigne, and since this was a personal word he would be obliged if Luigi would momentarily switch out the relay until the little *ting* told him that the private conversations were over; thank you.

Castang put the handset down, smoked his cigarette out, waited until Marcel was back; he was thinking about rabbits. He strolled across the square, busy now with midmorning activity, and down the fifty yards of side street to the primary Groupe Scolaire—from three-year-olds in the crèche for working mothers to the ten- to eleven-year-olds who next term would be moving across to the secondary school along the road, at the bottom of the Avenue Mozart. The midmorning break was in full swing: already on the square Castang could hear the thin shrill shrieking of playing children, one of the most attractive sounds on earth. As usual, it dug into him. Vera, Vera, why have we no children? Even when she was half paralyzed, and against her doctor's head-shakings, she had refused utterly to "take precautions." But she'd been trying well before that time, too.

Madame la Directrice was in her office and would be glad to see him, said the concierge. Up the passage, third on the right.

She stood up politely to meet him: a thin, pale, slightly faded blonde of fifty in an almond-green jersey, two-piece. Smart, bright, gentle, beautifully balanced: a perfect honey. Time for him, too, to meet a honey: the world, so far this morning, had been sufficiently cranky. What a joy to meet this delightful, nice-smelling woman who understood everything before any laborious explanations, and made brief, sensible remarks.

"Of course I know Mme. Delavigne, though I only know her from a couple of meetings: Rachel is a child who gives no trouble. A good judge—if I'm any judge of judges! Naturally, we share the same interests. We've had no professional contact. I have some backward or deprived or difficult children, as who hasn't, but so far we've managed to handle our little delinquency problems without recourse to the courts! A melting pot like all large schools, and since we have the old village with the modern suburb imposed upon it we're bound to have a few rough edges arising from the different backgrounds. On the whole, we're very fortunate. The district is wealthy, the mayor is reasonable—I've had his two daughters, and they're both at the secondary now—and we have the added fortune that this is a pilot school approved by the Ministry, so that we've two nursery classes in foreign languages, an English and a Spanish, and we're proud of them.

"Rachel—I know her fairly well. She's a withdrawn child, with a good moderate intelligence, no very great imaginative projection, well coordinated and well integrated. She plays, soberly and a bit stodgily, with the gang—oh, yes, I know all about the awful Jackie; she's a useful brake upon his wilder fantasies. She's very shy and has nice old-fashioned manners, curtsies like a little German girl. Quite plain, and no extravagant vanities. Rather too fussy and meticulous, perhaps a little too much cotton-wooled by her father, but on the whole robust and self-reliant. Certainly not the child to wander off irresponsibly or fall for any crude offers of lollipops. . . . I quite agree with you: if there was any trap, it would need to be skillful.

"No, we've had no trouble of that sort. We take no responsibility, of course, outside our gates. That main-road crossing is a perpetual anxiety but the mayor is good about having it properly supervised. Those alleys up the hill—yes, for a child like Rachel—where does she live? At the very top? Ah. I live halfway down, myself. As one gets up, there are fewer children, naturally, and those the richest, frequently picked up by car. She'd make her way alone quite frequently, the more as it is a solitary child, who stands and gazes at things and takes her time absorbing them. . . .

"I quite agree, and of course publicity wouldn't do us any good, either. I'll have a word with her form mistress at lunch. There'll be no drama. The sprained ankle will do very well for a few days. We'll add a few words to the children about exhibitionists and so on, though it's not a problem around here. Not so many little girls nowadays worrying about father's big hairy dangly thing. The town children take it for granted, and the country children are all used to the cock jumping on the hen. Among the little ones there's any amount of male vanity and boys brandishing their zizi in the lavy, and once that stage passes the natural modesty of the pre-teen years gives them a good protection.

"Not at all, M. Castang, a pleasure. And a pain, of course. I'll say a prayer. We won't dramatize. I've no doubt you'll have found Rachel in a very few hours, and I hope Mme. Delavigne will agree that unless there's been physical maltreatment—which God forbid—sending her straight back to us with the minimum of disturbance in her patterns will help the trauma heal the quicker. Children need patterns, you know. Above all, they need to know where they stand. Even a certain coarseness, a slight brutality, is preferable to well-meant wavering and shilly-shally. Goodbye, M. Castang."

A disciplined woman, as well as a sensible one. She had hesitated ever so slightly before her final phrase—but no, she wasn't going to meddle in police business. Neither morbid curiosities nor emotional displays of self-indulgent sympathy entered into this woman's patterns. He made his way out, through a faint, comforting, rather pleasant smell of small children's pipi, into the hot, dusty, still air, and a world inhabited by Pauls and Marcels and imbeciles. And mayors.

Castang called on the mayor, and the local police, and the local secretary of the Federation of Parents. He learned nothing new. By quarter to twelve—telling Marcel his lunch break did not begin before twelve, or end after two, and to leave the car where it was—he was following Jackie's gang at a discreet distance up the hill. Jackie had pocketed some chalk, and stopped —before three admirers—to draw a face on Élise's wall, add two swastikas and the slogan "Heil Hitlerin," and swagger on home. Castang walked quietly in at the garage entrance of the Résidence Dampierre just before the businessmen got home, and found Colette and Vera having a calm, respectable, bourgeois Campari-orange before lunch. Thanks, he'd like a big Suze with lots of ice, and might he have a wash? Yes, he did think poor old Luigi would like a pastis, and he'd bring it down with pleasure.

"Great hypocrite," said Vera when he got back.

"It was much better that you heard it direct from Colette."

"Sorry," said Colette. "I must go for a pee. Damn it, I think I've been every ten minutes, ever since breakfast. No, I haven't taken any pills, of any sort whatsoever. I did weaken around midmorning, but Vera stopped me. She's been marvelous," with tears brimming hatefully, "and M. Besson rang up very kindly, and so did the senior judge, and everybody's so kind, and you've worked like stink all morning, Henri, and Bernard's being absolutely controlled and utterly perfect—and, God— why don't I hear—where is my child?" And rushed head downward for the lavatory.

"Don't give me any more," said Vera. "Just give me some more ice to stretch what I have. She hasn't broken down a second, all morning.

"You're out working, at least," Vera went on. "You move

around, you talk to people. While the women have to find their own devices. They shop, they cook, they iron, they do some washing, they do the little jobs that the cleaning woman has dodged or forgotten—and they carry on a dialogue with themselves. I'm used, of course, to feeling helpless, whereas she's accustomed to getting things done; to giving orders and seeing them punctiliously executed."

Colette came back with her eyes carefully painted. "I suppose I've sent a lot of people to prison one way or another. The law prescribes such-and-such; one is there to administer it. There is no particular case of conscience. One examines each instance with care, naturally, to decide whether such a one will benefit from course A or course B in the pretty restricted range available. It can happen quite often that one decides with no hesitation that prison is the best choice. But after only one morning's prison I shall never feel quite the same."

She had fine eyes. She was looking at Castang with them, but not seeing him.

"I recall a seminar given in the magistrates' school, on psychiatry. The mark of mental health, said the good man, is the ability to repress our knowledge of the world's cruelty. Yes, yes, we all nod; it's obvious, the usual illustrations: animals tearing one another to pieces, abattoirs, going on to prisons and capital punishment. Followed by group discussion: yes, prisons dreadful places, very bad; the young criminal is corrupted and so forth, and of course all the little students have read Albertine Sarrazin between the doses of Hans Gross, and there's an outcry about homosexuality and the lavatory bucket, sitting there eating the ghastly noodles while some girl is pissing a few feet away. The man pulled us up right away. Read it more carefully, he said, and quoted a letter, a remarkable letter in answer to a boy asking Sarrazin's opinion on capital punishment. Three main points. First, it's infinitely better than life imprisonment. We fell on that, of course: just shows how bad prisons are, et cetera. It's a chance to finish well a life begun badly, a life that has been nothing but dirt and savagery. Another point one cannot, as a student, understand. Thirdly, quoting her directly, 'I have learned to accept this as I accepted all the rest'—a lesson we evidently had to learn, too. Finishing conversationally, the Herr Professor told us that when a patient walked into his office saying the world was too grim to bear, he treated him as a sick man. . . .

"The patient was right, of course, and saw life clearly. But he was ill in the basic immunological sense, having lost certain basic defenses—or, if you like, the illusions that keep us sane. . . . Now, boys and girls, chew on that."

"In other words, thank God for the opportunity to exteriorize —or is it externalize?" Vera's French was sometimes shaky.

"It's the old thing," said Castang. "The police are callous. But all the arguments are emotional."

"They are, aren't they?" said Colette dryly. "What happens if I'm called upon to judge the kidnapper of a child? I suppose I ought to be thanking God for sending me this unusual opportunity of enriching my experience."

The door opened, and Bernard and Richard came in, laughing heartily together. Hell, thought Castang, a clever bastard that Richard. Not only makes a good entrance but at just the right moment. And plainly he's a lot better at this than I am.

"Time for a drink," said Richard calmly, kissing the girls' hands in his carefully aseptic thirty-centimeters-away manner. "After which I make a small progress report and Castang and I go for lunch and plot."

"And I go home," said Vera.

"Certainly not; you're staying for lunch," said Bernard firmly. "I've seen nothing of you yet."

"We were just talking about Albertine Sarrazin."

"Albertine," said Richard, "delightful girl. No, I never knew her but she's a mine of home truths. In the provinces, she says somewhere, the judge, the President, the Proc, the director of the prison, and the principal commissaire are all cousins and in the clan. 'Maqués ensemble' is her vivid expression. Perfectly true: I've been at the Palais all morning conspiring. I won't go into details, Madame; you'll hear them all this afternoon. But to be serious, my report is briefly this—go easy with that whisky —we're inclined to treat this as an attack. We don't know yet what sort of attack, so we're being wholesale. All available resources of the magistrature, the P.J., the prison authorities— everything down to 'assistantes sociales.' We're looking at every affair judged or instructed by Madame in the last two years linked to mental homes, prison releases, provisional liberty, psychopathic anything—the lot. We're largely agreed that this is where the answer will be found."

"Somewhat academic," said Bernard mildly.

"Somewhat academic," agreed Richard. "You mean what are we doing to get your child back promptly? I haven't had a chance to talk to Castang yet: that'll be over the steak and chips in a few minutes. It's my main difficulty, to keep police procedure away from juridical entanglements without the one losing sight of the other. So we won't sit here chatting amiably, but we drink and run. Come on, Castang."

"So there's still nothing—except talk," said Bernard pathetically. Like a child whose birthday is on December 24th and has had only one present.

"I don't want you to give me time. I grudge every second of it. But time is what I must have. It isn't the serenity of the law. It's a matter of verifying factual detail. We keep the listening post, because we're convinced it will bear fruit. We keep what is vaguely termed a consort watch on your home and on yourselves, and we wait: we must wait; we've no choice. So, to work." Richard gave Vera an official smile. "I'll let you have him back by this evening, Madame—I hope!"

"Well," said Bernard solidly, "what's for dinner, so I know what wine to get out of the cellar? By the way, has anybody taken a drink down to the slave of the phone?"

"I did," said Castang. "We'll be seeing you."

"We eat down in the village," he said to Richard, crossing the road. "I've got the child's route, and I may as well tell you that even if we do a house-to-house we'll be lucky to get any witness. As you'll see for yourself. I want you to look at two points. Both are possibles. Neither shows any indications on the ground—though, if you agree, I'd like the technicians to go over both. I've one piece of totally unconnected evidence which I'd like the lab to look at this afternoon."

"Which is?"

"Shit," said Castang succinctly. "Rabbit shit."

"We've had every other kind already," muttered Richard. "Ah," with a passing look at the spot opposite Élise's house. "I'll hear what you have first." And "Ah" again, at old Léon's courtyard. There was still no sign of that worthy. Was he inside making rabbit stew, or was he content with a sandwich in some strange corridor of the Palais de Justice? A man with a grievance against the law. . . . It had nothing to do with a Judge of Instruction, who is not concerned with civil cases. But in the tortuous, obscured mind of an elderly countryman? Can't go too fast, thought Castang, reserving his fire for the twelve-franc-fifty "fixed menu" of the Hôtel de la Poste on the square.

"Rabbits," said Richard thoughtfully, unfolding his napkin.

"Raw salad and the steak and chips," said both men together.

"And to drink, gentlemen?"

"Carafe of Beaujolais and a bottle of Vittel," still together. They were accustomed to business lunches together.

"Rabbits," said Richard again. "It would be clever."

"To entrap a child," prodding about. The usual raw carrots, red cabbage, green peppers, tomatoes, cucumber, and a dab of mushrooms in the middle, "Greek style." The usual, in short. Police vitamins.

"I remember reading," said Richard, tearing a bit of bread in half, "an interesting footnote on the Boston Strangler." *Glug-glug* went the Vittel water, which was Évian, but no matter. "You recall perhaps? After a series of sadist murders, the prob-

lem was to persuade either young or old women living alone—
hey, leave me some carrots—that however determined they
were never to open their door to a stranger, it was in fact a very
simple thing to gain entry, even with a police lock on a top-to-
bottom bar. Red cabbage and tomatoes—you've noticed?—look
horrible on the same plate."

"Close your eyes."

"Exactly. The trick is to get the woman to open the door
herself, thereby nullifying all the bolts and bars. Now, you—too
much pepper in these mushrooms—as an experienced policeman, how would you go about that?

"I'd put on overalls and I'd say, 'Plumber, missus.'" Castang
was thinking of the Entreprises Paul. "Most women are so
happy to just get a plumber they don't stop to think of where
he came from."

"Not bad. In fact very good, because that was exactly how it
was done. But I was thinking of a demonstration made by a
police officer at a conference, which so frightened the girl secretaries present that they were paralyzed," spitting out a lemon
pip.

"Well, tell me—I may want to try it myself someday."

"You mew like a kitten. A lost and frightened kitten." Richard demonstrated, causing the people at the next table, tucking
into spaghetti, to look at him with horror, a rather repulsive
performance when busy eating spaghetti.

"Jesus."

"Now rabbits . . . it's even better, in a way. Trouble is, if it's
a real rabbit, it leaves traces. These traces you have found. I
think we'll have a talk to this old Léon. I say," plaintively, "talk
about false fillet."

"Faux-filet" is the French translation of a naughty kind of
sirloin steak, with all its gristle left on to make it look bigger.
The chips were not greasy—that is an English rather than a
French fault—but there was a large quantity of hard, tough,
twisted fragments.

"If you can't eat, you can always drink," said Castang cheerfully, filling his mouth with bread and pouring out an ominously purplish Algerian Beaujolais. "It's our fault—the smell of steak and chips, the sight of a menu, our extreme hunger—we salivate like a Pavlov dog when the bell goes. Irresistible—exactly like the kitten."

"Yes, the blood runs cold. So easy, so discreet, so incredibly simple. That case—terribly simple, a poor type. They put the whole resources of the city into it. War room, computers, the entire police, the F.B.I., Boston and Harvard Universities—all the brains; it's a classic in police procedure. Only a few years ago. If I eat any more salad, I'll turn into a rabbit myself. Turned up some extraordinary things. The fellow himself had a gag of measuring girls—'you'd make a good model.' Believe it or not, there were girls who ran to change into tights—there were girls who stripped naked!"

"You'd never get away with that now."

"I'm none too sure. Listen, they turned up a suspect, used to ring girls up. I'm Dr. So-and-So. I met you at a party, I was struck by your intelligence; can I come round and continue the discussion? You won't believe it but he bedded hundreds. And do you know what he turned out to be? A pickle salesman!"

Instead of being asphyxiated by a good meal, Richard was excited by a bad one. He pushed his plate away, filled the wineglass up with water, and pointed a finger.

"Fiction. But good. Psychopath wants to kidnap a pretty student. Stops her on deserted street and says, 'I've just run over a dog. It doesn't seem badly hurt but it can't move. Come and look.' Girl walks over, straight into a rag filled with ether."

"Yes—I thought of the rag filled with ether. But an old peasant—say—wouldn't operate that way. Like the old one the other day—locked the wife up in the bedroom because she talked all the time—gave her nothing to eat. Crème caramel," snapped Castang at the waiter.

"No—it was lousy. And a cup of coffee."

"Just coffee," said Richard. "Yes, we know, you're only the waiter. And I'm only a businessman from the town. But *if* I find myself complaining to the tourist board, tell your boss not to be openmouthed with innocent astonishment."

Richard sat back, not sprawling but properly fitted into the chair, head upright, his back very straight, the way he did in his office. He lit one of his cigars, exaggeratedly long thin things from Brazil which looked innocent until one had the imprudence to take one when offered: they kicked like an army mule, therein resembling Richard himself. He, too, was tall and thin and tightly wrapped; he, too, looked harmless. He had pale opaque skin which did not tan; regular, quite handsome features; hair of a distinguished silvery color worn short and flat. He had a quiet slow voice which he never raised or hurried. His clothes were neat and dull, running to gray suits, cream shirts, and dark ties. He never lost his temper or said "merde."

Yet he was feared, though it was hard to find out how or why. He was generally believed to be absolutely honest, and known as meticulous and painstaking. A good administrator and a dangerous policeman. As far as was known, he was quite unpolitical, but managed to be on good terms with everyone. Why did one never feel quite at ease with him?

Perhaps because nobody knew him. If he had friends, nobody had ever seen them: he was known to have a wife, but nobody had ever laid eyes on her, nor did Richard ever telephone her to say he'd be late for dinner, or to complain that there were holes in his socks. Even Castang, who as a senior member of the criminal brigade saw as much of him as anyone, felt slightly ill at ease in this distant presence.

"You're not very happy with this old Léon? Very well, run him to earth. Get to the bottom of this rabbit affair. And let me know; I'll be in the office. You'll want a search warrant: I'll have a word with the judge. One good thing about old Jérémie, he leaves one a freeish hand, doesn't tread on one's toes at every step. These young judges who insist upon controlling every step of an inquiry . . . Very well, Castang; let's hope it turns out this simple."

Bernard and Colette Delavigne were having a better lunch than the two policemen. To both of them, it had been a relief, and a pleasant surprise, that there are always so many stupid little details to take one's mind off a larger problem. Thus Colette's cleaning woman, at best a touchy soul, who had become filled with peculiar suspicions when she had come for the usual two hours' housework. Why was Madame at home? She wasn't sick or anything, was she? The notion had got lodged in the good woman's mind that Colette was checking up on her in some way, and had been difficult to dislodge.

It was quite pleasant to have time, for once, to spend on cooking. Magistrates' schedulers gave her an hour in the morning to get things prepared, but one now had a luxuriously large number of hours. She had had time to work out quite an elaborate and fiddly idea involving the trout, which hadn't been eaten the night before—and to get heartily fed up, and wish she hadn't begun—before Vera turned up. The right person to ask aid from—a much less brittle character than herself, with "moral resources." She seemed to have built-in shock absorbers: her whole face had stretched and wrenched with pain when Colette had abruptly emptied herself of the whole tale. But she had been so sensible. Not that she'd said anything particularly intelligent; in fact, she'd made several remarks that Colette privately thought rather silly, but even flat phrases like "Hard for poor Bernard to learn not to fuss" had been comforting, because Vera, somehow, was too generous and too broad to fuss.

"People show up well in crises." It was banal, yes. "I know that Henri, of course, is much more sensitive than anyone gives him credit for under that tough-cop act he affects, and so do you or you wouldn't have called him. He didn't say a word to me, cunning old devil, but that's a good sign. But I meant Richard, who isn't nearly as dry a stick as he seems; he won't just do all the obvious things. I've known it once or twice before. He's one of those people who can surpass himself—raise his game like a good tennis player. He doesn't operate all on one note, though you'd never believe so to look at him; you know, that air of only caring about keeping his out-basket empty is most deceiving. And that horrible old Besson . . . I don't know him at all except from seeing him in court a couple of times, but you said yourself you were astonished at how kind he was to you last night. I'm not astonished a bit, really: he's evidently genuinely fond of you and values you. That's very good for him—make him look at his ghastly job in an altogether different light."

"Very good for me, too, you mean?" Colette asked in an angular sort of voice.

"It would be atrocious of me to think of anything so vile," said Vera, upset at the idea of being so priggish. "Hell, my hair's awful this morning; I do wish sometimes I had a wig."

They were eating on the balcony; it was almost like a party. And just the two of them. An anniversary or something, thought Colette without sarcasm, but a certain tenderness: her poor Bernard, he was taking this awfully hard. Despite much gallantry from him, Vera had refused to stay: had a highly developed sense of making one too many. Men had a pleasant innocence: he was enjoying his dinner, and it was doing him good.

She had made stuffing for the trout, to stretch them a bit, with new vegetables and cream and stale bread crumbs, and had made a cream sauce to go with them. She had braised them with a glass of white wine, and added the reduced juice to the sauce: it had come out very well. Bernard was now eating Rachel's trout as well as his own: she had kept this for the slave of the phone, but Castang had said reasonably that the neighbors would think it very odd if they saw her carrying trays down to the cellar, and not to worry about the slave; young Marcel would bring him in dinner and a bottle of beer and in general all that the heart could long for, and she wasn't to worry. She had enjoyed her own trout; she'd remembered chives, and they'd made all the difference. The recipe, oddly, was one of Vera's. . . . And Bernard had gone down to the cellar with a drink for the slave, and come back with a nice bottle, a rosé Pinot, beautifully dry and flinty, just right with the cream sauce.

"Say what you like," said Bernard, polishing his plate with a bit of bread, "a good meal is a lift to the morale even in the most evil circumstances. Raspberry tart!"

"Vera made it. Her pastry is so much nicer than mine, and I never can understand why. I do all the same things. I watched her exactly through every detail."

"Those funny stubby fingers of hers," said Bernard affectionately.

Sidelong glance; was that euphoria, or did Bernard have a small sneaking regard for the amusing and sometimes very attractive Czech Mme. Castang, which secretly overstepped decorum?

"You fancy her, do you?"

"Good God!" said Bernard, shocked. Much too shocked. "Is there more tart?"

"Yes, there is, but it's for tonight, and you're not to go greedily stuffing this afternoon. Stay where you are, I'll make coffee. Would you like a little glass, since you don't have to work this afternoon?"

"No—there's a glass left here in the bottle. I'd only fall asleep."

She brought him his coffee, and one of his small cigars; he beamed like a baby, sitting there very happy in the sunlight dappled through the climbing plants—her cleaning woman was very good with climbing plants and brought slips from her own —which guarded the balcony from indiscreet gazers across the street.

At the moment when perfect content was about to descend like—as the French say irreverently—"the Child Jesus in little velvet shorts," there was a loud noise. The teen-age son of M. Robin, the technical director in the local office of Électricité de France, who lived just below them, was also sunning himself upon the balcony, and improving the climate with a transistor radio. Bernard's day was spoiled.

"One pays a lot of money to have some elementary comforts and even they are denied one. Illiterate bawling drool; might as well live in public housing if one's going to have that thought-substitute fed into one's digestive tube."

"He's only a boy."

"I'll damn well complain to Robin. Some people have no consideration whatever."

"They don't, do they?" said Colette. "Let's make a complaint to the police," in a colorless voice. Glance of fury at this betrayal.

The noise hushed abruptly: another neighbor had given a pained telephone call. Men—doesn't take much to upset them. As Vera had remarked, the row there was this morning when Castang found they were out of shoe polish! Why are men so inflexible?

"Everyone's windows are open—just think of the weekend. We can be eating behind the shack, without a sound," she said.

"Except airplanes. And the fact that by then it will be raining. And the small detail that our daughter is—God knows where."

"We'll be laughing at our own fright," said Colette, unconsciously quoting Vera. "Behind that pedantic manner, Richard is an outstanding police officer. And Henri Castang is a person in whom one doesn't just have confidence but complete unquestioning faith."

"You're very keen on him all of a sudden," with a nasty look.

"He's never impressed me particularly with his intelligence. Perhaps he has some appeal to women I don't know about."

"Bernard, please. . . . I must change, dear; it's time I started thinking about the office. Have a quiet afternoon. If you wanted something to do, you might look at the little washbasin in the lavy; it empties too slowly."

"Ah, yes, and I've got large amounts of paper in my briefcase. Oh, I won't be short of work!"

"There's still a cup of coffee in the pot," said Colette soothingly, whisking into one of the dark frocks suitable to Madame la Juge. "Zip me up, would you?"

Bernard stared gloomily out the window, determined to master his irritation and perfectly able to do so, but frenzied by female fiddle-faddle. Go and be done with it! Don't hang about powdering your nose. Ordinarily he enjoyed the swift deftness with which she "put on her face." But it was not until he heard the motor of the little car reversing up the slope from the garage and saw it swing to accelerate away down the avenue that he felt comfortable again inside his skin.

Odd sensation, being alone in the flat. Accustomed to the routine of commerce, to beginning early and finishing late, with those immensely long and lavish business lunches in between, it was rare that he got home before Colette, and when the lamp burned late for the Judges of Instruction, as sometimes happened, he had Rachel's company: they nibbled biscuits together, and he made fizzy drinks that she liked to sip from, and he played long absorbed games with the small supple body perched on the arm of his chair, making knots in her fingers and seeing if she could get her foot into her mouth, while she licked her finger and made comic patterns in his eyebrows, or borrowed his comb to give him new hair styles. He turned away from the window with a sigh, and went back again to undo a series of complicated knots made in the cord of the Venetian blind. Well . . .

It was nevertheless agreeable to be alone in the flat. One felt unexpectedly rich, like a schoolboy given a sudden half-holiday. He poured himself a second cup of coffee and, despite previous denials, a glass of the raspberry alcohol—and was going to steal another piece of the raspberry tart, but scruple overcame him. He carried cup and glass over to the armchair. The living room was becoming cooler and shaded as the sun moved around to the west: he could lift the blind. The room was trim and neat from the extra housework Colette had done this morning. Better than the hasty rigid tidying that betrayed the hand of the cleaning woman, who always put dusted objects down in irritatingly just-that-little-bit-wrong positions. Today the books were not forced too tightly into their shelves, or mathematically aligned, but breathing in a warm comfortable rhythm.

It was rare enough to be noticeable. Colette disliked antique furniture—"I haven't time to look after it myself and one can't trust the women to do it properly"—and had chosen everything here to be modern and labor-saving. He found it all rather lifeless, but he himself had no skill or taste for pottering about with carpentry any more than he had for going fishing: too nervous and impatient. And she was not a "femme d'intérieur," either; she cooked as a duty, sewed as a chore, stuck bunches of flowers in vases the way they were bought, and complained that she never had any time left for painting. Thoroughly efficient, yes. Always well dressed and a "credit"; meals were always on time, and he always had clean shirts and socks; for any friend or even business acquaintance, he could always count on a poised, intelligent, witty, and delightful hostess. The house ran like silk. He realized how lucky he was, and was grateful, and did his best to be considerate and unselfish. To buy her frivolous nightdresses and exotic dressing gowns and new sorts of perfume was easy; to take her out to concerts, which bored him stiff, to tête-à-tête restaurant dinners, which he detested, was harder: to cook a meal when she was kept late was an amusement that had palled—but he had acquired techniques.

Bernard picked up a book and prepared to make himself

comfortable. His content, painfully won back, was short-lived, because he had hardly turned three pages before the doorbell rang. A wild hope that this might be Rachel—or, at worst, Colette back with hot news—was dashed when he opened: the police again. Despite the hot day, Richard was as cool and neat as a slice of ham in aspic.

"Not interrupting?"

"No—no, I'm by myself. Can I offer you something? Coffee? A drink?"

"Thanks, I've just had some. Can I have a little talk with you, Delavigne? Completely informal, just between ourselves?"

"Of course. Please sit down. You prefer those cigars of yours? These are Cuban. . . . What exactly does it mean, a little talk? A sort of interrogation?"

"All police interviews are interrogatory, by their nature. A television interviewer, on the other hand, is trying to ask the questions whose answers will make a portrait of someone vivid, alive; isn't it so? It's a thing Castang's good at. But I didn't want to ask him to do this. After all, he's by way of being a friend of yours. It might have caused some embarrassment to both of you."

"You're being tactful," said Bernard.

Richard smiled.

"You want to ask personal questions and you choose this roundabout way of preparing the ground."

"Yes, perhaps a little more personal than a television interviewer."

"Well, I can't object, I suppose. I don't think I've anything to hide. I don't altogether see how it advances your inquiry—or mayn't I ask about your inquiry?"

"You may, and I'll answer because we can be quite straightforward with each other. The inquiry is official, which is to say we have by now grounds for hypothesis, a criminal complaint is made against X, the Procureur de la République has instructed the criminal brigade to use all means in their power and all diligence, a dossier has been opened and an instruction begun by M. Savornin, who is the senior Judge of Instruction—I don't really need to tell you all this, because you know through your wife how the legal machine works. To come down to what concerns myself, I am, as you know, the Commissaire commanding the criminal brigade, and we have an official inquiry, which concerns yourself. Good, you have every right to know all about that. It is, in a sense, three-sided. We have a senior officer examining and following up all possible physical traces —that's the affair of our friend Castang, and right now I may tell you he is busy with some promising material. I don't wish to raise your hopes unduly; I suspect this may prove inconclusive, but it must be gone into, and it may lead to other useful discoveries.

"Secondly, as you know, because of the particular position occupied by your wife, we have afoot a very deep-reaching inquiry into the background of any personage, normal or abnormal, who might be thought to have a sense of grievance against justice, and for juridical reasons this inquiry is being conducted by the legal authorities. This is, by the way, quite usual: all affairs conducted by any magistrate come up regularly for review by the Advocate-General.

"And lastly, parallel with the direction and administration of the local P.J. services, I like to conduct my own cases. I'm not just an unadulterated bureaucrat. I like to know a little of the human backgrounds to an affair as important as this, and that's what I'm here for. To fill in, if you like, the gaps in my knowledge of the characters and personalities involved—to ask some questions that may strike you as unpleasantly personal and indiscreet upon occasion, and you are of course aware that you have every right to refuse: there is no compulsion whatever upon you. But I cannot deny that it would help me, especially in as difficult an affair as this—a family affair."

"Smooth speech," said Bernard. "Sounds well practiced. I know now where I stand."

"Quite right. Between men. Not even businessmen, telling one another great lies and perfectly aware of it, enjoying themselves. You are lucid, skeptical, slightly suspicious—all of which is good. Tell me lies if you must; I'm used to it. Like a doctor when he asks how many cigarettes a day I smoke—he doubles the answer he gets."

"It's a psychiatric examination?"

"Something not too unlike. I want to get to know you."

"Sounds like damned nerve. You want to ask personal questions, and I'll put one to you. In what way does this advance your inquiry, as you put it?"

"Your daughter has disappeared, M. Delavigne. After considering what we know, we hypothesize a criminal attempt. Kidnapping is one of the gravest crimes there is, equivalent to a murder. At that moment we don't know enough. It becomes important to us to find out all we can about the lives and backgrounds of the persons involved."

"But, good God, man, you're talking as though I had murdered my wife and fallen under suspicion; it's preposterous."

"Look at it another way. You're a businessman: assume you are going to employ a man in a position of confidence. Before you give him that position, you want to know a good deal about him. Not only his curriculum vitae but his character. Things like has he ever had trouble with the law? Does he drink? Has he been divorced? Does he pay his bills? Is he thought of by those who know him as a stable and reliable person? Big firms think nothing of getting an inquiry agency to run a neighborhood check, of asking to meet his wife, of having his handwriting analyzed, even of psychological tests. The Americans went so far at one time as to insist on lie-detector tests. All that, it could be claimed, is an abuse of civil liberties and an invasion of privacy. But they still run security checks on everyone considered for employment by a federal agency, and that's a lot of people."

"I don't understand the allusion—I see no possible parallel."

102

"The parallel is in the justification for these actions, which is the security of the state and the safety of the people."

"But, good heavens, man, if I suffer a burglary and as the injured party make a complaint—I'm utterly innocent."

"That is only an offense against property. We're talking about a crime against the person. Try to understand—innocence has nothing to do with it. If you were in a car accident—even if the other party was openly, self-evidently at fault—in the case of material injury there would be an inquiry into your behavior. Had you been drinking? Were you preoccupied or absent-minded? Had you perhaps had a lapse of attention even if you were not actively negligent? It is our job to make these inquiries. We have to do it thoroughly. A court might demand to use our findings as an element in assigning a share of responsibility —which can amount to a great deal of money. The average person, protected by his insurance company, does not think a great deal about that. He doesn't think about crime, either, because the odds are he's never been involved in one. A crime of this sort could lead to something a good deal graver than even large sums of money. It leads to loss of liberty, imprisonment for perhaps many years, and that marks a man's whole life."

"Well, all right, all right," said Bernard irritably. "I know all this; I'm married to a judge."

"Just so," said Richard curtly, "and you're accustomed to thinking of it all as an intellectual abstraction. This isn't a game; this is real. So just forget all the detective stories full of bumbling Scotland Yard inspectors. Forget all the gangster films full of Hollywood Indians getting shot and falling down. Forget the prison movies with a phony wrench at the emotions when the fellow gets guillotined at the end. This is for real. I'm being patient, M. Delavigne, because you have suffered a very severe blow. Also because you are an intelligent, educated, sophisticated man. Also because you are a prominent citizen married to a magistrate. So I treat you with every possible courtesy and consideration. The poor don't see me that way. They see me with fear and hatred, because I'm a cop, the fellow who can take them by the collar and put them in the jug, the enemy. They think there's another law for the rich, because they don't distinguish between the law and the application of the law. The law confers upon me the right and the obligation to put such questions to you as I see fit, if I think that justice will thereby be served."

"Oh, all right," said Bernard sulkily. "There's no need to make a speech. I'm sorry," with an effort. "One just doesn't realize. It's true—the police are like road accidents: they always happen to other people. All right, go ahead," wearily. "Put your questions."

Castang was thinking somewhat the same thoughts. One does it every day: one goes through the same motions and it's all routine, all meaningless. One is a cop the way one is a plumber: it's just a job, and the fact of being blunted by the distrust and dislike shown all day makes one more insensitive still. Even now —a kidnapping. Which means there's an extra panic on. And, lordy, it's the child of a magistrate. Double the panic, for the Proc and the Judge are affected, and they'll, by God, see the screws are turned. And we'd still just shrug and grind on because one does one's job, more or less well, as circumstances permit. Oh, sure, sure, it's watch your step, don't fall asleep on this one; these are highly placed people and if you do anything stupid it'll be your neck. It still wouldn't make that much difference, seeing you're a conscientious cop, and vigilant and diligent and blah. Not even that I know Colette and Bernard, or that she's a friend of Vera's: I've been involved before in inquiries concerning people I knew. Hell, one knows a lot of people. But a child . . . a child is altogether different.

Not just in the emotional sense—innocent and vulnerable and all that. A child is special because it is free of human degeneracy. Even the most vicious, brutalized child is not yet defiled: it has a sort of purity. The public has become so apathetic to violence and brutality that it shrugs at a road accident and drives on fast for fear of being involved, for fear of being given forms to fill in, for fear of being deprived of pleasures. When there's a holdup nowadays, the witnesses look round skeptically for the television cameras. "I thought it was for a film." They can't switch the bloody box on without seeing a lot of oafs brandishing guns and slugging whoever stands in their way, which is all right because it's a baddy. We've seen so many joke policemen that the real ones become a joke, too. It's like naked girls: they're just so much dead mutton. So to excite and tickle the public one has to push further and further, reaching out more and more desperately for a devalued exoticism. Getting more and more unreal in the name of realism.

A child is the only human being as yet uncorrupted.

Old Léon had proved tiresomely elusive. At the district law court he was well known: oh, yes, crazy old man with delusions about justice; he's always around. Haven't seen him today. To the clerks of the local notaries' office, he was midway between a standing joke and a dreaded bore. He was a bore or a joke everywhere. Castang wasn't sure it was either that dreary or that funny. He slammed back into the car.

"Palace of Justice," he told Marcel tonelessly.

The Palais is a really terrible building, and nowhere can the crushing bad taste of the eighteen-eighties be studied to greater advantage. Slab after slab ad infinitum of moldy travertine—the same that Robert Browning's bishop was worried about when he ordered his tomb in Saint Praxed's Church—lines the hall, so excellently named "salle des pas perdus." The vast unwieldy double staircase and the soot-caked ceiling, the long claustrophobic passages, the rows of top-heavy oak doors with bare wooden benches outside—give the worst possible impression. From the pompous pillared entry, where flimsy yellowed carbons of legal notices, all several years out of date, curl their corners behind a massive iron grille, to the fire escapes leading to the bare and dusty courtyard, there is not a scrap of art, not even the monstrous pompier art of the eighties—unless you count the two immense sphinxes in petrified margarine that guard the bottom of the staircase. And not only is there no art, there isn't a scrap of color, of greenery, of the sootiest or most depressed of flowers: it is far worse than a graveyard. In all this chilled and congealed gray grease, the message "Abandon Hope" can clearly be seen written.

Castang was so accustomed to it—it was, after all, only a very little worse than the grim building which in Napoleonic times had been a military hospital, where the P.J., along with a thousand other municipal administrative instances, was lodged— that he rarely noticed the horror. Perhaps he noticed it today because just before arriving they passed the Hôtel de la Préfecture; an elegant eighteenth-century palace, classically simple, light and elegant, in warm red stone, with a fountain sparkling on the lawn and flowers massed upon every balcony. Now if the Ministry of the Interior has money to pay gardeners, why has the Ministry of Justice none to buy dynamite? As for Colette, who worked there daily, she had come to accept it with stoicism, the way a polar explorer learns to accept the existence of blizzards, or eternal night in the wintertime. She spent a good deal of money on flowers, but, as she said, "It is the fires of heaven must cleanse this place," and it was indeed difficult to see what a human agency could do, short of a few parachute mines. Certainly this much was obvious: that long, excessively flowery, rhetorical speeches about the reform of the magistrature were not going to alter this monument in a hurry.

As usual on a hot sunny June afternoon, there was nothing happening at all. The hall had its customary smell and color of long-dead chrysanthemums and there was not a soul to be seen. In the corridor outside the offices of the Judges of Instruction there was the usual sediment of hangdog witnesses on benches and a few brisk gendarmes, amazingly smart in pressed summer khakis and polished black belts, with mournful criminals tacking along at the end of handcuff chains. Outside the "grande instance" offices on the floor above, an advocate came sidling along crabwise with a stiff neck and a gown almost as rusty as his hair. Two more pleaders with waxy complexions and brightly polished shoes were chatting on a bench with piles of paper between them. At the corner, two very smartly dressed and highly painted bourgeois women were evidently trying to "wake the place up a bit."

"The judge doesn't really seem to understand" went the voice, full of money and assurance, as he passed.

No sign of anybody like old Léon. He went all round the far side, past acres and acres of judges and greffiers to the civil courts: Marcel, working the other direction, came suddenly round a corner and shrugged.

"Try the Parquet," they both mumbled.

The magnificently named Offices of the Parquet of Monsieur the Procureur de la République were on the top floor—a thing M. Besson complained about more than the need of a coat of paint. "The serenity of justice implies a certain austerity." Such had also been the opinion of the sphinxes.

Prowling noiselessly up and down, tacking off at angles to hug the wall, dressed in a Sunday suit with a gold watch chain in the waistcoat, a little old man crackling with energy and frustration stopped to rehearse grievances in the window-bay before darting on again. Castang watched him for a moment. The uncoordinated movements spelled insanity clearly enough, even if not really certifiable. He nodded to Marcel.

"M. Martin?"

"You don't hurry yourselves, I'm bound to say."

"We are officers of the Police Judiciare. We have some questions to put to you."

"I've got more than a few to put to you." A fierce look from the light prowling eyes. "I can only hope you're a bit more conscientious and less frivolous than some of these quill pushers, because if I don't get some satisfaction around here pretty soon, I'll be taking this matter to the Cour des Comptes in Paris, and they'll be combing out a few of these provincial magistrates' wigs for them, I can tell you. The waste of public funds in this place . . ."

"Let's sit down. You're M. Léon Martin? And you live at Number 1 Rampe Notre Dame, Samois les Roses?"

"And let's see your identification, young man, for a start," Léon said.

It wasn't easy. The old boy bristled like a hedgehog with procedural points and rights. He knew, apparently, all the codes by heart; from Public Health and Social Aid right through to Criminal Procedure. In order to stop young Marcel giggling, Castang had to get quite hot himself on everything between Article 224—outrage or insult to an agent of the public order —to Article 230—threats and menaces addressed to same. The reservations of Article 64, which states that there is no crime or felony when accused is in a state of dementia or constrained by an irresistible force, were of small help to him. The racket at one moment reached such proportions that a variety of typists got sent popping out of the mattressed doors to inquire what the hell was going on, and finally a youngish substitute came busting out himself.

"Oh, it's you, Castang. What the devil are you playing at? . . . You start making scandals here, my friend," to Léon, "and I'll have you down cooling your heels at the Dépôt in no time at all. . . . Well, if you've got a warrant, Castang, why in heaven's name don't you execute it? . . . Any more lip," to Léon again, exasperated, "and I'll instruct the officer here to put you in handcuffs. . . . Get him out of here, Castang, or we'll have the Proc out complaining."

There was a moment when Castang got seriously worried at the old boy's excitement, and Marcel was plainly wondering why he didn't take the man downtown for a cell and a psychiatric examination. They got him out at last and slapped him in the car, where Castang explained that by right of the mandate duly signed by Monsieur le Juge, et cetera, they were going to search his house. More legal outcry. They could only do so in the presence of the Commissaire and his own legal representatives, and so forth. It all made for a tiring afternoon.

Old Léon lived, and slept, and ate, and washed, in the kitchen. The rest of the farmhouse was strongly Miss Havisham, and the cobwebs had not been disturbed in at least ten years. There was no sign of Rachel anywhere. Nor was there any sign of rabbits. In, on, and around an old writing desk there were papers and letters dealing with half the laws of the Republic, and Castang had to go through them all. But there was nothing remotely to do with any criminal affair, or with Mme. Delavigne. And the cellar was full of coal, wine bottles, potatoes, and broken furniture. Castang felt an acute frustration. Damn it, it had looked promising. Quite apart from physical opportunities and possibilities, a man with this much grievance against the law had an adequate motive. But there was not a shred of evidence.

Now that he had a splendid new grievance, of course, he was talking about suing all and sundry for false imprisonment and unlawful constraint and arbitrary search and Lord knew what all. He was also exceedingly gleeful. Whatever it was the police thought they were doing, they now cut a lamentable figure; it was a massive and total victory. Castang cursed his own clumsiness, feeling sure that somewhere at the start he had taken the wrong line. Could he not have cajoled, enticed, enlisted sympathy, gradually coaxed the recalcitrant old bastard into being forthcoming? Perhaps he could; he had tried. But to old Léon he was just another proof of the law's injustice, one more rusty spike in the iron maiden. No use insisting or explaining. Castang would always be "them" who are against "us." It is a daily part of the experience of any policeman, and there's nothing whatever one can do about it. They were, as near as makes no matter, seen off the premises with the shotgun, amid exultant toothless grinning.

"Thought you could come and push me about," he said. "Not the first. But I'm still here—and I'll bury the rotten lot of you." To the end of his days, old Léon would be convinced that this had been one more effort to strip him of his property. He would tell tales in the café about it, and only the old civil servant from Hanoi would add two and two, and hug his silent enjoyment.

"Got our heads washed there," said Marcel, who had rather enjoyed seeing his superior officer with soap in his eye.

"Yes," said Castang briefly; "pity I can't take it out on you." It is painful to be completely helpless in a situation one would have been able to handle if one had just been a little bit better collected.

Mme. Delavigne—unaware of the drama raging over her head outside the Parquet offices, where old Léon, tired of making complaints about crooked notaries in writing, had come to have it out man to man, and would have, too, if they hadn't with that typical cowardly brutality put the cops on him, which just showed how frightened they were—Mme. Delavigne was working on an equation similar to Castang's. Whatever she did, she reflected sourly, magistrates had a trick of seeing it as a manifestation of oppressed feminism, and were quick to band together against any women's-lib nonsense. They see an able and energetic young woman, who carries out her legal functions with competence, and does not pester them with any damned biological functions. When secretaries or typists get a bit emotional about their men and their hipline, it is put tolerantly down to silly girls of inferior intelligence and faulty upbringing, who stuff themselves with low-fat foods but are too stupid to see that women's magazines are a far more indigestible diet. Little Mme. Delavigne does not pester us with untimely displays of knee and bosom, does not spend interminable hours in the lavatory, leaves us mercifully free of boring involvements in her menstruations and fornications and lactations, has a good little head screwed on her shoulders, and still manages to be pleasantly feminine. But now there's a drama about a child throwing the whole place in an uproar: somehow one always knew this would happen. Colette sighed. Liberated women, she suspected, will always be deeply neurotic.

Commissaire Richard was in his office. However incompetent the prevention of crime might be, the administration had to be kept running. He emptied his pockets of a variety of old envelopes with remarks and reminders scribbled upon them, as well as a good deal of neatly noted agenda, and summoned a technician.

"Daniel, find out what you can about this."

"What is it, rabbit shit?"

"Unless," said Richard patiently, "it's hare, or peacock, or maybe a walrus."

"You mean what it had for breakfast and whether it ought to have its appendix out?"

"Be witty upstairs."

The phone rang. Castang at the other end, being toneless about his frustrations with old Léon.

"Very good," said Richard, also tonelessly. "We were, of course, bound to check up on it. I won't say I expected no better. No rabbits, by the way? Mmm; we'll see what Daniel has to say about these rabbits. I want you to move over to the cheese factory: I think it's time we knew a little more about M. Delavigne's background. As for the lady, I don't want you to allow your wife's friendships to color your judgment, but we'll discuss that when you come in this evening—shall we?"

"Understood," said Castang briefly, and rang off. The Commissaire went on with his paper work. In parallel, his mind dwelled upon little Mme. Delavigne. These emancipated women, his inclinations told him, had a built-in tendency to neurosis. That Czech girl of Castang's . . . No fault of her own, of course, and none of his. A delightful, interesting, and attractive woman. And stable; she didn't throw strains upon her man —not, at least, such as to diminish his work performance. But it alters him, no doubt of that. Quite a complex situation, and one that will take some careful attention.

It had happened to Richard in the past to find a member of his staff entangled by personal relationships in a criminal investigation. It had even happened to himself once.

Not his wife, thank goodness. She was—he thanked heaven for it—a comfortable and satisfied woman who was quite content to stay at home and do the housekeeping. Doubtless it was very regressive and reactionary of him, thought Richard dryly, but he was profoundly grateful for the fact. His own tastes did not run to frustrated women. He liked his roses full-blown; large comfortable girls unworried about their hips and unimpressed by the floor needing scrubbing, who weren't ashamed to get down on their knees to it. A woman's body needed that. Cooking, scrubbing, lifting heavy children, plenty of shit and lots of sex, and you had a thoroughly used, contented woman on your hands. And that, thought Richard, grinning, will be denounced as "sexual fascism" by a pile of constipated men who are run by their wives. Hmm, little Mme. Castang was an artist. And little Mme. Delavigne a lawyer, and the two women were friends. And both were very nice girls. Artists. M. Richard liked artists;

they were necessary animals. But if he had been an artist, the women Rembrandt or Renoir liked would be the ones he would choose to paint. And shall we now join the ladies?

If you started keeping an eye on Castang, it would be very quickly noticed, since he is not at all an imbecile, and anyway he might be waiting for it, laughing. And if you let him see it and let him know that you know he's seeing it, that's the kind of thing which might in some circles be thought clever, but in Richard's book wasn't in the least clever, because if you didn't trust people you'll never yourself be trusted. It was that simple. No, trusting Castang is a thing that we will not fall down on. But trusting Mme. Delavigne is a different pair of shoes.

Richard rang for his secretary, who was young, Italian, quite voluptuous, and mercifully liberated, with the utmost contempt for notions like being seduced by her boss: her sex life was her affair, and she didn't worry him with it.

"Fausta, my dear, have you any cold mineral water?"

Castang had made a stop in the café, with the same thought in mind. The big café, this time, since the lavatories had been modernized, and there was a reasonable chance there of a good wash in reasonably civilized circumstances.

He could see easily enough why Bernard was proud of his "cheese factory." True, it was nothing but a kind of cardboard box, painted a rather horrible bluish gray and looking as though it were constructed of packing materials, standing on a relatively quiet side road halfway back toward the town, but it looked smart and neat, with quite a wide strip of mowed grass and a screen of poplar trees. All very hygienic: the refrigerated van being hosed down at the service point had been scrubbed spotless, and a glass panel in the wall on his way to the offices gave a glimpse of pastel-green tiles, stainless-steel tubing, and girls in bunchy white overalls. And the managing director, a quiet man with very little hair left on top, but a generous distribution on his bare arms and open neck, confirmed the good impression. "Certainly we're proud of it, but it's the result, you know, of some rigorous self-discipline. We plowed every penny back for ten years: what would you say if I told you that neither of us took a penny home and that even now we live on salaries no bigger than those of the accountant and the chemist?"

"I'd be impressed and I am interested to hear more."

"No paper work, no secrecy, nothing in compartments. This door is open. Anybody, the girls or the drivers, can walk in here if they've a problem and tell me about it. Well, what's your problem?"

"I'd be glad if you'd close the door now, because it's a secret. Personal and confidential."

"Aha. Well, we've no tapped telephones here." Castang forebore to tell him that he was in error.

"M. Delavigne's in some trouble. He's receiving a certain amount of unspecified menaces: there's been, as yet, no overt blackmail demand, and we're in some perplexity as a result, because the threat and the hostility may be aimed at him personally, or perhaps at his wife."

"Yes—he was looking seedy. Went home at lunchtime. That it?"

"So I come to you in confidence, and I hope you'll be open with me. I don't wish to pry into your affairs, but I'd like to know whether all is well between you, and whether in your knowledge all is well between M. Delavigne and everybody else."

The man put his bare arms on the desk, joined his hands loosely, and thought carefully before answering.

"Of course you can smoke. Thanks, I don't. I'll try to be brief. We're very open here. Bernard and I have a good, loose, complex relationship. We don't have rigid limits to our responsibilities, though I handle most of the financial details and Bernard does most of the marketing: we interlock on most things, be-

114

cause of overlap. I daresay I don't need to tell you that a business of this sort is very competitive, and that a constant effort is needed of imaginative vision. Production is dead simple: a question of turning out yogurt, and maybe the chemist worries about putting avocados in it without losing the nice fresh green color. Where the shoe pinches is packaging, distribution—recall we're up against gigantic enterprises like Saint-Gervais. So that I see Bernard constantly, and of course I know him very well. Now, how to answer your questions simply?

"I'm, as you see me, in shirt sleeves. You'll find me everywhere, down looking for ways to make the girls' work less monotonous, trying to load a truck with less waste movements, quite as much as going over figures with the accountant. I'm totally involved; this is my entire life—my secretary here is my own wife. Very humorless and boring you'd find us, solemnly talking about yogurt at our own supper table. Now, Bernard . . . he runs the sales staff and talks to buyers. He wears a smart suit and a tie. I do a lot of traveling—but he goes to the meetings and the lunches. I'm a very outgoing, freespoken, spontaneous personality; I like to think I'm very uncomplicated. Bernard is, too, in a way, and at the same time he has a secret side, closed and sealed off. There's a lot goes on in his mind I don't know about, whereas I'm an open book. I am the son of a small farmer, a country boy. My wife was a country girl. She can make Camembert; she made our first batches of yogurt in our bathroom. Bernard is a city boy, infinitely more sophisticated, and his father was in textiles—he's a third generation of bourgeois commerce. I'm a first. There alone is a very considerable difference. I don't mind telling you that I never read anything but technical literature, don't know anything about music, and my notions of art are nice pots to put the stuff in. Bernard likes books, novels—Jesus, *The Count of Monte Cristo*'s good enough for me. So I don't move in his circle. Above all, not in his wife's. I've met her, of course. She comes to dinner with us twice a year, and we go to them twice a year, and we all get on well

115

together, and I find her a very nice, quiet, polite girl. Yes? Very simple terms, very childish, I use to judge her, huh? I'm like that. It's all I know about her. I'm not her speed. I know nothing about law, save trying to keep inside it. Ethics and morals and philosophy . . . I mean I'd bore a woman like that stiff. A magistrate, from a family of magistrates. 'Noblesse de la robe,' as they say; a legal upper class: her family has it in the blood, where mine were just Limousin yokels. What have we in common?"

"Good," said Castang, "that's all clear." It was, too, because he knew most of it already. Bernard talked about his partner freely enough. With respect, and affection, and with humor.

"So you know nothing about his home life?"

"Good heavens, no. And less about his wife's, if that's what's bothering you. If, on the other hand, there was anything that created troubles here at the office, then I would know. I can see you coming; has Bernard been a naughty boy? Well, I'm not going to peddle any stale gossip; it's not my style. I don't allow any malice and backbiting around here; it interferes with the running of the place, and I'd get rid of anybody inclined that way. And my wife keeps an eye on the girls. All right, so I'm puritanical, so I'm old-fashioned, so I'm a Jansenist old bastard. But no bloomers-down-in-the-storeroom around here: out, even if they're good workers, because it just leads to trouble. What they do outside is none of my business and I try to be Christian; pregnant girls make good yogurt and I'm not asking to see their marriage lines."

It was all a bit too good to be true.

"One doesn't sack a partner," gently. "One wouldn't even sack a good accountant or a good chemist."

"Sorry, my dear man," flatly, "no soap. I'm not gossiping about my partner, or my senior employees. The furthest I'll go is that I know of nothing—repeat nothing—that would give rise or has ever given rise to any troubles here in the factory, and I know of nothing—I'll underline that for you, *nothing*—which might have landed anybody here in a blackmail demand. As for

Bernard, he's my partner—my junior partner, if you like—but his contributions to this enterprise have been and continue to be highly important and exceedingly valuable. He doesn't let me down, I won't let him down, and that's the secret in a nutshell of why we are successful. Sorry, Inspector, I can give you no further help. What goes on outside these doors is not my affair and I know nothing about it. Inside, everybody here reckons with me. You question anybody you want—outside. Here you'll find me tough. I don't permit you any inquiries, not without a mandate from authority. Okay? Is it fair, is it clear, is it understood?"

"Yes, but don't get tough. There's no need and it doesn't impress me. I won't try any backstairs politics with you, and I'll take your word that you know how to handle what goes on in your premises. Just don't try to tell me you run a finishing school for young ladies."

"My dear man," suddenly very human, "one has to close one's eyes from time to time, and the hard part is to know when."

"People being more difficult than yogurt."

"I'd rather my job than yours."

"And, oddly, I'd rather mine than yours. Even if it doesn't smell as hygienic."

The man studied him with his head a little on one side, shrewd-eyed. "I'd like to get one thing clear," suddenly. "You're acting upon a complaint by M. Delavigne in person? You promise me that? Does he know you're here?"

"Not in as many words. He's well aware that a bright light might get poked into all sorts of corners, and he has accepted that."

"As a man with a singularly boring and unscandalous private life, perhaps I have the right to say that I would have very little enthusiasm for anyone looking at mine."

"I wouldn't want anybody looking at mine," said Castang mildly; "it's a matter of not having too many illusions, or maybe changing the pattern of illusions. As a state official, whose job

117

is investigation, I might feel obliged to keep my life free of scandal, or I might feel that even if I was subject to scrutiny I could rely upon the solidarity or even complicity of my superiors. Imagine for a second that you were a highly placed official in, let's say, an American national-security program, and you knew that people had turned over every page of your past and were observing—and recording—every detail of your present. Maybe you'd feel that you just didn't care: you might go living a flaming varied sex life in broad daylight knowing perfectly it would never be publicized. How do you imagine the people feel who direct these surveillance operations, knowing that they themselves are under the same examination? Or do they think that whatever they do it will always be covered by higher authority? Permitting themselves every kind of corruption and finagling, telling themselves, and maybe even believing, that it's all in the sacred name of state security and the national interest."

"You seem to have given the matter some thought. I confess I haven't."

"I don't suppose it makes much difference. You or I are both condemned to the possibility that at any moment our private life might not exist any more."

"I would answer that, perhaps, by saying that I am a small businessman and, as such, enjoy no protection in high places. And that you were a relatively minor official, and, as such, the protection you would enjoy was limited. Everyone knows that corruption—and, if necessary, protection—exists at higher levels and that if you, for example, discovered a damaging fact about an important personage you would report it to your superiors, knowing perfectly that it would there be smothered. You would be told to forget it."

"And," said Castang smoothly, "you're suggesting that I might forget it officially but pursue it privately, just to round my income out a bit."

"It's been known," bleakly. "There's no reflection upon you, since I think we were both speaking impersonally."

"And do you think M. Delavigne enjoys protection in high places?"

"Knowing nothing about his private life, M. Castang, I really couldn't say. It is not my business. And if you'll forgive me we'll put an end now to this discussion—personal or impersonal—because I have the peculiarity of businessmen, which is that they're frequently busy."

"I'm much obliged to you."

Richard was initialing reports on his desk.

"Well? Sit down."

"I saw Delavigne's partner. Interesting man. Huh? What motivates businessmen, makes them a success. It got quite complex."

"Come to the point."

"Maybe there isn't one. Cagey, of course, and prickly. Made a big thing out of not knowing anyone's private life and not saying if he did. Is himself a peasant, a farmer's boy worked up out of the ruck by talent and determination. Got the characteristic suspicion and dislike of the bourgeois. Couldn't quite stop himself voicing his feeling that things were different for them. Thus, outside the office, where he says—and I believe him—that there's nothing, he claims he doesn't know what might happen. True up to that point, because he feels that Delavigne, and the wife, are sophisticated people with whom he has little in common. Bernard works hard, produces results, dovetails in well, is good at the smoothy commercial stuff this man feels he hasn't the time or the talent for. There is some buried resentment. Bernard has an easy assured life, and is married to a magistrate, which gives him a free ride all over the shop. When I did a bit of coat-trailing, he hinted fairly broadly that if there was a blackmail attempt they'd both know how to cover it up. Anything scandalous would be smoothed out in the old-boy network. One interesting point that might appeal to you: Bernard worked for some years without taking more than a nominal salary, but has a big expensive flat and a country cottage. This fellow's wife is a peasant girl, she works with him as his secretary, they have two children who live back on the farm with the family; themselves they live in a dreary little flat in quite a poor quarter, where they've been ever since they started, and don't entertain. A couple of years ago, they bought a piece of land out in the valley, and they're going to build a house, because the business is beginning to pay off. An architect is busy with the plans. It isn't at all grandiose. No secret about any of that; it's common knowledge. Still no phone calls?"

"Still no phone calls," said Richard. "A peculiar pattern. Nothing comes to light at all. The Parquet has been checking those dossiers all day, and so far with no result at all. Twenty-four hours, and nothing whatever. There's no sign of the child anywhere. I'm putting a man over on the house, for what good that may do. It begins to look like a sort of torture, a deliberate intention to create pain. Or else," unwillingly, "a brown paper parcel hidden somewhere it won't turn up for a few days. In which case . . ."

Neither man cared to spell it out.

"Go home. We have to try and rethink it all from other angles. Here's your rabbit report. It's meaningless to me, even if it had anything to do with the matter in hand. Go home and knit socks."

Castang, who had his report to type, cast a sour look.

"And don't think paper work is any pleasure to me," said Richard in a flat tired voice, slapping a pile of folders still waiting to be read.

The report was brief, technical, and as unhelpful as Richard suggested.

1. Yes, this is rabbit.

2. Adhering dust and grit suggest urban or suburban area. Conclude caged or tame animal, whose owner lives within reach of country district. Analysis shows animal to be nourished on fresh greenstuff as gathered in any field. Traces also of dried material; i.e., hay.

3. Animal appears healthy and free from parasites.

4. We're not really experts on rabbits. From the material available, the subject seems to be the ordinary domestic species.

5. The excreta are fresh, dating from between twelve and twenty-four hours. Sun-hardened, but interior moist and undecomposed.

Conclusion: on this amount of evidence, nothing can be put forward with certainty. The best that can be said is that in probability the subject is the ordinary brown short-haired animal, well-nourished and undiseased, which enjoyed a moment of liberty sometime yesterday, and anything more than that is conjecture.

Castang went home.

Colette had left the Palace of Justice a little earlier than usual and, her shopping done, found herself in the worst of the rush hour. It was very hot: flocks of men in flocks of cars creeping along the dusty grilling roadway glared resentfully at this cool, self-possessed, superior young woman, so elegant and unruffled in her expensive little car. She felt very far from what she looked. A sense of depression invaded and possessed her; she felt terribly vulnerable, as though these hostile and grimacing faces were the masks of wolves.

Ahead of her, a vast lumbering truck belched smoke at her: the traffic was too dense for her to overtake it. As they were turning on to the main road and preparing to speed up a little, the lights went amber. The truck accelerated to try and steal the amber light, and she with it. The light went red a second too early. The air brakes of the monster stopped it dead, and her own with her hood an inch from its license plate. Another truck behind, thundering up with an excess of idiotic optimism, braked furiously with a loud inefficient squeal. She glanced up into her mirror and shuddered violently at the sight of the huge radiator grille ready to bite the Alfa's trim little behind off. If his brakes had obeyed a sluggish boot and a dozy brain a second slower, she would have been pulverized between the two masses of steel. A thing that had happened a day or two before to a twenty-two-year-old girl in a deux-chevaux: it had been in the paper. The sense of vulnerability swept over and engulfed her. Men, said the psychologists, felt so safe inside their little mobile tin womb, projecting aggression around as though it were a safety barrier. And a car was so fragile: it took so little to crush one inside in the sort of horrible weld of bright flesh and bright metal—a crumpled paper tissue—that she remembered from the traffic seminar at magistrates' school. In the ravine between steel cliffs held immobile by the red light, she had all too much time in which to recall a shakingly vivid experience.

The introduction had been bad enough. Thin, elderly, silver-haired law professor accustomed to rule coughing, shuffling classrooms, with no need to raise a thin, elderly, academic voice above a dry conversational level, as though he were discussing Aristotle.

"Before these films are shown, I want you to think back to what we have come to accept as the limit in human degradation: to wit, the photographs and newsreels taken in the death camps, to which one might add, by way of contrast, the pictures shown to Herr Hitler of the conspirators in July, 1944, strangled with piano wire and left hanging on meathooks, and perhaps the official photograph, released to the glee of numerous millions, of the row of Nazi chiefs left hanging in their turn. To the younger among you, that will seem very ancient history."

"Napalmed Vietnamese children," interjected a sarcastic student voice, "are slightly less ancient." The professor was unperturbed.

"We are not discussing politics, M. Massillon, and I need only remind you that every generation has its horrors and refer you to the drawings of Goya. Man's cruelty to man is less our theme than man's indifference to man.

"The man who took these films will show them to you himself. I asked him to; I wanted a living link between the camera, which is often indifferent and impersonal, and the audience. I will introduce him very briefly. Herr Ahlers is German, served through the Russian campaign in tanks, became after the war a news-agency photographer and, at my age, has seen everything two generations of war and disaster have to show. I might add that he has worked in Vietnam and filmed napalmed children there. In the discussion to follow this screening, he will answer questions.

"A word now about the films. They cannot be shown to the public without causing hysteria. They were taken for the Police School in Fontainebleau, and will be screened for you by the courtesy of an instructor there. When I saw them, I asked for them to be shown to you. Your careers will call upon you to judge life and death: it is even possible, in the present state of the law, that at least some of you may in the course of your functions be called upon to witness the supreme moment prescribed by the criminal code—I mean the death penalty. Furthermore I have thought proper to use these pictures to illustrate the differences between English law and our own. You have learned a good deal about English law, and I have been present at discussions where its superiority in many ways has been advanced. Like most arguments about the biggest and the best, these arguments are in general futile. The law is simply different. Evolved over the years in pragmatic style, it suits the English very well. We have adopted another system, and time has shown that it suits us well. One of the principal differences, as you are aware, is the way judges come into being. As you know, the English choose their judges among barristers.

"Pleaders, who are well equipped to weigh the arguments of other pleaders. A good system. Our studies—I might use the

123

word today—are more clinical. We do not want our judges to be like generals who have never seen a shot fired in anger. We are concerned with the study of the human being: today we look at the pathology. These films are the result of the human being at work, inspired by vanity, by unbridled impatience, by aggression born of misery and frustration, by fear, by what you have learned to recognize as paranoia. The springs of crime. It is very easy to commit a crime. As you will now see."

The light had gone green at last. It had been a long wait.

The German cameraman had been standing patiently with downcast eyes, an elderly stocky man of a faded khaki-gray color, informally but smartly dressed in a neatly pressed, unfaded khaki safari suit and sandals. Oddly—perhaps cleverly—he chose to disconcert his audience with a low-clowning act, pretending to write on the white screen with an imaginary chalk as though it were a blackboard, dropping his chalk, using the pointer instead, getting flustered, covering his pretended confusion. He did this well, with rapid supple timing: even priggish students laughed, and all relaxed and stopped being bored.

He banged his pointer and poked it at the screen. Nothing happened: he did an act of angry frustration. He was a driver. At last he got a picture. A publicity still of a beautiful shiny new car.

"Cocorico," he crowed triumphantly. When the laugh died, he spoke in French with a clown-German accent. "Also meine Damen und Herren," the very voice of Chancellor Adenauer, "we look at dirty pictures." Appeared a lot of naked bodies in laborious copulatory attitudes. "Oh," hiding his eyes and rubbing his crutch like a chimpanzee, "bad picture, put to make police laugh. Ah, we make girls laugh. No, no, not emotions. Not laugh, not cry, ce n'est pas à faire pleurer Margot. So, you know me already, I am old man, tank captain Russia, also desert, hot sun, tank go *plouf,* burned inside, smell bad. A beginning, isn't it? Holding nose. Now more pictures, Norddeutsche Rundfunk, we make the reportage worldwide, here nice animals Lake

Rudolf, pretty flamingos, here Alaska, pretty Eskimos, here Bali, pretty naked girl, sorry mistake not Bali, Greek island, naked Mrs. Kennedy. Now Vietnam, go very fast, Phantom fighter, that me inside, go too fast to have political opinions. So here, this Vietnam baby all burned, and this soldier-boy from Iowa impaled on bamboo spike. Neither very nice. Here tank run over little boy, any tank, tank got no political opinion either. So now very important cameraman, film everybody, here Mr. Nixon laugh, here Mr. Brezhnev laugh, both very funny men, very nice, make joke. Here Lyndon, very sad, go to funeral give widow medal. Here English big statesman, Sir Ranthony, he tired, rest James Bond house Jamaica. Here French big statesman, grand Charles, secret army shoot his car, he not impressed, give sack like intendance, all incompetent. All done same camera, I hold up, my baby, old hand camera fifteen years I got him, but you bored, finish all this boredom. Now color movie very brilliant, you see, you wait a second, here, fine autoroute, very fine shiny car, publicity Mercedes-Benz, I chase. I lean out of window, like to film fine impact like gangster movie. Sorry I miss impact, got fly in my eye. So here after impact, bad imitation hamburger, no good for bei uns zu hause, even cat's-meat man no want. Here gendarme, blow in mouth to resuscitate but, hell, where mouth? Can't find. Here doctor, good surgeon, please cut there with little sharp knife, but little knife no good, better get circular saw. Aha, come sapeur-pompier, good idea, oxyacetylene cutter, no much like, cut metal but first burn meat, smell like tank. All that work, here, this he get out, one hand to put in coffin, small problem for undertaker, coffin much too big, never mind, we fill up with roses."

The students had by now realized the reason for the clowning. The light went red for the Avenue Mozart. Colette was pleased, this time. She felt that while she was on the road, sealed away from telephones and doorbells, it gave time for things to happen. News, and it would be good news. Already she pictured the beaming faces: a grubby, excited, disheveled Rachel.

"Mama, I went on a horse and we galloped!"

"Hallo, darling, have you had a happy time?"

A paternal brigadier of gendarmerie, very neat, cap-à-pie in his smart khaki summer uniform. And the child's much-loved German uncle, with a delightful ability to clown, and keep little girls amused. Now a bit sheepish and shamefaced at being thoughtless and causing a drama.

"Ach, Colette, I sorry, I make you anxious, but everything now okay, she come with me, we make nice ride, eh, fifille, on a rigolé ensemble, pas vrai?"

"No, no, it was very irresponsible of you; you clown but we were out of our minds with misery."

From the side street down to the village, a silly boy on a ridiculous little firecracker bike made a dangerous turn right in front of her and accelerated frenetically up the slope.

"Boy take wings here," said the voice of the kind uncle. "Bike make like rodeo cow down there, you see, I take zoom lens, there. This distance he fly, so-o-o, and here gendarme measure, he not believe, is seventy yards on wing. Here is boy, very good, all still in one piece, big surprise, how come? We look, he got one-piece leather suit, we find everything inside, nothing missing, even head still in helmet. But better not unzip suit. Put like so in graveyard, because inside, soup. Like making apple sauce, very fast centrifuge mixer, done in a second, so *brr-brr* and is ready—purée." And a photograph of the eyes, which finished off one or two budding magistrates for the rest of the day.

"God," said Colette out loud as she parked her car, "send us a deliverance."

"Why does he talk like that?" asked several students.

"International pidgin," said the world-wise Massillon. "They talk English and Russian the same way, and they don't even notice what language they're operating in."

"I think, too," said the professor, "that he wanted to emphasize the extreme infantilism of mentalities unable to distinguish between the Keystone Cops and a shattered child."

"Have you brought anything for dinner?" asked Bernard anxiously.

"Dinner, yes, dinner—oh, yes, I've been to the butcher. Didn't see anything that pleased me. Bought hamburger."

"Hamburger," disappointed.

"Yes, very dull I'm afraid. I'm sorry; I know it must have been horrible for you, shut in here all afternoon."

"I passed away an hour being questioned by Commissaire Richard. Disconcerting individual. One goes to the cinema and the cops are all unsuccessful wrestlers of impenetrable stupidity blowing smoke in the suspects' faces. You're accustomed to them, of course; I'm bound to say I found him disconcerting."

"Don't tease me, Bernard, I need a moment to recover; I had a horrible nightmare in the car. What is she called by day, the nightmare?"

"I've no idea; I'll look in the dictionary," glad to seize on a distraction. "Very odd: 'cauche,' old French, and 'mare' from the Dutch, a nocturnal monster. Surely it's just a female horse? Unhelpful, the etymology. Hmm, the English is just as bad, says it's an incubus."

"The pale horse, perhaps, in the Apocalypse. I don't care; she comes by day, too, and she's diabolical in origin."

"I see her dark, but with pale blue flame where her breath ought to be. We'll ask Vera, she's the graphic artist. But what about dear old Freud?"

"I'll tell you what Vera would say about dear old Freud," said Colette, grateful to him; "she'd say he was a solemn imbecile."

"What form did it take?" asked Bernard, interested.

"I was crushed between two big trucks. Stay with me here in the kitchen. Just talk to me, talk about anything at all."

"Have we what you'd call a reasonable marriage?" His mind was still running on Commissaire Richard.

Colette took her dress off, hung it up, and put on a smock, glad to find her mind running on cold soup again. "Huh?"

"What is our solidarity worth? I mean when we are attacked, as we are now, does it weld us closer together, or tend to split us apart? If, for example, you were one of these liberated women?"

"Am I? I don't have the impression."

"Well, are you?"

"You mean you don't know?"

"I've occasionally wondered."

"Wondered what?" the judge's mind exasperated by this vagueness.

"Whether you had lovers, for example."

"Liberated women don't have lovers. It's unworthy of them. Afraid of being pawns in a sex war, of being denigrated. Very dull for them. And exceedingly boring for everyone else."

"Well, have you?"

"Odd question for in the kitchen. What would your opinion be?"

"I don't want to sound complacent. I'd say there were a few strong factors against. You are strongly fastidious. All right, leave that aside for the moment. You come of a family with a long tradition of scruple and integrity."

"Which I revolt against most obstinately."

"Very Catholic."

"Me, or my family?"

"You refused utterly to sleep with me before we were married."

"What would otherwise be the point of marrying? Concubinage in law confers the same rights."

"One can't have concubine magistrates," comically.

"I really can't see why not. Except that 'concubine' is such a ridiculous word."

"And if you had a lover you'd need to be appallingly discreet. Not one's close friends: one just doesn't choose lovers among really close friends."

"I can't think of any friends who're that close." She was beginning to feel cheered. Despite everything, it was somehow comforting that poor Bernard, too, should have felt the breath of the nightmare. Even the shaft of keen hatred toward that prissy old-woman Commissaire Richard came and went in a flash. An irresponsible gaiety began to bubble up.

"And not casual acquaintances," Bernard was saying earnestly. "I should think the men—the magistrates, I mean—choose their mistresses among careful, respectable married women, not a rackety nightclub gang."

"Well, who do you see as suitable among the discreetly married men who can be counted upon not to compromise the magistrature?" asked Colette.

"I don't know who we know," said Bernard laboriously. "Henri, perhaps."

Loud, slightly tinny laugh. "I see. A policeman would only compromise himself. Anything to reinforce this suggestion?"

"I've watched him looking at you sometimes."

"How does he look at me? Lecherously?"

"Not quite the right word. I don't know. Perhaps 'concupiscent.'"

"A magistrate's word, that," the laugh unforced this time. "As long as he doesn't start looking possessive. And if you're going to be liberated and start asking questions about my lovers, I take it you'll accept that I can do the same."

"That's reasonable," said Bernard, sounding downcast. I'll teach us both to have nightmares, thought Colette.

"What are we having to drink?" she asked enjoyably, tasting the meat for seasoning. "I'd like a big serious Bordeaux, since this is an occasion. And does the slave of the phone like his hamburger underdone?" Bernard trotted off; Colette blanched her tomatoes and threw them in the mixer bowl.

129

"The slave says he'd love a drink but no food, thanks; his wife will be cooking a smashing meal and he wants to do justice to it. The other old one will be here tonight. I asked what he thought about no calls at all, and he said in his experience it was odd, but the job stayed the job and whether there were dramatic developments didn't alter the case."

"There are going to be dramatic developments," splitting a green pepper and throwing it on the grill.

"That's what I thought, so I brought two bottles of Bordeaux."

"Very sensible."

"Covers a lot, that word. Shall I make salad?"

"There are still a few chives, and there's walnut oil if you agree, but don't overdo it. So you don't mind if I search you a bit in a magisterial way."

"I daresay," chopping chives carefully, "that you don't expect all your suspects to tell all the truth the whole time. Anyway, isn't it privileged? I've no lawyer present. Abuse of inquisitorial powers vitiates the process. There. Small Suze?" running the cold tap on ice cubes.

"Large Suze. I'm ready, too," sitting on the sofa and stretching her legs out comfortably. "Very well. We start with the office, but I think we eliminate that, because dear Jérôme is so fussy about sex in the office; there's probably more in the Palace of Justice. I have the utmost difficulty in imagining him and poor Anne in bed together. On the other hand, you've always been given to casual approaches to kitchenmaids."

"There, if I may say, speaks the young lady from at least four generations of snobbery."

"I agree, I suppose. I daresay I am a snob, though sleeping with policemen doesn't sound like it. But so are you, you know. You are extremely irritated now and then by my bourgeois ways, and relieve your tensions by bundling secretaries. Not your own, to be fair. Distant ones who act lordly. Still, you're a sensitive and vulnerable person, and you try to form permanent

130

relationships. You need reassurance and you want a woman you can rely upon. Is that fair?"

Bernard tinkled his ice cubes and said nothing.

"To do you justice, there's a great deal more in you than a crude need to assert yourself, and you would be very quickly bored by physical satisfaction if that's all there was to it. Bundling a secretary after too much lunch in a moment of irresponsibility is more a revolt against that deadly seriousness Jérôme brings to tinfoil lids on pots than against me; am I right? Your grievances against me are more important, without trying to flatter myself."

"Go on," woodenly.

"You are conscientious and meticulous, but it is a strain, because while you bring a strong sense of scruple to work you are still ashamed because you feel a dilettante by comparison with Jérôme. Give me a cigarette."

Bernard was enjoying himself by now. He no longer had that strained, glaring look around the eyes.

"It's not intended to be in the least insulting," she went on earnestly. "You were brought up, after all, in a family with a gift for commerce which had got wealthy thereby, and you were full of resentment. Lord, I remember you in your Stalinist phase, fulminating, when I knew you first. Fearful porcupine you were about parental indulgence and the easy ride you'd had in childhood, and so uncomfortable about being nouveau riche. Ashamed of your laziness and ashamed of your own facility—oh, the attitudinizing that went on."

"But I wasn't complacent, I hope."

"No, but don't be now, because you were not at all pleasant: detestable to your own family, who were really perfectly inoffensive, and amazingly aggressive to mine, whom you still detest. The grill ought to be hot by now: I'll do the hamburgers. You can be monstrously egoist of course, and the combination of indolence and impatience can be very unattractive."

"I'm going to need the second bottle," drawing the cork of the first. "I'm beginning to feel overwhelmed. Is there more?"

"Oh, yes, lots. You were very nice to me—horrid conceited little doll that I was. Spontaneous and generous. I found you good-looking, too."

"Popeyed."

"Well-made eyes. An open and attractive expression. Vile, often, but never mean. And, despite your frightful temper, seldom rancorous. Shall we go to the table? Yes, in answer to your question, I think we have a good marriage. I often think I don't appreciate it as I should."

"I don't think myself I'm any great catch," he mumbled with his mouth full.

"Very splendid, this," draining her glass.

"Palmer. Old firm. Very snobbish."

"I can't think of anything much more snobbish than drinking Palmer out of a Baccarat glass while eating hamburger. I love you very much. Yes, give me more, a lot more, I'm going to get gently drunk on this. Already my tongue is far too loose for a magistrate's. I love you because I'm a great disappointment to you but you rarely show it. You find me rigid and artificial. You loathe my being a judge and you resent the clan intensely; all that tight-knit family of lawyers, with Besson at the head. Like Bordeaux growers. Or shippers, who are, if anything, even worse. Little provincial aristocracy with far too much money, sending their children to Oxford and pinching their accents to sound English. My family's like that. I suppose it's why I married you, really, because you were rather odious."

"We'll drink Burgundy from now on," beginning to wonder uneasily what all this was leading to.

"Exactly. You often make these snide little remarks they go in for in Burgundy, like if it smells of the cork it's a Bordeaux, and down there they all die of diabetes."

"Why?" puzzled.

"Because they have to put in so much sugar, imbecile; you know how astringent that cheap Bordeaux is. And bourgeois policemen like Richard—you can't stand him and he sees it, and it isn't very clever to show it. Whereas a man like Henri you approve of because he got somewhere without any inherited positions, just by the force of his own two wrists—I don't blame you, either." She only stopped because her mouth was full. Colette never spoke with her mouth full. Incapable of it, just the way Robert de Saint-Loup was incapable of saying "William" when talking about the Kaiser. Being well-brought-up, he always said "the Emperor William."

Bernard filled up both glasses, pursuing the train of thought. "Charlus," he said.

"What?"

"You remember how nice Charlus is, getting cross with the French in wartime for being so crudely and so stupidly anti-German, and laughing tremendously at M. de Norpois for being such a pompous old imbecile, and never reading the reports of criminal cases because he's so sorry for the condemned man, and one likes him so, and then the next minute one finds him in the bordel being chained up and beaten by the soldiers. Only, how complex people are. I don't know you at all, really. I'm a bit shaken by the bombardment. Are there still frightful revelations to come?"

"There haven't been any yet," said Colette tranquilly. "Everything I've said has been quite superficial and obvious to anyone who takes the pains to look at you. Richard, for example, or Henri."

"There was a lot of loud talk earlier about my mistresses."

"If this person, this hypothetical observer, who is not all that hypothetical just at present, were asking himself a question like that"—taking a little rest before helping herself to salad and urging him to have the last hamburger before it got cold—

"they'd start by looking at me, wouldn't they? Or he. They are, believe me."

"Both your thought and your syntax—getting kind of tangled."

"Sorry. Give me a bit more of Mr. Palmer's nice juice."

"Mr. Palmer's nice juice. He'll be most indignant."

"They'd look, I think, for someone you felt thoroughly at ease with, which isn't the case with me. Someone a little timid, perhaps rather reserved and uncertain of herself. And someone with a lot more warmth and spontaneity than me. Someone who shared your interests in literature and art, less narrow, unadventurous, and boring than myself. And someone quite attractive, because you have high standards of presentability. I haven't thought of it often enough, but I'm very dull. You find me very dull."

"Not just now."

"Oh, that's only because I'm getting drunk. And how often does that happen? You're too nice, as a rule, to tell me so, but secretly you do find me very dull. I am dull. Oh, to be sure, I do my duty. Unselfish in bed, and I look after my appearance and wear nice underclothes and so on. But it isn't at all interesting."

"And where are we to find this paragon? It sounds a rare bird."

"Oh, I think that Vera would offer possibilities."

"Vera!" Startled, Bernard knocked his glass over, caught it in midair, and looked at it astonished by the rapidity of his reflexes. Luckily, it had been empty.

"Yes, Vera. Were you surprised at my catching that, or at your catching the glass?"

"But good heaven," grasping at the first argument he thought of, "she's half paralyzed."

"She was," blandly, "but I notice she gets around."

"But she's a friend of yours."

"Certainly, and a good one."

"She's not even attractive."

"Don't play the imbecile, Bernard, she's magnificent. The slight difficulties of movement make her, if anything, more so."

"You mean you find her attractive."

"Intensely so."

"Odd expression for a friend of yours."

"You're defending yourself very feebly. You'll be suggesting we're Albertine and Andrée next. I'm not lesbian, you know. Nor, I'm very sure, is she."

"You astound me."

"Really? Just because I'm a judge and have some training as an observer?"

Bernard meditated all this while unwrapping the foil and pulling the cork—making rather a thing of smelling it—of the second bottle. The wine waiter's act went on while he wiped the neck of the bottle out with a corner of his napkin, poured a bit out, held it up to get the light through it, swirled it around, and smelled it.

"Now drink some," said Colette a bit too curtly.

"You certainly got your own back."

"No. That's not one of my characteristics. If I sleep with Henri, it isn't out of any revenge feelings."

"I only meant a heavy return of service. You turned the tables neatly on me," finally getting around to drinking some wine. "Is it better than the first, or not quite as good?"

"Tastes to me exactly the same."

"Very well; suppose we accept your hypothesis, which I don't grant, by the way, and we were to assume all this to be true. Where do we go from there?"

"Ring them up and ask them round," as though it were the most obvious thing on earth.

"Just like that? What about the slave of the phone? I mean I know he's not supposed to tap outgoing calls, but . . ."

"Don't be idiotic; of course he listens to everything, but what's wrong with that? Henri is supposed to be detecting;

he consults us or, anyway, we consult. Vera is a friend; she was here this morning, holding my hand. Tranquilize yourself, we weren't making love: the idea wouldn't have entered my head."

"But it does now?"

"And then?" with an uproarious guffaw.

"You're drunk."

"Slightly. Going to get slightly more so, by the look of it. I'm like the man in the Thurber story—I'm sitting in the catbird seat."

"Tell me—what are you suggesting?"

"A party."

"You're not serious," said Bernard, much more shocked than he had thought he would be.

"Who's bourgeois now? Cheese?"

"Du Roquefort d'abord, d'accord."

"And then you can go and get up a bottle of champagne," she said gaily. "Don't be so silly; they give this stuff to babies."

"Will you ring?" asked Bernard politely. "Or shall I?"

"I'm nearest. What odds does it make? . . . Hallo, Henri. You've had supper? . . . Had a rest? Feel relaxed? . . . Listen, we have ideas, plans, various proposals. We'd like you to come over. Would you like to come over? . . . Oh, yes, quite indispensable to bring Vera. Yes, positively so. . . . Oh, yes, I agree, in your private capacities. Oh, absolutely. . . . Yes, of course Bernard's here with me. He's all for it. . . . Yes, yes, I quite agree." Great carillon of laughter.

"You haven't any bugs fixed here in the living room, have you, M. Castang? . . . No, of course I'm joking. Isn't it a good moment to joke? . . . What do you want, then? That I should sit staring out of the window with the tears trickling down? I've had a horrible day. So has Bernard. So, no doubt, have you. So has Vera, who played Sister of Mercy all morning. Before I face another day like this, I'd like to loosen up completely. I also think this will serve several purposes. . . . You will? Champion, champ." She put the phone down. "And, talking of champ, whip down the cellar."

Bernard, with an air of digesting peacefully, was eating Roquefort and finishing the Bordeaux.

"Come on," said Colette, "we want to get all this rubbish away. Don't want the place smelling of hamburger."

"What are you going to do?"

"Change. Put on a nice frock. Have a shower. As I say, unwind. Tomorrow is a holiday. No need to go to the office. I have shelved—ha—my current affairs. So we weekend. Exactly as though we were going to the country with a couple of friends; and the town, and all concerning it—work, and formal manners, and the whole law-politics-commerce syndrome—is laid aside, and all those topics of conversation are taboo. Forgetting the electric light and the central heating, and just have the oil lamps and the firelight."

"And play sardines."

"And play sardines," said Colette perfectly seriously.

And Rachel? Was she forgotten?

No, of course not. But nobody can go on speculating on a painful theme. By a tacit agreement, neither of them mentioned Rachel.

Where was Rachel? She was not happy. Neither, really, was she unhappy. She had made too many discoveries too fast to be able to do much thinking about whether she was unhappy or not. Just so, when in wartime one was suddenly whipped into the army, even those accustomed to all that was most idle and luxurious in a carefree existence, even men who had led a Noël Coward existence ("Whose yacht is that?" "The Duke of Westminster's, I expect. It generally is") were not in the least worried or disconcerted at the new preoccupation with boots and keeping their bed space clean and finding their entire life held in the hollow of an illiterate Welsh corporal's stubby grubby hand. Just so could a noble lord, heir to an immensely wealthy estate in one of the most historic, picturesque, and protected corners of England, when suddenly put in prison under conviction for a criminal offense, keep his balance and humor:

"Well, how do you find prison?"

"No worse than the Guards Depot at Caterham, thank you."

And the Guards Depot had been just like going to school again. Painful, to be sure, because one does not know the rules, and gets whacked for unconsciously disobeying an immense multitude of incomprehensible shibboleths. But a child as young as Rachel, who was not yet nine, is accustomed to severe rules in large quantities, even those laid down by persons quite as arbitrary as any fierce brick-faced noncommissioned officer. Children like rigid laws, and discuss them with as much solemnity and respect as any magistrate.

"On a le droit . . ."

"On n'a pas le droit . . ."

Young as she was, it was not the first time. The school playground, the lavatories, the class, the mistress. Silence periods and rest periods, moments of immobility with arms folded and hands and feet still, when chattering and tics and grimaces were severely reproved.

"We do not mill aimlessly about."

"We do not rush screaming through the passages."

"We stand up when an adult enters the room. We say 'Bonjour, Madame.' We do not make a Schweinerei with our play materials. We learn self-respect. We do not blow our nose on our sleeve. We do not have the right to jig about madly when we need to do pipi." Now that there were suddenly a million new rules, all perfectly incomprehensible, Rachel was not as disconcerted as she might have been had she gone to a "free-expression" school instead of a classical "maternelle" at four, and the "big school" at six.

"Acceptable work," read Rachel's first report. "One might reproach Rachel with being a bit too head-in-cloud." Un peu tête-en-l'air. And the odd blot in her exercise book severely ringed in red ink and the remark "Étourdi" with an exclamation mark. Unconcentrated!

Rachel found these people singularly ill brought up.

In the car, she had been very frightened. The young man was so violent. Not that she had been really frightened by the knife. He had opened it, and laid it on the ledge of the dashboard, and glared at her.

"You see that? That's to open the tripes of the animals. So you'll know that you keep quiet. If you don't keep quiet, you know what will happen." She didn't believe in the knife and its fearful threat. Indians on the television had such knives. They got struck down by arrows and bullets and fists, and collapsed in a heap.

"Hollywood Indians," said Papa. "They die every day for ten francs a time." She understood perfectly. They were actors. And the cowboys often spoke in those menacing tones, and despite the most appalling socks on the jaw, they were never hurt. "They are cascadeurs," said Papa, "professional fallers-down." She knew how to do that, too.

She had been much more frightened of the brutal way the young man drove the car, accelerating furiously, noisily, from the red lights, muttering threats at all who passed. A car, she knew, was much more dangerous than a knife or a gun. Mama had a gun in her handbag. Papa had a rifle in the country. Everyone in the country had guns, and these were plainly country people. But he drove much too fast.

They drove a very long way. Up hill and down, through innumerable villages. It was terribly hot in the car. She fell asleep.

She didn't know whether she had walked, at the end, or whether she had been carried. There had been such a hot smell of hay and animals. Now there was a country smell, which was familiar but somehow different. Wood smoke she recognized at once. Sour milk. A tarry smell of sun on creosoted wood, which she knew and loved. Other smells not particularly countrified but still familiar, like the smell of Marie-Line, at school, who was negligent, and whose hair was not always washed and who didn't change her underclothes every day. The smell, highly disagreeable, of stale sweat and musty clothes, which was that of the dirty-laundry basket. And a close stuffy smell of chicken feathers. But it was not dirty. The tiled floor was scrubbed, the enameled stove was clean, the window curtains were white. The people were poor, because, as Mama said, the poorer the people the fussier the lace window curtains, and these were extremely fussy. She was in the hands of peasants. She was not particularly frightened of peasants. There was also a smell of potatoes, wine, and whitewash, exactly like the cellar in Aunt Elizabeth's country house.

It was the kitchen. They all sat at the table, a big table with an oilcloth cover. She got a chair by the stove. They looked at her with curiosity.

"So you got it?"

"Like you see, no?"

"No trouble?"

"Why would there be trouble? Easy as winking your eye. I always told you it would be easy."

"But will it stay easy?"

"Sh-h-h."

"You hungry, eh? You want bread and butter?"

She was hungry. "Yes, please, Monsieur."

They were delighted. They all burst out laughing. What had she said that was funny?

"Yes, please, Monsieur!" But the old woman got up and cut a big piece of bread, twice the size she would get at home. She didn't mind; she was hungry. She could eat all that. There was no butter. The old woman had a stale smell, but her apron looked clean. She smeared the bread with jam, sickly pineapple jam, which Rachel did not like at all, but she did not think of making any complaint.

"Little pitchers," said the old man warningly.

"Ach, what?" said the old woman. "She doesn't grasp. Nor will she. No risk."

"Anyway," said the young man, "who's going to be dictated to? Had enough of being put down, right? Not having any more of that, right?" They seemed very angry. But not, apparently, with her. They all broke off to stare at her, not unkindly. They seemed to approve. She ate her bread in small mouthfuls, and tried not to drop crumbs on the floor, which was freshly swept.

"Been brought up right," said the old man.

"What do you know about it?" said the old woman. "What, brought up? They're allowed anything. But she'll learn."

"She'll learn," said the young one approvingly. "We'll train her. Dress her. Teach her what's what. How decent people behave."

"She don't answer back, anyhow."

"She better not. Soon see what she gets if she do. Back of my hand." She could understand easily enough. It was French and not patois. They had a rough peasant accent, but it was recognizable. It was like the carpenter, in the country, who said, "Eh, fifizou," when he saw her, and gave her a sweet. But he had a soft voice. Why did they shout so? Were they angry with each other? The old woman had teeth missing, top and bottom, all the way round the sides. Two big snaggle stumps in front. Rachel was fascinated with those teeth. The old woman had a way of sucking at them.

"What you staring at, eh? Don't you know it's rude to stare at people? Where's your manners, eh?"

The old man was small and thin. He was an ordinary countryman, such as Rachel was quite familiar with, and was not afraid of, except when they killed pigs or birds, which they were always doing; they seemed to enjoy it. He had an old beret pulled on very tight right down over his forehead, making his ears stick out. Didn't it hurt? He had very tiny eyes, which glared at her and looked very frightening, but she wasn't frightened. The eyes were somehow not vicious or cruel.

She didn't think the old woman was so dreadful, either, despite all the yelling. She seemed very worried. There was a perpetual anxious frown on her face. But when she sat at the table and started to clean a pile of green beans, the frown cleared, and then the eyes seemed placid and quiet.

"Shall I help?" asked Rachel timidly.

The eyes swung round and the puzzled glare that made them look so angry came back for a moment. The old woman seemed to think she was being mocked.

"What you say?"

"I know how. I could help."

The glare went out and for a moment the eyes looked quite benignant; the pursed mouth relaxed its suspicious pucker. "Well, that's good. Why not? Yes, you can help. Look in the drawer. Get a little knife. Don't cut yourself."

"May I bring my chair?"

"You may." A pile of beans on a sheet of newspaper was pushed over. The old man sat immobile, watching her. The young one lit a cigarette, a yellow one with maize paper and very strong black tobacco. He had black broken nails, and the skin seemed impregnated with dirty grease, as though he were a mechanic. He was very sullen; Rachel did not care for him at all. She did not understand how it was that she had thought him nice when they met by the roadside. In the car he had said nothing, except for the savage muttering at other drivers. Rachel had not been worried by that. Papa did it, too, occasionally when they went out to the country and he was particularly tired after a hard week. He was "énervé." He had that sort of impatience at home, too, quite frequently, roaming nervously about the flat—what Mama called "polar-bearing." It was quite true: she had seen them at the zoo and on the television, walking continually about in a gruff nervous way, looking for something to criticize. It was at these times that he grumbled about the food, or said he couldn't find any socks (they were there all the time in the drawer, under his nose: it was as though he just hadn't wanted to find them), or complained she hadn't brushed her hair properly, or made mean remarks about Mama's clothes. He could be most irritating, suddenly switching the television set off, punching the button far too hard, as though he wanted to break it, just when there was a program she wanted to see, muttering angrily and saying one of those horrid things that could be so hurtful.

"Sitting there on your passive bum, gazing aimlessly at that spineless trash."

Mama got upset sometimes, and there were rows when she was tired and what she called "ragged." She did not often look at the television, but sometimes she liked to sit and sew: a dress whose hem needed letting down, or some broken shoulder straps.

"I like sometimes just to sit and be female," as she said—a thing Rachel understood. Men always had to be doing things. Papa read, or wrote, or "thought," sitting with a lot of papers, twiddling his fountain pen round and round in what really was a bothersome way. Or shutting himself up in the spare room to paint—he painted landscapes in watercolor which Rachel was not allowed to touch (anyway, she liked her own box of gouaches much better; they were far brighter), making pencil drawings when they were in the country, with the margins full of neat little notes, and "working them up," as he called it, on a drawing board at home. Rachel admired them, but he always laughed at her and said they were no good.

The young man, now, did nothing, but somehow this was much more ominous and troubling. He sat sprawled in an arm-chair, and Rachel was slightly shocked at this, because the two older ones—could they be his father and mother?—sat on plain wooden chairs at the kitchen table and Rachel did not think this right. He was very much the king of the castle around here, it seemed: he sat slumped, with his long legs sprawled straight out. He was quite handsome, Rachel thought, but there was something wrong with his looks. Vulgar, she thought: it was a word that she did not really know the meaning of but that Mama used often for things she did not approve of, and Rachel understood why, though not quite how. It was hard to pinpoint. But he was scruffy, that certainly. He had thick brown hair, which should have been nice but was matted and dull-looking, and he had one of those checked caps on—in the house, too—like the grocer's boy had. And he had very long reddish "sideboards," and his chin was badly shaved; it gave him a dirty look, and sort of scruffy. He bit his nails, too, which was foul. Jackie bit his nails, and his hands were horrible. He fidgeted and sighed and shifted about. Why didn't he do something? The old woman sat placidly doing her beans. The old man hadn't anything to do, but he sat quite immobile and peaceful with his hands folded, seeming quite content.

Rachel sat with her head well down, top-and-tailing conscientiously at her pile of beans—it was a very big pile; she guessed there must be at least two kilos, if not more, and wondered why they needed so many. But she could not stop glancing up at the young man, because he fidgeted so dreadfully. And she was feeling fidgety herself. She hadn't gone to the lavy since leaving school, and was beginning to need to very badly. She didn't want to irritate him, because he seemed so uncertain and this she felt as a danger, but she couldn't help it.

"What you staring at me for, then? Just keep your eyes on your work. No call to go staring at me in that insolent way. Snotnose." She felt dreadfully crushed and humiliated, because she hadn't really stared, and certainly not in a rude fashion.

"Leave the child alone," said the old woman. "You've got her and now you've got to know how to handle her."

144

"I'll handle her," muttered the young man fiercely. "I'll dress her. She'll learn how to behave properly."

"You better take it easy," said the old woman. She had a funny way of talking, at once drawling and spitting, because of the lack of teeth. It was odd, with the drawn-out singsong peasant accent, but Rachel did not dare look up. "She's working, and that's all right, and she didn't need telling, and that's all right, and she's only a little one when all's said and done."

Rachel felt a bit indignant at being called a little one, but did not dare say anything. Thank heaven she was nearly at the end of her beans. It had been a big pile; she was getting very tired. And what about her homework? She hadn't seen her schoolbag since the young man had snatched it and flung it in the back of the car with the animals.

The young man seemed pleased, despite the reproof, which didn't worry him. He took his fingers out of his mouth to snicker.

"If you bite your nails like that when they're so dirty," Mlle. Lassagne said to Jackie, "you'll get worms." Rachel had been terrified at this horrible notion. Jackie hadn't minded: he never did. Ough! She shuddered. But she certainly wasn't going to worry whether this nasty person got worms. She rather hoped he did!

"The judge's daughter!" said the young man, snickering again. "So high and mighty, and look at it!" She felt angry. What was wrong with doing beans? She often did at home. She wanted to say so but didn't dare.

"I'm against," said the old man suddenly. "I have been against all the time, and I still am."

"Shut up, you." Rachel was again shocked. Even if it wasn't his father, one should not talk like that to older people. The young man had said "tu" too. Well, one said "tu" to one's parents, but not in that tone of voice; one would get clipped over the ear. Though she didn't see who would clip this one over the ear; he was too big!

"I won't shut up," said the old man, suddenly bawling very loudly. "I've a right to my opinion, and I say it's a mistake, and could lead to big trouble."

"Who's to know?" scoffed the young man. "Who's going to tell—you? No! Who else? Carney? Marie-Thérèse? Don't be so bloody stupid."

"And if someone saw?"

"Nobody saw. And nobody's going to see. We keep it indoors, right? We don't ask for money, right? We don't look for trouble. We keep our mouths shut. And so do you."

"I don't go boasting in the bar about how clever I am!" yelled the old man. "But what I say is keep your nose out of trouble. And trouble there'll be. There'll be cops smelling about. I've said so all along."

"You're so shitty you see cops under the bed in your pisspot," jeered the young man. "Cops." He spat, outrageously, on the clean floor. "I know something about cops. You don't know nothing."

"Proud, now. Something to be proud of, having been picked up before. Sung small, then, you did. They could peg you then, just by smelling your breath. And you were lucky to get off with it as you did."

The young one was all red, and absolutely flaming, like Jackie when he got into one of those awful tempers. Rachel felt frightened that they would come to blows. And if they did the old one would get the worst of it. He was so sort of scrawny. But the old woman intervened. She hadn't budged at all, just shoveled the beans into the pot and gone on sitting there massive with the huge pale face unwinking. She didn't raise her voice.

"Shut up, the both of you. You, old man, you talk about what you know. You never had no trouble with the cops because you're too bloody scared: you knuckle down and take your cap off to anybody, bowing down there like you was a serf. Like the boy says, you're shitty. And you, Pierrot, you better pipe down, too; your mouth's too big. What the old guy says is right. You think you can handle everything because you took them before. We can take them again, right, but we have to be smart and keep it quiet. We're the bosses now; we got them where we want them, all right, but no showing off. One thing we can't do and that's let anybody see we got them by the balls. It's enough we have, and it's enough we know it."

Rachel found nothing odd about this. She hadn't grasped a word, except to know that somehow it involved herself, but she was impressed by the old woman. She was, in a sort of way, a judge. Like Mama. If there were quarreling men in the court, Mama made them shut up. She had never been in the court, but she knew. Jackie knew all about it.

"Your ma's a judge. She sits up there on a special chair, and if they've been pegged for speeding she dishes out the fines. I know because Pop had a thing with a cretin who bumped him, and the insurance wanted to make it just knock for knock." The all-knowing Jackie. "But he wasn't taking that, and he shoved in a complaint for criminal negligence, and he went to court, and the judge told him he was right, and the other bugger lost his license three months. That's what your ma does."

"Well, you're just all wet, so yah," said Nathalie. "Rachel's ma doesn't do that one bit and you're talking cock. She's the Children's Judge and I know because my father told me, and what she does is she'll have you if you get caught pinching those pears, which everyone knows come out of old Léon's orchard and he's mad about it, and Ma said if I ate them it was as bad as pinching them and I'd be brought in front of Rachel's ma, and then she'd have to pay damages, because old Léon is always in and out of the court. And what's more, Jackie Sillières, you better watch out, because Rachel's ma could send you to the Assistance Publique with the Arab children and that's what'll happen to you if you pinch any more pears."

Jackie had been very noisy and aggressive, but they all knew Nathalie was right. Rachel had kept quiet because she was unsure. The Assistance Publique sounded very threatening, and

147

Arab children did get sent there, though she was not quite sure about it. It wasn't a prison. She had been there. She gave toys to the children, and wrote them letters: to Claudine, who had hair that did up in thousands of tiny curls all over her head and was nice. It was an orphanage. Jackie would not go there. She didn't really know where he would go. Perhaps to the Bon Pasteur, which was a very severe convent, where the teen-age prostitutes went. She was vague about what it was that teen-age prostitutes did, but it was pretty wicked and it was like a prison. Come to think of it, it smelled rather like it did here.

But if Mama caught this young man? He had certainly done worse things than Jackie. Because he had stolen her, and that was worse than stealing pears. But the Bon Pasteur wasn't the place. Neither was the Assistance Publique. And she didn't think he'd get sent to prison. She had heard Mama saying often enough that this was to be avoided. But the young man seemed too old for Mama, anyway. Mama did children, and this was no child. He had whiskers. Perhaps he *would* go to prison. Adults went to prison. It was not Mama's affair. She herself had never been in the prison but she had seen it from outside, and very grim it was, worse than where the ogre lived who roasted little girls on the spit and ate them, though that was, of course, just a story. Mama said it was Victorian. She didn't know what that meant, either, except it was antique, and very primitive. You had to go to the lavy on a bucket. She felt that this would be suitable for the young man, and recollected with a shudder that perhaps they went on a bucket here. He wouldn't mind. She would. And she'd soon find out, because she couldn't hold out much longer.

"What you fidgeting for, eh?"

"Please, Madame . . ." She didn't want to say in front of that horrid young man. At school one didn't mind. Anywhere else she wouldn't mind. It was, as Mama said, a natural function and nothing to be ashamed of. The Queen of England had to sit on

148

the lavy, too. What was hers like? Not a bucket. "May I whisper?"

"No you may not. No hole and corner here."

"Bad manners," said the young man ominously.

"Wants to piss," said the old boy, coming to her aid. She was grateful. She nodded at him. "All right, little rabbit, that's okay. I'll show you."

An evil sort of scullery. And one couldn't even lock the door.

"Used to have to go down the garden," said the old man, giggling. "Modern now." If that was what they called modern . . . But she felt so much better when she had finished that courage remounted.

"Want to come with me, eh? Feed the beasts? All right, you can."

"Don't let her outside!" screamed the old woman down the passage.

"Just the shed." But he winked at her. "Fussy, eh? Can't let you be seen. Do you no harm. There, that's rabbits. That's a guinea pig. You seen that before? You can pick it up. That's right. Watch he don't piss down your front. Outside's the chickies and the ducks. There's baby ducks, too."

"Can I see them?"

"In the kitchen, maybe."

"Hey, oldie," came a bawl down the passage, "fetch me a beer."

"Fetch it yourself, lazy sod," bawled the old man with a surprising force of lung. "I got to do the chickies out."

"Tell the kid, then."

"Here, see that door," said the old man. "That's the cellar. Don't fall down the steps. There's crates on the floor. You know

what a bottle of beer looks like? Fetch one. Better fetch two—
Carney'll be back soon. When I've done the chickies, I'll show
you how to draw a jug of wine from the barrel. You got to learn.
That's a kid's job. Make yerself useful."

Rachel was not frightened of cellars, even strange dark ones.
There were cobwebs and big spiders, but she was not frightened of them. She got the beer without trouble.

"That's right," said the young man sourly. "Don't shake it
then. All right. Learn to obey, and then you won't get locked
in the cellar. Because that's what we do, see, with kids which
are troublesome or cheeky. And that's what you are, a deal too
cheeky."

"She ain't been fresh yet," said the old woman. "Here, kiddy,
you come help me fold these clothes. I got to iron, see? Can you
iron?"

"Only dollies' clothes. I tried but I burned my arm. You can
still see. There's a mark."

"Got to learn, and that's the way. Burn once, you won't burn
a second time. That's the way we teach 'em. Pull it, then, kiddy,
pull it."

"My name's Rachel." She detested being called "kiddy."

"Fancy name," said the old woman with a snort. "Christine'll
be back soon. You can play with her. You can watch the television, too. Nobody means you no harm. You just watch yer step,
you'll be all right. Teach you how to live is all. You don't know
nothing. Need educating. Never seen the way real people live.
Judges!" with immense contempt.

"My mother works very hard," said Rachel, stung. "And I'm
not frightened of work."

"Here, watch it. No cheek. Glad to hear. You'll get plenty. As
well as having a nice holiday." The old woman's chuckle was
sinister.

"How long do I have to stay?"

There was a guffaw through beer from the young man. "Just

as long as we thinks right, kiddo, and that's all you need to know."

Rachel's heart sank. Nobody could possibly know where she was. Mama would try. Papa would look. Mama would tell policemen. M. Castang, for example. He could come, and he could put the horrid young man and the old woman in jail. But he wouldn't know where to come. She had no notion where she was. None of the roads were familiar. What she had seen of the village . . . She had seen nothing. In the car, the young man had picked the knife off the dashboard and told her to get down on the floor, and to stay down, if she knew what was good for her.

The clothes folded, she was allowed to go back to her chair. She looked at the clock, which was comforting, because at home in the country they had one like it, in a wooden box with a glass front, and a brass dangler that clicked rapidly to and fro. It said ten minutes to seven. She looked at the television set, which she had admired. It was very large, encased in veneer of extreme glossiness, which she found splendid, and had a brass trim and brass buttons.

"May I see?"

"Yes, youngster, but you mayn't touch." The old woman waddled across the floor and switched it on. The evening programs were being announced by the usual vapid young woman who didn't know her lines. The sight flooded Rachel with joy and relief; the busty, overdressed figure with the painted face and silly voice, ordinarily greeted with groans, was of a sudden infinitely dear and cherished, like a doll one has had a very long time (which it much resembled). So in a far-flung country, surrounded by avaricious natives, the heart of the depressed tourist floods with sympathy at sight or sound of a fellow countryman. Rachel followed every affected gesture with warm love and tear-filled eyes and intense homesickness.

The loud noise of a car motor reversing with a roar made her look up.

"There's Carney," said the old woman between thumps at the ironing board.

Rachel was afraid. She had had time to get accustomed to this kitchen, and felt familiarity—almost affection—for it. The first shock of unhappiness had worn off. It was quiet here and somehow cozy, with the television going, the old woman ironing (a peaceable and reassuring set of movements), and the old man again sitting quiet in his chair with a jug of wine and a glass. Even the dreadful young man had calmed his restless fidget, or the beer had calmed it for him. He was sitting apathetically, gazing at the screen with slumped limbs. The noisy sucking way he smoked a cigarette had ceased to scrape upon her ears. At least he was no longer showing violence.

But now anxiety surged up and she tried to make herself smaller, crouching stiffly in her chair, dreading the moment when the door would open, as though when it did it would be to give passage to the executioner and his assistants. She felt the pains of foreboding and anticipation, often much keener a torment than physical pain.

There were loud laughs and noisy voices. They were so noisy, all these people. The door was flung open with a great unnecessary bang. Except for those of the old man, who, she had already realized, carried little weight in this extraordinary household, all their movements were like that. The beans had been thrown in the pot like fagots of wood flung upon a stone hearth; the lid had gone on with a crash; even the water from the tap had gushed with violence. When the tap was closed, it gave loud shuddering jerks for no apparent reason, and a series of small explosions seemed to take place in the piping.

Yet it was a perfectly commonplace pair that entered, a man and woman of harmless and conventional aspect, and, most commonplace of all, they were pushing a young child in front of them, a little girl younger than Rachel.

The "man"—for so Rachel continued to name him, even after discovering that he was the young man's elder brother and that

152

"Carney" was a family form of Claude—was not a fearsome figure. Rachel saw at once that he was the type Papa described as "rickety": a thin thing with hollow cheeks, hollow chest, bent legs, and round shoulders. Once extracted from his car, in which he was the terror of the highway (his lifelong dream was that he could—if he had not been dispossessed and pillaged and trampled upon by the rich—have been a successful racing driver), he cut a pathetic figure. He did not wear a working outfit but a demoted Sunday suit, looking the more wretched because neither its exaggerated cut nor its cheap synthetic fabric had resisted six months' wear on best occasions. He would always have that draggled look of someone who has fallen in the pond and been put out to dry on the clothesline while he was still inside his garments. Perhaps because he was aware of this, he carried himself jauntily, with the bobbing movements of a marvelously articulated and skillfully manipulated puppet. He always performed complicated movements; a perpetual cigarette jiggled in his bony fingers and flicked from one corner to the other of his mobile mouth. As he came in he was juggling the car keys on his palm, tossing them up and catching them, flicking back his long dark hair, stroking his small mustache while his eyes jerked and snapped from side to side, with the effect of a match being struck on each bony eye socket. Where his younger brother had the big slab-sided Flanders-mare build of the old woman, who, though she was drowned in pale cool fat, still had the solid muscles given by a hundred years of buckling into the beetroot harvest under the skies of Artois, he had the loosely jointed clotheshorse look of the old man who, in his sleeveless vest and bib-and-brace salopette, had the scrawny neck of a plucked turkey and whose puckered blue jaw moved awkwardly and woodenly to and fro in an uncertain wobble the whole time, rather as though a wasp were buzzing about just at the back of his neck and he was trying to catch a glimpse of it, to know where to launch a smack from the desiccated forearm.

His wife was a different sight. Quick, alert, pretty, well cared for. A tall, slim, and shapely figure. A cascade of thick rich blond hair with a natural wave, a well-turned pair of fine-boned and suntanned legs, a lusty look of life enjoyed, an upright healthy physique, with a strongly shaped head poised on a fine neck. Isn't she pretty, thought Rachel, with a touching belief that a pretty and healthy young woman will prove to be a kind and gentle young woman. It was sad indeed that the illusion lasted so short a time. What had gone wrong? What unhappy handicap so marked and marred this pleasant, good-looking, still youthful female and turned her into a spitting viper? Even her name, Marie-Thérèse, should have been that of a gentle, pretty, and kind girl. An awkward poser it would be one day for a Judge of Instruction.

Had she been born with that voice, or had she acquired it after years of embittered suffering? It was the first thing, after the initial impression of health and vivacity, and the gift of physical good looks, to strike the onlooker.

What sharp, agonizing, penetrating pain had so struck and bitten into this strong young body? This perhaps unintelligent, but quick-learning, responsive young mind?

Something could still be seen in the face: a bright and sunny disposition checked and warped by misery. Turned violently in upon itself. Worse still; writhed and knotted into a wound that had festered, that had turned with adulthood into a well of poisonous hate.

That is a hard and bitter thing, which even an adult finds difficult to grasp. Why is the world so full of malice? Why are we so evil?

To a child it was simply a harpy, in a simple literal sense—the classical Virgilian sense. Nec sævior ulla pestis: flesh-tearing carnivore, yet a woman. A young pretty woman. Tristius haud illis monstrum: a sorrowful fact of existence.

Rachel was to learn that all her dread, of the thick floundering old woman, of the toothless old man who could still bite like the netted weasel, of Pierrot, that suffused, stupid young bull (and there are paper bulls as well as paper tigers), and even of the jaunty Carney, manipulated like dough by his fearful consort, and dangerous because of this: all dread would be insignificant before that of seeing, hearing Marie-Thérèse. And, for an eight-year-old girl, being touched by her.

Melodrama. Yes. To be sure. A generation afraid of blowing its cool despises melodrama, and is the more frightened of it. But a police officer, and especially a P.J. officer, is not contemptuous of melodrama. He comes to know, too, if he has any taste for reading, how oddly true to the facts of his existence are the nineteenth-century novelists. It is Stendhal and Balzac, Dickens and Dostoevski, who give him the visions that to him are anchored in reality.

Thus Castang, who would come one day to see Marie-Thérèse as part of Victor Hugo's family Thénardier. A Punch-and-Judy show, a Grand Guignol. Certainly. But alive, real, present, dangerous. As Thénardier lands on the ground from his prison break, breathless, giddy, nearly dead with fear, he picks himself up and says, "Who shall we eat?"

Marie-Thérèse perhaps, by paradox, resembled the most melodramatic of all nineteenth-century figures—Beethoven's Leonora. The examining magistrate, an opera-lover, came eventually to this conclusion. It was not in the dossier sent to the Chambre de Mise en Accusation; it was not mentioned to advocates or written on any official piece of paper. But in his private notes it went down: "An evil Leonora—if such a thing is conceivable."

The moment she came in the door, she broke out into a croaking shriek of laughter. "The judge's child!"

Rachel shrank away before the gloating face, stunned.

An officer of Police Judiciaire does not make anything to boast about in the way of a living. Even with a few years of seniority, he is at a modest clerkly level, and Castang lived in a street so apparently beyond his means that he had been suspected betimes of taking bribes. This street, besides being relatively close to the center of the town, and a small pleasant bike ride from the office, was much sought after: an address with considerable standing. There were three reasons for this, all good. The street led nowhere in particular and was not much used by cars. It faced a disused canal whose water ambled at foot pace between grassy banks, with towpaths from the old horse-drawn barge days. It had an unusually wide pavement on which residents could park their cars in comfort between splendid big poplar trees of much age and beauty: these on the canal side. On the house side were planes. This was all very nice.

When Vera had had the accident that left her legs paralyzed (not a road accident, not even a ski accident, but—even more dull and boring—a stupid fall while catapulting off the parallel bars used by girl gymnasts: Vera as a teen-ager had been a competition gymnast), they had been forced to conclude that she would be in a wheelchair for the best part of her life. No operation was possible. Nearly a year of physiotherapy—including a long and horrible stay in a re-education center full of pathetic boys who had been in motorbike accidents, and a grandiose sea-water cure where her roommate was an international ski champion with a ruptured Achilles tendon (amazingly patient on her crutches, the child was only eighteen, had nothing else to live for, and this had given Vera a new lease of fortitude) —had made no improvement in her condition. Her top half was better-looking, firmer-muscled than it had ever been, but the sad wasted legs just would not obey. Castang had determined that if she was never going to go out much any more she was at least going to have a flat with a view, and a quiet street where she could sit on a balcony and draw trees, for Vera had been to the Beaux-Arts school as a teen-ager in Czechoslovakia, and even made a small amount of money as an illustrator, which was very good for her morale.

Professor Rabinowics, the doctor at the University Hospital who was her specialist and had become a friend, had pulled strings to find them this flat. He had been pessimistic about the future.

"Medicine has done all it can. But it has been known for these things to get better, not altogether spontaneously."

"You mean I should go to Lourdes or something and pray for a miracle?"

"Well, I'm far from despising that: it's a therapy like another, but it's not quite what I meant. I've no judgment to make about supernatural resources. The Madonna might cure you, and so, come to that, might a witch doctor; I know one or two—alas, the Social Security Office won't repay them. What I wanted to say was that I may have exhausted my resources, but I'm not altogether convinced that you have exhausted yours."

And in the end Rab had refused to give an opinion. Was it physical or metaphysical? Had Vera simply been her own witch doctor? And—she was a baroque, Jesuitical sort of Czech Catholic—had the Madonna lent a hand?

"More than likely," said Rab. "The X-rays are exceedingly difficult to interpret, but something happened to the lesion." All that had happened perceptible to the human eye was that Vera went on stubbornly exercising her legs for nearly eighteen months. One day she stood up, upon the pins, and didn't fall down. Some few days later (this had all been kept a dark secret), she had taken a wobbly step, and still hadn't fallen down.

Vera now walked, in a shuffly way; a bit odd. She couldn't keep it up for long. But she got around the flat, she limped through the shopping, she could get into and out of (which was harder) a car. And the muscles of the legs were no longer wasted. As good as new, said Castang, contemplating them with pride and satisfaction.

Neither the Madonna nor the witch doctors had been efficacious in her attempts at having a baby, but this was a problem dating from before the fall.

She had wanted to give up the flat, which drained their resources. They never had anything in the bank.

"Not on your life," said Castang, imposing a thoroughly male decision. It was a very small-bourgeois existence, with a canary and a little orange tree.

Vera looked up as he came in, tired, sweaty, and bearing marks of discouragement.

"That was a long day."

"Very long, and singularly useless. I've nothing to show for it."

"Do you want dinner now, or wait till you get it?"

"I'd like to wait a bit. Does it matter?"

"Not a bit; it's stew."

"I must have a shower. A drink first to get up courage. I need to feel comfortable, but first I want to feel at home."

"My poor boy."

"You know, I'd like very much to bust this. I feel deeply involved. Implicated." His hands sketched folds. "Emberlificoté."

"Yes. I can understand. I'm very fond of Colette; she's a good person. Since I feel bound with ties of affection as well as sympathy, I don't feel able to make anything of it. I just sit numb, wondering how it must be for her. I can't arrive at seeing it from outside."

"Better," drinking half a glass of red wine and topping it up from the bottle. As cheap wine went, this was honest. It was almost honorable. He got it from the grower. One doesn't have to take bribes to be able to enjoy privileges. "Throw me the matches, would you? Richard asked this morning whether I'd perhaps let myself get overfriendly with Colette."

"The ideas he gets!"

"Yes, well, it doesn't do to take him too literally. More a way of telling me his own mind was cantering around, wondering whether either of them would have a motive, say, for using the child as a weapon."

"Meaning that she wasn't kidnapped at all?"

"I think she's been kidnapped, all right. But Richard's a cautious bastard. He thinks about possible knowledge, eventual connivance, a conceivable obscure device or even plan."

"That sounds plain silly to me."

"If one just supposed, for example, that Colette had a lover, would you know about it, do you think?"

"Good heaven, are you serious? You think we go about whispering teen-age confidences into one another's ears? You can't be that naïve surely. Nor Richard, for goodness' sake. If he thinks Colette tells me about her private life, he is imbecile, and if he thinks I'd spy for him on a friend—assuming she had given me any confidences about her personal problems—then he's infamous."

"You wouldn't even tell me? Assuming I needed badly to know?"

"My poor wolf, I suppose I tell you pretty well everything I know or hear, since you're my husband, poor you, and I suppose if I came into possession of any knowledge involving a crime or a possible crime, or even just a felony, I'd tell the police. If it were a case of conscience, you know, the professional secret or the confessional secret, I suppose I'd be in a dilemma. It's never happened to me, so I don't know. I imagine that it would worry me very much. I think, though, that if Colette had given me a personal confidence, feeling sure I would respect it, I'd hesitate a long while before blabbing, even to you. I'd want to feel strongly convinced that you had the right to know."

"And that only the existence of a crime would give me that right, is that it?" finishing his glass and his cigarette.

"I suppose so. I haven't thought it out."

"Do think it out—while I have a shower."

"But, my darling, I don't have any such knowledge, believe me, so don't add to your anxieties, I beg of you. Anyway, if

Colette's lover is you"—laughing—"presumably I'd be the last person she'd confide in. But surely I don't need to tell you that we're friends but that doesn't mean she confides. In any case, she's a secret person who doesn't gush about her innermost. It would be very dull if she did. Does anybody? Adults don't, surely. They may be transparent persons, but they still have all sorts of secrets, or they wouldn't be adults."

Castang, wearily, was undressing. He threw his dirty clothes on the bedroom floor, sighed, picked them up again, and put them in the basket. He kept the bathroom door open to avoid a lot of stuffy condensation from the warm summer evening. He could hear Vera talking, but not what she said, because of the rush of water.

"Anyway," Vera was saying, scooting her wheelchair across into the kitchen, which was a lot quicker than walking, "as Colette herself says, it's not what you do that counts, where the police are concerned; it's what it can be made to look like in a court."

She put a flame under her vegetables and gave the stew a stir to be sure it wasn't sticking. He had forgotten—or been in too much of a hurry—to get any clean underclothes. Men! They left the bathroom door open, made a lot of noise and splashing, left water all over the bathroom floor—she did wish she could afford something better than beastly cheap plastic shower curtains—and then came rolling out all bare and hairy complaining that there were no clean underclothes. She went patiently into the bedroom to get them. A shirt button was off; she got a needle and thread. He was jumping about and yelling because he had turned on the cold water. The underclothes were old and worn thin, patched across the seat. The shirt collar needed turning. She could thank God it hadn't been her hands that got paralyzed. She made virtually all her own clothes, and mended all his. Hmm. One could always find excuses to be grateful for not having children.

He appeared with a wet towel; also a thing worn thin and

needing replacing. Warmth and moisture made the hair on the stringy forearms fluff up; his legs were still plastered. The big stitched scar on his back, running from the bottom of his ribs up to the shoulder blade, was white and crinkly: he had been ripped by a shell splinter and sewn up casually. Every time she looked at it, she couldn't help thinking she would have made a better job with a needle and thread than that. Still, field hospitals in Indochina . . . not exactly proliferating in creature comforts.

Face hollowed by fatigue; muscles sunken, queer nose a bit flattened by boxing. The hair, when wet, could be seen getting thin on top. Too young to be looking that middle-aged.

Vera thought that if he were Colette's lover Colette had made a good pick.

He was in no hurry to dress: he sat there contented, waiting for the warm evening air to dry his skin thoroughly. The chair, which was rattan and had a washable cushion, would take no harm. He took a second drink, a thing he rarely did. She bit off her thread and tossed him the shirt.

"Photograph," she said, giggling. "Unbuttoned policeman."

He laughed. "Yes, one's there all day, neat and functional— the severity, you know, and the official importance. 'Now, Mrs. Whozis, I want you to think carefully. Police Judiciaire, just answer the questions.' I suppose some take it home with them. Bullying their wives, having the children brought up with military exactitude. Law and order in the home. 'Go and get your hair cut. Show me your school exercise books, and if your marks fall below the acceptable level I'll deprive you of pleasures: no going out, no television; watch it or I'll take the belt to you.' There are some like that, too weak to be able to take the uniform off; they have to be wearing it even in bed. And there are some one knows of who go bloody near the limit of what is officially permissible, and even beyond it, at work. Abattoir types. Always talk in a yell, always got their hands loose to make some boy's ears ring—nastily expert in giving a slap without its leaving a mark. They're not bad, most of them, just coarsened, just naturally bastardly, but I think a lot go home and are perfectly reasonable and quiet with their family. Nearly all get pretty calloused. So do doctors, or dentists, or whatever. Make up your mind not to get calloused and it's one long grind."

"And poor."

"And poor. Come home and your wife goes on about turning a shirt collar and you start thinking of all the nice contributions you could be getting for turning a blind eye. Half the time you're turning a blind eye anyhow, and it eats in to think you could be getting paid—and pretty well paid—for doing nothing. You don't need to connive at any crime; only the very stupid ones do that—you know, taking a kickback from the sale of drugs in a café. All you need to do is take the borderline stuff, the old-fashioned misdemeanors. 'Well, Mr. Thing, you do realize that it's a technical infraction, it's in the code, but since it's not really a moral issue nowadays, in these changing times, I'm prepared to be indulgent; and now what about our widows and orphans?' A good P.J. cop doesn't have to take any bribes at all. He leaves that to the municipal small fry, tapping the businessmen in exchange for not making a fuss over illegal parking on the pavement. In the P.J. you don't need anything crude like money changing hands. I do you a favor, you do me a favor. See that the children get good marks at school, see that my wife gets her hairdressing free and her clothes at sale prices. See that I get a good buy on a watch or a car or a suit. All you need do is respect your own standing at your own level. Once you're a commissaire, it becomes a bit more sophisticated. Make certain I have a surefire stock-exchange tip. I'd like to join the golf club, but I find the dues kind of high. I like to go to starred restaurants, and don't give me that crap about the tables all being reserved."

"And you had to go and marry a Czech Communist."

"Come off it, Communists take far more bribes than we do."

"An artist, then."

162

"That's better. If I started playing the golf-club game, it'd just make you sick."

"So petty. I'd far rather be poor."

"I'd like to be rich, for a change."

"Make up to Colette, quietly. A Judge of Instruction can do a cop a lot of good, on the quiet. See that he's well noted with his superiors. That the Proc thinks him a good fellow, in line for a few rewards. That he'll get transferred to a good district in Paris."

"Most of the Paris cops I know have requests in to be transferred to the provinces. Too far to go to get home when off duty."

"Those are the stupid ones. The good ones have unobtrusive flats in historical buildings where the rents are frozen."

"I know one who has a flat in the Rue Bonaparte. Building is classified—there's no lift. And not much space. But there's a garden behind the house. And I know another, on the court-yard, an hôtel particulier in the Rue de Sèvres. Both work in the sixth arrondissement. Five minutes' gentle stroll to work in the mornings, stopping for coffee and a couple of fresh croissants. They don't need anything old-fashioned like a car to get to work, and they don't climb into a Métro, either. The rent's peppercorn, with antique furniture thrown in. They've never taken a bribe in their lives."

"And yet you're clever enough. It's your wife who is stupid."

"All she has to do is accommodate. Like if her husband is friendly with a magistrate, see that the magistrate's husband is kept happy."

"Yes. It all goes nice and smooth. And then the stupid magistrate's stupid child gets itself kidnapped. So, you being a pal, they ring you up quick to make sure that a press blanket is put on and all the scandal stays inside the family."

"That's right. But I've got to be very careful that that bastard Richard doesn't get into the act, because he wants to make quite sure the Proc won't get cross with him."

"Children are very embarrassing."

"One does far better not to have any."

"Poor Colette. She's under considerable strain," went on Vera reflectively. "She is very tense under that relaxed exterior. Eaten up by all sorts of anxieties. Worries about how the child sees her, and how the child judges her. My mama is a magistrate. That's bad. My mama is a bit of a whore, really. That's not very good, either. She's far too fixated on the child's opinion of her."

"You think she'd better have another one? By me, maybe?"

Vera looked at him wryly. "That's a bit like saying I ought to stir my stumps, isn't it? If I can't manage with you, I'd better jog Bernard into collecting his responsibilities. Vera thinks herself an artist, silly bitch. Restless dissatisfied woman: give her a baby, do her a world of good. And Henri will know perfectly well, and it gives him a good efficient lever. Make Castang a commissaire; we'll find someone who is decidedly superfluous to requirement. Uh—prompt me."

"Sallebert. He's a lazy bugger; Richard does all his work. Adjunct commissaire is a good job to have: the pay is reasonable and the responsibility minimal. Post M. Sallebert to Pézenas and give me his job."

"Can I get the dinner on the table? Put your shirt on, do; I'm not having men with hairy armpits at the dinner table, even if you aren't even an adjunct commissaire. Really, it is the child who is the great stumbling block."

"You're telling me. Bernard becomes thoroughly unbalanced. Colette can't be relied upon. What does she do? Flies into a panic and phones me. I'm involved right from the start. If anything goes wrong, Richard blames me. If I get it sorted out, Richard takes all the credit. Because, either way, the Proc is breathing down his neck. I'm in the middle getting screwed. And the worst is, first, I'm intensely worried about what happens to Rachel. She's my mistress's adored only child. Second, as a police operation, she's turning out singularly difficult and ungrateful. Where is the child? What has happened to her? Nobody has the faintest idea."

"Nobody?" said Vera, ladling stew. Not even the faintest? Because these tirades were not unknown after wearisome days, full of a lot of futile stumbling about. When they had been newly married, she used to have horrid visions of a husband sacked for incompetence, or transferred to some barbarous hamlet in the extreme backwoods of the Massif Central. She no longer took the tirades quite that seriously.

"Throughout the entire day, I discovered one grain of fact—literally the size of a pea. Which isn't linked to anything, may be sheer coincidence, and even if connected—and that remains pure speculation—isn't helpful, because what is the rabbit population of France? There's no evidence that any kidnapping ever took place. Which balances us between two uneasy notions. That a dangerous maniac somehow gained possession of the child, which would mean giving what we know to the press and appealing for information. Not a happy thought, and we labor under the tremendous handicap of twenty-four hours lost. Or that there never was any kidnapping, that either Bernard or Colette—you can take your choice—has been playing an immense comedy, in a quite unbalanced and dangerously irrational fashion. Richard has been toying with this notion—how seriously I don't know. Nor what—if anything—he might have to go on. Are there any more beans?"

"Didn't he give you any instructions?"

"He just went enigmatic. Told me to continue probing the background. After all, what do we know about them? Precious little. What do you know, even?"

"She's a good judge, I should think; I've never seen her at work."

"She bears that reputation," said Castang.

"I only know her outside, and then she can say things of startling silliness. What are you going to do?"

"Go over there after supper, in the role of family friend. They haven't realized it yet, but the police can put a searchlight on one's private life which is unpleasantly bright, upon occasion."

"Think if it were us," said Vera softly.

"I am," he said, "but the point's got to be cleared up. Startling silliness, you said. Like for instance?"

"Are you examining me?"

"Yes," briefly. "Look, of course it's never very nice to be in an investigation of a serious crime against the person. You have to go trampling in on people's privacy. All sorts of little details that aren't necessarily damaging but that they'd rather keep to themselves or that they wouldn't mind telling a doctor inside his professional secrecy, but having it typed out and read back to them makes them wriggle. A magistrate—or a policeman, too —has his own professional secret, too, of course. But these dossiers are seen by a lot of people: the smallest of details might come to acquire importance; it might be something the president of a tribunal decided to bring out in open court, that you'd been sleeping with your sister or something. We get pretty depersonalized about this, even brutalized. But it still comes as a shock when it happens to oneself, or to one's friends."

"Yes," said Vera unhappily.

"You don't really understand, do you?"

"Not altogether."

"This—Colette's a magistrate; she knows all this. So like a good magistrate—or a good policeman—she keeps it all compartmentalized. Her professional mentality doesn't leak into her private life. If she's examining the parents of some child that set the place on fire, she doesn't stop to ask herself 'Suppose this were me.' You do that because you're an artist, but justice —or police work—doesn't get done that way. I might be underestimating her, I don't know. But I don't think she's grasped the fact yet that this time it's her under the lamp, and that if Richard wants, he can reach a long way into her privacy. Including that of her friends."

"You're saying—if I've understood—that if the hypothesis is

166

correct, and you're her lover, it would come out."

"Yes."

"And if Bernard was my lover—that, too."

"Correct, Madame. For all I know, Richard's got someone watching this house."

Vera took a cigarette, a thing she did two or three times a week. "Colette has never told me anything like that," she said slowly. "When I said she was capable of silliness, I meant quite commonplace things. She has a weakness for astrology, and fortune-telling, and magic—she has a childish side. And foolish notions. There's no harm in my telling you."

"Whether there is or not—you better bloody tell me."

"Oh, well, the other day we were talking about holidays, and she brought up that old gag about having separate holidays. You know the theory. Saturnalia when the law does not run. One is happily married and one has a good husband, but when one goes on holiday one puts the wedding ring in the handbag and goes looking for adventure, and the husband goes off on his side, and this is simply lovely, and very adult and mature and an enriching experience and all that, and nobody tells and nobody asks—oh, you know."

"A vulgar, silly, and dangerous fantasy."

"That's what I told Colette," said Vera dryly.

"Does she do things like that?"

"I don't suppose she does more than toy with them. If she did them, she probably wouldn't tell me. Or it might be her way of setting aside the hidebound bourgeois traditionalist upbringing she's so ashamed of."

"Stupid cow," muttered Castang angrily.

"She's vulnerable. Needs constant reassurance. Tense under that air of relaxation. Look how she drives that car. Too fast."

"But well."

"Sure," said Vera. "Familiar syndrome. When women are good drivers, they are very good, equal to any man. Same with magistrates."

"But she's perfectly aware she's good, and accepted as good. It's ridiculous; she doesn't need to go proving it to herself the whole while."

"She always wonders whether she's taken seriously. Always oversensitive to a suggestion of humiliation. She feels that at present. I got a long tirade this morning. All about she knew it was absurd but she couldn't rid herself of a feeling that this had all been arranged to discredit her."

"Now, that is interesting."

"It's idiotic. I told her so."

"Bernard's more the one really to have secret feelings of inadequacy or notions of being humiliated. Being sensitive about commerce, or anxious lest people find out about the yogurt and start laughing."

"But it's perfectly honest to sell yogurt."

"Of course it is. We're accustomed to being despised by the neighbors for being in the police. It's thought of as a dirty job. Yogurt sounds to me like a paradise of healthy clean living." And he couldn't resist laughing at himself. It was true, ridiculous as it sounded. Several of their neighbors felt that having a cop in the building lowered their standing. Even when they themselves worked in insurance companies and, as Vera remarked, there's nothing lower than that.

"What are you laughing at?" she asked, relieved.

"Oh, just that this afternoon I was interviewing Bernard's boss. Partner, by courtesy. Now, there's a fellow who's quite single-minded about his yogurt. Thinks of nothing else. Humorless. Rather admires Bernard for being sensitive and all that. Poor old Bernard, who is sensitive all right, about not taking yogurt seriously enough. And has some resentfulness at his being sensitive about Colette being a judge, while he's just a dirty little sales manager."

"Something the way I'm sensitive about you being a P.J. cop and a good one? Whereas I'm a draggy little Czech peasant with broken legs. A bloody hindrance, and can't even give you a baby."

He looked at her across the table, face emptied of expression.

"Sure. Like I'm sensitive about being a dirty little muckraking cop, sniffing at old clothes through a magnifying glass, and getting very humiliated about my wife being an artist."

"So we both try not to pity ourselves. Looking it in the eye, you rather fancy Colette. I'm unsurprised. She's exceedingly attractive."

"Maybe—when I'm very tired; like now. Discouraged. At that moment she might make my head swim a bit."

"Not an open-air object, like the rustic wife smelling of sweat and cherry orchards. What perfume does she use?"

"How should I know?" He laughed. "Chamade, probably."

"What does it mean?"

"Medieval term for surrender," grinning at her.

There was a small awkward silence.

"I wouldn't altogether feel surprise or grievance," said Vera, "if you were her lover."

"As Richard thinks I am. What would you feel?"

"I'd think it my duty to keep my mouth shut. What is unsaid is better left unsaid. Even if what is thought cannot be unthought."

"A policeman finds the same. One starts turning up things that had been better left unturned."

"Everyone, however placid and serene their life, needs a lot of courage to keep it running. Without grief and pain. Without thinking a lot of things better left unthought."

"Colette is wondering whether this hasn't all been arranged to discredit her. Richard's little theory begins to gain ground— that Bernard is capable of cooking up a drama to sabotage her."

"Why do people take lovers?" abruptly. The sudden naïveté —Vera's speciality. The only way to take it was seriously.

"They haven't enough illusions?"

"A sign of fundamental feebleness? Piffling? Except for the very young."

"Yes—at eighteen, cocufying some pompous bore is the ideal."

"After that, surely, a sign of stultification. Prolonged immaturity, like Louis Quinze. Hmm," said Vera reflectively, "I'm stultified, all right."

The telephone rang. Castang picked it up languidly. A small frown formed between his eyes. As the voice went on, now and then suddenly too high and too loud, forcing him to make a face and hold the receiver away from his ear, Vera watched. She was too far off to pick up the spare earpiece and listen in, and it was too much trouble to satisfy her curiosity, even though she recognized Colette's voice—or, rather, intonations. The voice itself was shrill and edgy. A drama? She watched Castang's face changing from irritation to boredom, then to a sort of good humor, and gradually back to a kind of interest, going a bit further than just curiosity.

"She's pie-eyed," putting the phone down. "Come to our party."

"Party's well on the way, to judge by her voice."

"Mmm. In a mood to do silly things, all right—risky things, too. And Bernard's in no condition to stop her. She wants me to bring you."

"You're going to the party?"

"I was going anyway, as I told you: detecting to do. I was putting it off. Waiting another half hour won't make me any more thrilled. But what about you?"

"I'm more than game," said Vera enigmatically. "Help me change my frock."

They got into the car together. Castang had put on a seersucker shirt, and after some thought a linen jacket to conceal the fact that he was wearing a gun. Taking one's gun to a party, thought Vera: hmm . . . She was wearing an ankle-length cotton dress. Loose enough for her, too, to wear a gun. But it would take a lot of time and effort to get at it. Unless somebody strips me, she thought. Perhaps I should take my bow and arrow. Will you show me how to put my fingers on the string? Emma, came Mr. Knightly's voice, you are behaving foolishly.

Castang drove, always very serious and deliberate at the wheel of a car, and looking both ways the whole time. This extreme caution struck her. She remarked on it jovially.

"I've my wife with me," said Castang in a toneless grunt. It didn't sound as though he were warming up to enjoy himself. Colette carried a gun in her bag. She had told Vera a rambling tale of bringing it out the other day, for the first time, to point at a nighttime lover-boy. As long as this doesn't become a habit . . .

The street was deserted, the Résidence Dampierre wrapped in discreet bourgeois tranquility. Whether or not the inhabitants had peace of mind, nothing must be allowed to show. Broad deep generous curtains of full-length velvet drawn across their windows. The windows themselves firmly shut, even on a June night. The night air is noxious, pernicious, most unhealthy. The sounds, and smells, and dusts and din of traffic must be most painstakingly excluded. And to be sure, anything going on within must be kept in. Not just an eye patch, thought Vera, but a nicely cut, pretty velvet mask. Mask!—a whole veil. Our velvet hand adjusts our veil. The countenance must not be seen to be distorted by pain or fear. The screams must be stifled.

A line of verse came from somewhere into her mind. What had brought it there? Velvet, perhaps. "Peace of mind becomes me . . ."—yes, of course—"As soft white velvet hands become a man . . ." Oddly touching scrap of verse. The silent scream of Albertine Sarrazin at the barred window of Amiens prison. She'd had no velvet curtain there.

"As on half-healed wound a dressing— A dressing of diamond." She said it well, thought Vera. The softness of gauze and the hardness of the hardest grit: abrasiveness of diamond dust. No mere grindstone could cause such exquisite pain to the film of new, tender pink skin. And yet precious, that pain . . . precious as diamonds . . .

What had kept Albertine going? Not her pride in herself, in her writing. Simple. Simple love, pride in her man, love for the man who had not had soft velvet hands.

Soft and delicate this interior. Not velvet but beautiful lined linen curtains of a soft straw color. Vera had never been able to afford any curtains at all in her own living room, and had to be content with Venetian blinds; she really rather wished that Henri would pick up a few bribes from time to time. And shantung lampshades of that same straw color, with lines like straw in the weave. And pale beautiful straw-colored champagne. Oy! Krug 1966. No less.

And even soft straw-colored music. Bernard's immensely expensive high-fidelity record player, and one of Colette's delightful collection of "nostalgia" records. She had something for every mood. Noël Coward's song about the room with the view. Hoagy Carmichael—Lauren Bacall's song from *To Have and Have Not*—ha. The vintage of 1944: hadn't that also been a good champagne year? And "My Defenses Are Low." The hell they are. All we need now is Richard Tauber to sing "You Are My Heart's Delight." Colette had that, too. As well as Tauber singing Mozart: better and more bitter. And playing at present she had Nelson Eddy and Jeanette MacDonald giving their wildly laughable version of "The Indian Love Call."

"Why'n't you take off your jacket?" asked Colette in her soft, party-slurred voice.

"Because I'm wearing a gun underneath," crisp.

"And he can't take his trousers off for the same reason." Bernard being funny. This piece of undergraduate wit went down badly.

"Go sniff some glue or something."

"Oh, come, Henri, darling, don't be acerbitous."

"The people are nice and the drinks are good, but the kind of party where the women get shrill and somebody ends up yelling, 'Let's all sleep with one another's husbands,' is just crappy."

"Henri," said Colette, "that was rather a wounding thing to say."

"Where did this elaborate fantasy start? Don't think I'm against; I thought it funny. Just that if we end up believing it's true we can hardly be surprised if everybody else does, too. There's no rumor so tenacious as the one you start yourself."

"What on earth are you making such a fuss about?" asked Colette languidly. "Who has to go running to disprove rumors that don't even exist? You're being a self-important prig."

"I'm a cop," said Castang, "with enough experience to know there's another cop outside."

"You mean the slave of the phone down in the basement? That he really is listening to all our conversations?"

"I don't know whether he is or not," tranquilly. "It would be perfectly possible. I doubt it, because you're a magistrate, and other magistrates might not take kindly to the idea of eavesdropping: it might happen to them someday. And because you're a magistrate, you're entitled to a good deal of protection, and by the same token you'd be unusually vulnerable in the case of anybody cooking up a rumor about you. As for me, I'm unimportant; nobody much cares who I sleep with. But it would be enough to have a suggestion made—say, that your husband was friendly with my wife—for a lot of people to conclude that I was conspiring with you to cover it up."

"But this is preposterous—you don't mean to say Richard imagines that. . . ."

"Why not? You did."

Colette looked at him with a sort of weary disbelief.

"My dear boy," she said. "I don't know whether the imaginative M. Richard is trying to protect his department from any eventual criticism, or is setting you up as a scapegoat in the event of M. Besson taking a dim view, but I don't know what you're using for brains. I am, despite my youth and innocence, aware of the dangers of a magistrate having things in his or her life—even private life—that he or she would prefer to conceal. And I'm aware that cops very easily get frightened lest even their wives' friendships should compromise their career. I suppose I shouldn't be surprised that an old wife like Richard has the mentality of the John Birch Society. I had thought better of you. I had imagined Vera's husband capable of understanding that a time sometimes comes when one just doesn't give a damn; when one wishes to give way to feelings that were originally those of a spontaneous and generous character. When one feels so hemmed about and encompassed by malice that one wishes to break out."

She was taking deep breaths in order not to yell. "I don't have much experience as a magistrate, or of life, but quite enough to know that the whole of society is based upon thinking ill of others, and that the chief pleasure of the human animal in all walks of life is backbiting." She was working herself up now into a fine rage: what Bernard—who was wise enough to keep his mouth shut—called "lashing her tail."

"So that as one small section of educated persons we try to have a belief in civilization. Which is what? Perhaps a tiny effort now and again to raise ourselves above the level of plant biologists and fortune-tellers, to believe that we aren't just animals concerned with nothing but fear, aggression, and the satisfactions of the belly."

Castang was just thinking that a university education served this much purpose at least, that emotional problems always got placed at the level of intellectual argument, when abruptly she came down again to personalities.

"You're such an imbecile that you can't even see why I wanted to get drunk. It wasn't just for crude oblivion, you know.

174

And I suppose I can't blame Richard if he has so little understanding as really to believe that Bernard or myself would use Rachel as a weapon against the other, whatever dirty tricks we may be capable of."

"Good," said Castang. "I suppose you're right and I am a horrible prig. In all justice, though, don't believe I'm bothered by every evil notion Richard gets into his head. I came here to tease him a little, it's true. You alarmed me because I thought you were getting a bit too reckless. The press is like a champagne bottle: if you want to get the cork off without noise, it's as well not to shake it too roughly. You don't want to go to bed with me in the least; you've a vague notion of humiliating yourself and punishing Bernard for getting you in the shit, and punishing yourself for wanting to give him pain, and we were handy bananas."

"Bananas?" asked Bernard, puzzled.

"Back in Cayenne—the Islands of Salvation, well named—the executioner used to test the guillotine on a banana stalk. Right thickness, right resistance."

"Henri," said Bernard softly, grinning, "tell me one thing honestly. Did you believe—put it, was there a moment you believed—that I was sleeping with your wife?"

"Oh, if you want me to be quite honest . . . I'm a policeman; do you really believe I'll ever be that honest?"

"Wouldn't do you any harm to try," said Colette.

"All right, then, if I'm going to be absolutely honest—for an instant. A very fleeting instant." All three were laughing at Vera's outraged face. "I would be readier, on the whole, to believe myself Colette's lover."

"The wish being father to the thought," said Vera tartly.

"Because we're really more reckless. Artists never are, really. They pretend to be; big bohemian act of utter responsibility to an irresponsible ideal."

"Huh?"

"All that asserting of their independence, pretending the

175

rules don't apply to them. But unless they're very stupid there's generally a cold cunning little mind working away there, well able to judge what they will and what they won't get away with."

Colette burst out laughing. "So much for you and your kitchenmaids," she told Bernard.

"Crime," Castang told her meaningly, "is only committed by the bourgeois."

"You're calling yourself a bourgeois now?" Vera asked, interested.

"All policemen are bourgeois—conditioned by the rules of a bourgeois society, the principal characteristic of which is, as Colette pointed out, the willingness, readiness, and insistence upon thinking ill of other people."

"Did you come here thinking I'd go to bed with you?" asked Colette curiously.

"There was a moment when you felt quite ready to," he told her.

"That's not an answer to my question," said the magistrate.

"No, Madame la Juge. Put it that I was aware that the moment existed."

"Touché," said Bernard.

"You conjugating that in the masculine or the feminine?" she wanted to know.

"I'll get you off the hook," said Castang. "I really came here to do a bit of work. As your partner Jérôme puts it succinctly, no bloomers-down allowed in my factory."

"Now who's touché?" remarked Colette.

"I came to the conclusion I hadn't done a proper day's work."

The whole atmosphere changed. It was like a refrigerator that has had what technicians blandly call the "intelligence" to find itself constipated with masses of ice, and switches itself on to defrost. At a certain moment, it decides that it is sufficiently purged, and starts freezing again.

"I want to put a certain number of questions." Even the

record player in the corner, coming to the end of its meal of disks, fell silent.

"Your country house."

"It's not really a house," said Bernard automatically. "It's still just a shack, really. We own a certain amount of land, that's all. Why don't you come out and see this weekend—when we have Rachel back?"

"I may be out there even quicker."

"But this is very odd. Are you thinking it has anything to do with—?"

"I don't know. It's been an odd day. Richard, as you know, has been mucking about—I suppose that's the right word—at the Palais all day. Looking at dossiers. Wondering why."

"It is the right word," muttered Colette. "Shit-shoveling."

"I spent the day hereabouts, tactically—huh—working out how. Going up and down the hill. Somewhere on that hill . . . She left the school. She set out for home. Carrying her bag. There's no doubt about it. The alleyway from the village— doesn't matter which, because they both meet at that ramp."

"It's odd; I've hardly ever been that way—I suppose because we don't do much in the village."

"I shop there occasionally," said Colette, "and take the short cut home. But I've never noticed it particularly. One doesn't, somehow, living up here."

"Exactly. It's part of the village. Whereas you're townspeople, living out here by accident."

"It's a sort of playground for the children."

"And where—this preoccupied me—would she have been momentarily out of sight and away from the attention of the other children, the people who live there, all the potential witnesses to anything outside the ordinary pattern? There's precious little. There are just two places that form cul-de-sacs, which might be fertile ground for the criminal attempt we now feel sure has taken place. I went over them very carefully, because I have the absolute conviction that she passed by there.

Nothing else makes any sense. There's not a shred of any suggestion that she deviated from a familiar path. I'm not going to bore you with a round-by-round commentary. I brought a boy with me who had a camera, and he took pictures—a great many in close detail. There's nothing in them of any interest. Confused traces of feet and tire tracks, too blurred to mean anything on that dry ground. The usual litter—well, that's police work; photos of old cigarette stubs and chewing-gum wrappers: one just does it to be thorough, because somewhere, sometime, one might find a link.

"In one of these blank corners, we found a very promising suspect: crazy old boy with delusions and grievances about justice, quite unbalanced, lives there in ambush. For a moment, we thought we had it taped, whipped along to your colleague, Colette, got a search warrant, and came up with a handful of dust—nothing, a dud. Well, one's accustomed to that.

"The other place is as likely; children play forts there, and Indians, and probably father-and-mother—sort of overflow to a building site. But less promising, too, because overlooked by a nosy old biddy, and I'm witness she doesn't miss much. Technically less possibility. Good, I'm beginning to sound like Richard but it started giving some outline of the person—or brain, if there's more than one—we have to deal with. Someone cunning, sly, and who'd thought out a clever trap. I don't mean intelligent in an intellectual sense—more in a military way: someone who knew how not to be conspicuous, how not to attract attention. I'm sure, too, it was planned, thought out by someone who took a good look at the terrain and knew instinctively where best to place his ambush. A country man, I'd bet, because it's not an urban landscape, it hasn't the characteristics of an urban ambush, and also because there's a piece of physical evidence; it's not connected in any way, but neither is it connected to anything else around there."

"And this is?" inquired the judge coldly.

"I said a handful of dust; should have said rabbit shit. A rabbit was wandering about there. I make three conclusions. People have rabbits anywhere, also there, but nobody lets them loose, because, as it was put to me flatly, there's too many cars and too many boys. Now that's, you'll agree, a good bait for an eight-year-old girl. Ambles about and hops. Cuddly. No urban—I mean flat-bred—child resists that. Because it's the most satisfying sort of toy. An urban mentality could perfectly well think of it, it seems to me, but where would he get the rabbit, how would he handle it, where would he keep it? It's the weak part, which stinks of contrivance and fiction, in *The Hound of the Baskervilles*. Fellow—I forget his name—had to invent a whole enormous melodrama of pathless bogs and abandoned moorlands and unworked mines and whatnot because of where to keep the bloody hound, which is a hell of an awkward thing. He's a sort of undersized harmless-looking butterfly chaser, and how does he organize this savage beast, painting its muzzle with phosphorus and all—it's just idiotic, unless of course you happen to fall under the spell of all that Sherlock crap, which needs, to be at all convincing, the assumption that all policemen from start to finish are totally cretinous as well as craven. The Scotland Yard inspector, when he sees the hound, gives a yell of terror and falls flat on his face, though a moment before he was making with the big pistol. That's typical faking. In real life, of course, the slowest and most rustic village cop would have: one, cleared the whole job up in three days; and, two, told that great bullshitter Holmes to fuck off out of it and stop his fancy posturing. Sorry, Mister, the law enforcement around here is me. Now, sorry for the parenthesis, the country cop here is me, and the hound's a rabbit, and that's a thing a countryman thinks of and uses because he can handle it effortlessly; it's unforced, it's natural. Sorry, I'm getting heated. Richard doesn't see it because he's full of fancy Freudian notions about Bernard having cooked this up as a fancy way of punishing Colette's clever little adulteries. Which is, if you'll forgive the expression, a load of rabbit shit."

"Prolix," said the judge, "and you could have spared us the fiction bit, but a cogent argument."

"Somebody whom nobody'd notice, in what is, after all, a kind of no-man's-land but has a village atmosphere still. Somebody who could park an old car there with a bit of hay and some rabbits in the back. Somebody who could talk to a child without arousing automatic fear and distrust. Young, old, male, female, crazy, sane, a howling psychopath, or just a dimwit peasant with a grievance, which is all old Léon, the suspect I mentioned, is really. I haven't a clue, but I'm interested in your neighbors in the country."

Bernard looked at him blankly. I can see, the look said, why you're barking up this particular tree, but there's nothing in it: I've climbed it.

"Well," politely, "of course it's true that you've never been out there. I mean to say, yes, there's a tiny one-horse dorp, which overlooks the valley, and of course all the peasant houses are built carefully facing away from the view, and then there's a bum road that makes a big loop and rejoins the main road about five kilometers farther, and up there it's even prettier. The view's getting spoiled, of course, because people are building. We have a big field, and a few trees, and a big brambly hedge that shelters us from the road. It's all very humble—just a prefab wooden chalet. But we've managed to get a well sunk, and a septic tank, and electricity, and we'd like to build, but keeping small and very simple: fieldstone, and a terrace for looking at the sunset."

Castang nodded.

"And as for the neighbors, there aren't any, because one side is a sort of broken ravine and the other is a dentist from the town, and we've no troubles there, because we agree to disregard each other and we both put up a belt of trees to form a hedge."

"And the people you bought the land from—no grievances? No dispute about the boundaries?"

"No—all marked clearly in the cadastral survey."

"And Colette's never had any legal dealings with the villagers or even in the district? Drunk boys beating up the local dance hall or whatever? Or even just local rancor?"

"No," she said. "Villagers—you know . . . As long as one doesn't pretend to ostentation or airs of superiority."

"And, above all, not mix in local politics," added Bernard.

"Just a question of tact, really. Be polite to everybody, the more so when they're a bit sour, buy a bit from the local shop, let them cut the hay on the field."

"Mmm," said Castang.

The telephone rang.

Rachel had watched the television with Christine, who sat quiet and said nothing, and didn't even show much curiosity. But Christine was much smaller than Rachel, and a year or more younger. She still had all her milk teeth. Or "all," thought Rachel, is a manner of speaking, as Papa says. Her mouth smelled, and Rachel tried not to get too near her. The teeth were discolored, with sort of blue patches. She knew about that, because Papa went on at her about eating sweets, and had terrifying tales about English children, who all had false teeth. It was more disgusting than terrifying: like here. She went to M. Combes, too, who was not at all terrifying, though Mama pretended he was, calling him "the anticlerical" and making jokes about pulling Jesuits' teeth out, which Rachel failed to understand because M. Combes was the gentlest soul alive, spoke in a soft whisper like Mère Marie-Dominique (but she rather hated her, because of a slimy way of talking about "the dear child"), and above all was always honest.

"This won't hurt at all"—it didn't.

181

"This might hurt a little—tell me if it does and I'll stop"—and he did.

"This will hurt a lot, but only for a second." He didn't tell lies.

Time passed not unpleasantly. The young man, and the atrocious Carney, and the old man, too, sat watching the television, drinking beer and a jug of wine, sucking their teeth (M. Combes would be anticlerical with them, all right; all rotten, noted Rachel, scandalized) and saying nothing. And the hideous young woman sat smoking like a chimney, looking at the television, and looking at her—Rachel—a lot. Rachel tried not to look, not to see, and not to think.

The old woman put big black frying pans on the stove. The food smelled good, though it looked queer whenever Rachel dared give a round-the-corner glance. When it was ready, the old woman gave a sort of grunt, and they just all "drew up," as they were, around the table. It wasn't cleared or anything: the beer glasses and the jug of wine and the ashtrays (stolen, she knew, from cafés, because they had "Cinzano" written on them) stayed as they were. Greasy steel cutlery got handed out; soup bowls were slapped in front of everyone. Nobody paid any heed; they just went on looking at the television. The soup was bouillon gras with white beans and bits of carrot. It looked horrid but tasted good: she was hungry. It was the kind of farmers' soup Papa always said he loved. Everyone tore off great hunks of bread, and they all soaked that in the soup till it was like porridge, and then sucked that up: bouh.

There was a lot to eat. There were pancakes, very big thick ones, with bits of bacon in and onions, and big pieces of parsley. They smelled simply delicious but were very clawky. She couldn't finish hers, and was frightened, because at home she had to finish her plate no matter what. But she was—unexpectedly—supported by Marie-Thérèse. She didn't finish hers, either.

"Those things would choke an elephant," she said in her hoarse growl. And Christine didn't get any, and left half her soup, and was not punished. The men ate all theirs, and a big panful of sauté potatoes, too. Rachel loved sauté potatoes, and didn't get any, and didn't dare ask.

Then there were beans; the beans she had helped with, and in them she felt a sort of proprietary pride, so that she ate them gladly, though she had hardly any appetite left, and was glad she did; they were delicious—one had to be fair, much nicer than green beans at home—cooked just right, still all crisp and crunchy and with a marvelous flavor. She knew this was because they were out of the garden, and it was like that special restaurant she had once been taken to where Papa and Mama went once a year to eat asparagus because it had just been picked.

Then there was cheese, which she didn't get offered and was glad of it because she didn't like cheese, and couldn't eat any more anyway. She hoped there would be fruit—in the country there generally was—and was disappointed because there wasn't any, not even cherries.

"All right," said the old woman when they were finished. "Go play with Christine." She was relieved, for she had wondered whether she shouldn't volunteer with the washing up. In the country, she always did it with Papa; there was no machine for the dishes there. Papa washed—very careful and exact, everything in its proper place—and she dried. She couldn't wash, since the water was too hot for her hands. Mama "cleared." Papa said that women had no notion how to wash up properly, and Mama said in that case why didn't he cook, too, and sometimes they got heated and exchanged insults, but it never lasted long.

"Don't ever let the sun go down upon your anger," as Mama put it.

Christine was not much fun to play with. She was passive, as Mlle. Lassagne said about fat Véronique. And there were so many things that weren't allowed. She wasn't allowed out, but Christine wasn't, either. It was unhealthy. Children needed fresh air. That was perhaps why Christine was so puddingy and had rotten teeth. And she didn't know how to skip or how to play with a ball. They played "marelle," where you mark squares with chalk and hop on one foot and nudge a stone from one square to another, but Christine was no good. Too small, anyway. And she kept showing off.

"You haven't got animals in your home." "You haven't a garden." "You haven't even got dogs."

Well, one wouldn't want dogs like that. There were three, and they were shut in a sort of wire enclosure, which was very dirty, and they'd done caca all over the place, and they smelled simply horrible, and they spat when you went at all close. She got a bit of beastly saliva on the back of her hand and rubbed at it as though it burned: bouh. And that stupid Christine seemed not even to notice how they smelled. She was snoof. Papa's word for someone who can't smell: like deaf. But she was too little: she didn't understand. At the same time, she was quite clean. She had a checked smock as an apron. Rachel wished she had an apron. She'd left hers at school, because it wasn't the day for changing it. Her skirt was stained, and her top grubby, and Mama would be cross, and Rachel understood that because she wasn't happy about it. She wished she were at home, and could have a shower and get a clean dress. No shower here. Not even a bathroom. No wonder everything smelled so.

Marie-Thérèse suddenly appeared. Rachel winced because she thought she would get a slap. But it was Christine that got the slap. For no apparent reason. She didn't seem to mind. Used to it, perhaps. She didn't even cry. Sniveled a bit, but Rachel knew perfectly well that one can always produce a snivel; it doesn't necessarily mean one is hurt or anything. She sniveled herself, even though Mama said cuttingly that snivelers were to be despised. But she wouldn't snivel here: she'd rather die.

"All right. Bed." And they went. Just like that. They didn't have to wash. Their hair wasn't done. Christine had hers cut short in a mop, but it was dull and dirty. Rachel's was long, and had been loose all day. It had gone strangely. She would have liked to brush it. She couldn't plait it by herself, or put it up. There wasn't a brush. There wasn't even a comb.

They went to the attic. The attic was nice, with rough boards and a good smell of hay. Christine had a wooden bed. Rachel had only a folding canvas camp bed on a metal frame, but she didn't mind that: it was much the same as she had when they were in the shack. But there were nasty features. The blanket smelled musty. The sheet was clean, though. And that beastly little Christine had a pot to pee in, filthy little beast. She wasn't going to pee in any pot! The lavy was repugnant, but she'd rather go down two flights of wooden ladder and stairs, and go out near those horrible dogs, which barked and threw themselves against the wire grille and spat through it: anything rather than pee in a pot which one kept in one's bedroom all night; that was the pink limit, as Granny said. Granny was Mama's mother, and had a country house with a marvelous smell outside Toulouse, and when they were there Rachel got a bedroom with wonderful faded flowers printed on cotton, which Granny called "chintz"—a funny word that made her laugh.

She wasn't frightened of a strange bed. She had slept in many odd hotels, and in the country she had camped with Papa, on a bed made of freshly cut spruce branches. Under the sky, even. There was a "chouette"—a barn owl—which was frightening; Dracula might come. But Papa had his rifle, and a tomahawk.

Nobody came to "border" the two little girls. Mama came— not always, but regularly—to "tuck one in": this was a female ritual, which men did not understand; Papa did not know how. She didn't care. Nobody would want to be bordée by Marie-Thérèse: thanks, one would rather have Dracula. Come to think of it, Marie-Thérèse much resembled Dracula. She had white teeth, at least, but such biting teeth.

The worst of all was that the little pig made such a fuss about the window. It was only a skylight, but it would open, and

Rachel wanted to open it. And that idiotic baby pig Christine yapped and cowered and complained and said she'd call Ma. It was dangerous, she said. Dangerous! As though Dracula would come. There wasn't any Dracula. Rachel knew that perfectly well. One was frightened of him, but he didn't exist, which was silly but there it was. There were plenty of things that didn't exist but that one accepted. To set against Dracula, there was the guardian angel, and the Sainte-Vierge, the Bonne Mère who looked after small children. She had never seen them, and plenty of people said they didn't exist, but they kept Dracula off.

"Yah," said Rachel silently. "Beastly baby." She began to cry, rackingly, but stifling it under that musty blanket. Christine might not be asleep, and she wasn't going to cry in front of that rotten-toothed snot. Anything rather than alert that horrible Marie-Thérèse.

She wished Jackie was here. He'd open the window. She wondered for a long time whether she dared. Finally she crept out and opened it. Bouh, it was stiff. But she managed it noiselessly.

Deathly tired, aching, crying again a little, Rachel fell asleep, with a sense of triumph despite everything. She couldn't get away, but at least she'd got the window open.

The cock woke her up, crowing, in the morning.

She dressed as quickly as she could. The house seemed still but she couldn't tell; somebody might come creeping. The old woman puffed and grunted, and the stairs creaked under her weight, but she had noticed that the young woman could move catlike when she wanted, perfectly noiseless. Very like a cat, too, that evil, unwinking green gaze. Only she couldn't stay still like a cat: she fidgeted and picked at her fingernails.

186

Rachel was worried about her clothes. Her undies were not too bad, and would do another day at a pinch. And it was a pinch. But she had tried her best not to get them grimy. Mama would certainly have made her change her pants, but Mama, desolatingly, was not here. Mama would be very worried. And Papa would be upset, and when he got upset he was liable to get very cross with her. How to make them understand that it wasn't her fault? And that it was even very unfair. She hadn't done anything that was forbidden. She had followed the usual path: well, not perhaps quite the usual path, but she hadn't been in the mood for playing with Jackie. He was so noisy sometimes. And she and Véronique had had a tiff. Not really a quarrel; they'd "had words" and Véronique had "boudé," gone off without speaking to her.

Perhaps she was being punished for being nasty to Véronique.

She had been stolen. People did steal little girls sometimes, and did horrible things to them. Such people were not in their right mind. That was one of the reasons why one had to come straight home, and leave a note if one went again out to play after having one's goûter. And the principal reason why one must not talk to strange men or even women, nor let them talk to one.

Well, she hadn't. It wasn't for that she was being punished. She hadn't done anything, truly. She had only looked at the rabbit. Had it been wrong to pick up the rabbit? It was from that moment on that things had gone wrong. But the young man hadn't been cross at her picking it up. On the contrary, he had seemed pleased. Surely it wasn't that which had made him so cross and touchy. Later, she knew very well, he was cross and nervous because he had stolen her, and was afraid of being seen and noticed. Did he know that Mama was a judge, and could send all the police in the town after him? Rachel was sure she had, too, but they hadn't found her. She was well hidden. She didn't know how far they had come, but it was a long way.

The pants had to do. What she would do tonight she didn't know. Perhaps Papa, or the police, would have come by then. But they would need to be strong.

She had had to sleep in her shirt and underpants, a dirty thing to do, but she had no pajamas, and no nightie. Prisoners—and she knew she was a prisoner—got given special clothes when they went to prison. Rough scratchy prison clothes, because they were being punished. Would she get given prison clothes. She hoped so. She wouldn't mind their being scratchy as long as they were clean. This house was so dirty. Not really dirty that there was dust everywhere and a filthy mess and everything slummy and untidy. But it did smell so.

Christine slept with her underpants on under her nightie. A dirty thing to do. One more reason for despising the little horror.

Rachel's socks were very dirty. They would just have to do.

She crept downstairs very softly. In the kitchen the clock with the loud tick and the vulgar bonging chime said twenty to six. Early. There was no sound in the house. She put on her shoes carefully, not to make a clatter. She wanted badly to do pipi; she tried not to think about it. That place was so horrid and stinky. And it would make a noise. She would put it off as long as she could hold out.

She studied the door that led outside. There was a big lock, and the key in it. There were big bolts as well.

Suddenly a wild flutter of hope rose in Rachel. The door led to the street. Not far away, she knew, was a village. How far? She didn't know. But even if it was far, a kilometer, she could perhaps run. If they were all still sleeping. A kilometer was no farther than the distance to school. She could run. It was downhill, too. By six there would be people, a baker open. In the country people were early. But would the baker perhaps be friends with these dreadful people? In the country they were all in clans. Papa always said that one must never get involved with the village people because they were all cousins or cousins-in-law. And they stuck together, to their wife's cousin as to their own. But surely there'd be someone who would think it not right to keep little girls prisoner. Somebody would agree to phone the gendarmerie. Perhaps the gendarmes would be still in bed, but they'd get up for sure when they were told that a little girl was held prisoner, and had escaped. Come quick before the dreadful people find out and chase me.

Very softly, Rachel took a chair, climbed up, and tugged at the top bolt. It was oiled; it came quite easily. So did the bottom bolt. That left the lock. She wrestled with it. It was very stiff. The big key gave plenty of grip, but she was not strong; it didn't turn easily. She got up on the chair to get more leverage.

It turned: it was coming.

Behind her a harsh voice cackled with laughter.

She turned in a great hurry, terrified that it was the cat, the dreaded dreadful Marie-Thérèse. It wasn't, thank God. It was the old woman. Rachel had been so concentrated on wrestling with the horrible great key she hadn't heard anyone. And the woman was all dressed, too, in her skirt and her apron, and the wooly bedroom slippers she wore all the time. She was angry; her hand went up. Rachel cowered, but she did not get the smack she expected. The old woman laughed again, hoarsely.

"Thought you'd run away, eh? Thought you'd open the door without making any noise. But I was watching. It wouldn't work even when I wasn't. There's a bell on it outside, see. Can't open it without the bell rings."

"But there wasn't—last night, I mean." Again the cackle.

"We put it on at night, we do. Can't nobody open the door without I hear." And suddenly angry, "Fresh little bitch."

The hand swung up again, but Rachel was a quick learner. The hand flew up, but it didn't always fly down. It was a menace, no more. She had seen the hand fly up to cuff Christine for whining. Christine was a great whiner. Papa, who was peppery, would have cuffed Christine a few times. Even Mlle. Lassagne, who never cuffed anyone, would have become impatient.

"Now, Christine, stop pitying yourself. That's the way to earn a slap." Since Mlle. Lassagne virtually never gave anyone a slap, this was the ultimate menace. Even Jackie dreaded a slap from that thin hand with its sparkly diamond ring. ("Mademoiselle has a boy friend!") These great meaty hands flew up far more often, and somehow the menace wore off. Devalued, as Papa said, laughing.

"You watch it, and no fresh stuff, or you get the back of my hand." Perhaps they weren't "in their right mind." Or Rachel didn't think so. The young man, twitching and muttering. Maybe he was out of his mind. And ghoulish Dracula-Marie-Thérèse. She could well be out of her mind. Still, she hadn't hit Rachel yet. Christine had got slapped. Four times: Rachel had counted. For not having poured milk for the cats. (The animals here seemed to have a much better life than the children.) For wailing when the television got switched to another channel. For having dirty underclothes (but they still hadn't got changed, and Rachel had really found that difficult to understand. "You just go on wearing them, dirty pup, or I'll rub your nose in them." Rachel had cowered under her blanket). And for talking late at night. Marie-Thérèse had come creeping.

"You keep your mouth shut, now, hear me? You get a clip round the earhole." And she'd got it, though mostly on the hair, and Rachel had been ashamed for her. To yell so hard for so little—though it would hurt, that bony knuckly hand.

She got breakfast. This was nice. A big bowl of milky coffee, and she only got coffee at home on Sundays. It wasn't as nice coffee, having a strong taste of caramel and chicory and not really very much taste of coffee, but it was recognizably coffee, and not just baby cocoa.

Carney appeared, unshaved and horrible, sullenly sour, saying nothing but unlocking the door.

"Hey. The bolts are drawn."

"Yes. The young'un thought it'd make a getaway."

190

And two thick satisfied cackles of laughter. But not really cruel. More just brutal.

"Is brutality worse than cruelty?" Mama asked Vera one day. Nice and pretty Vera, who taught her how to dance and do gymnastics, and whom she was allowed to call "Vera" and not "Mme. Castang." Vera who had bad legs and limped, but who had such finely shaped and terribly strong pretty hands: short and somewhat stubby but somehow beautifully shaped, too. Vera who had made her such a lovely drawing of horses playing and prancing, which she had pinned up in her room. Her eyes filled with tears.

"Stop sniveling, little'un," the old woman said to her.

"No," Vera had said. "Surely brutality can never be as bad as cruelty. Brutality is just stupidity. I ought to know. Once I had a cruel schoolmistress. She made us suffer in a quiet voice."

Oh, Vera. Even with her limping legs, Vera was very tough. And Vera was a gymnast and knew judo, too. "Next time Jackie is horrid to you, you catch him so, and drop your shoulder and swing your hip so—oh, you, you've too much tummy."

"Do it again," laughing to find herself on the floor.

"So! You try that—that'll astonish Jackie's weak nerves!"

All dirty as he was, with black bristles all over, Carney went out, and she heard a car start noisily, and he was back a few minutes later with wonderful big country bread smelling good: "miches," big round blackened loaves. The old woman cut them in thick slices in the old-fashioned peasant way: clutching them up to her huge solid apron-bosom, and making a sign of the cross over them with the fist holding the knife, and cutting them in to the apron.

It did not astonish Rachel. Mama did the same thing, in a different way. Sometimes laughing a little, but always really serious, "because I come of a bourgeois family." Mama always made a cross, too, over bread, with her finger, the way Papa with his thumb made a cross on her forehead when he said good night. Rachel was never allowed to waste or throw away bread. "But why?" "Because it is our daily bread," said Mama, quite fiercely, "and we ask God daily for our bread, and we are grateful, because you know very well how many children have to do without. And because it is the greatest of all symbols; Christ chose the bread to be Him, and it is our promise and our hope." Which Rachel understood perfectly well. And whether they were brutal, or cruel, or both, it was somehow less bad.

And it was nice bread, too. And she could dip it in her coffee, which was forbidden at home.

To her infinite relief, Carney took Marie-Thérèse away "to work." And to her infinite surprise and anger with herself, they took away Christine. She cried, and was ashamed. Christine was such a drip, and a dirty little thing into the bargain. But Rachel had looked forward to playing with her. And was jealous, too, because Christine was bumped into a smock, and had her face scrubbed (but her hair wasn't properly brushed, and she didn't do her teeth), because she had to go to school; and at that minute Rachel wished she was going to school with almost as much heart as she wished to be going home after an ordinary, quiet, rather boring day's school.

The young man wasn't there, either. It was midmorning before she plucked up the courage to ask the old man where he was.

"He's at work."

"But at night?" puzzled.

"Sure. They're on shift. He's on nights this week. He'll be back," with that toothless sly giggle, smelling brassy of old wine and nasty old corks and reminding her of the horrible coppery taste of the thick little pot which Mama used for making sauce hollandaise on fish days and which always had to be so particularly scrubbed and polished. But the morning was quiet. The old ones pottered about. Only once was Rachel harshly treated, really imprisoned, when the butchers' van suddenly parked and tooted just outside the door, and the old one suddenly took her

192

by the collar and pushed her in the larder and locked the door on her. Rachel decided not to kick at the door, and not to scream, because the hand which went up would, she knew, this time come down hard.

"You make a noise, and I'll . . ." She was quiet, and she was let out within a quarter of an hour.

She was not allowed outside. She would have liked to go out and do some gardening. At home in the country, she could do gardening. She had a garden, with snowdrops and crocuses in spring, and different things in summer. (This year she had orange and yellow and red nasturtiums, and taller, elegant, feathery blue flax flowers, of a very lovely blue that Papa said was like her eyes.) And for the autumn, at the back of her border, there were orange and yellow chrysanths, but a totally different orange and yellow from the nasturtiums, much deeper, much more autumny, and also tall rain-smelling Michaelmas daisies. It was dreadfully much work, because there were so many weeds, and there were slugs and other nasty beasts, and sometimes she rather hated the garden and was bored with it. Here she would have gladly gardened, but it was not allowed, and she had to peel potatoes, which was not nice, and courgettes, which had a rough unattractive skin, and aubergines, which were lovely, so dark and blue-violet and beautiful, but beastly difficult and slippery and tiring.

The old woman would have helped her, she thought, because rough as she was she wasn't really beastly, but just at that minute the young man appeared. He was beastly. She had to fetch beer again, and minister to him, and put away his boots, and peel the vegetables alone, and she didn't cut herself, but the knife nicked into her finger at the side and the thumb on the ball, and made them sore, but she had to do it.

"No lazing," he said. "Get on with it, and if it's not properly done you get the stick across your arse, understand?" She didn't think she would be beaten, not really beaten on the behind with a stick. But she wasn't going to risk finding out. Being beaten would be fearful enough, but being beaten by that horrid man would be the most horrible thing she could imagine. Even being beaten by Marie-Thérèse would not be worse. Still, she wasn't beaten, but only because she worked terribly hard. After dinner, thank God, she was allowed to lie down on the bed and sleep. The young man, as well, went to bed. Thank God. She didn't sleep properly, because when she woke up it was the same time as the day before, when she had been stolen. The young man was not there with his hot greedy not-right-in-the-head eyes, but she had been prisoner a whole day and a whole night. And Papa had not come, nor had the gendarmes, and she was helpless, and the kitchen floor had to be swept and washed, and a sort of dreadful routine had set in, and soon the filthy Carney would be back again, and the dreadful woman with him, and that horrid Christine, whom she no longer looked forward to playing with though she had been longing all day, and her undies were filthy now, and so was her frock with no apron, and what was she going to do?

The day passed quietly enough, and even quickly, because there was lots to do. The house was much bigger than it looked. At the back there was a warren of rooms, in one of which the old ones slept, in the middle of a strange heap of tools and flowerpots, and upstairs a kind of flat where Carney lived. These rooms smelled of Marie-Thérèse, a sort of shrill scent in which the only element Rachel could distinguish was the smell of carnations, and she loathed carnations. She didn't know why, but they were nearly her most unfavorite flower. She was afraid to go into these rooms. There was a hairbrush with a lot of hair caught in its bristles, which made her shudder. She had to sweep the rooms and dust them, which was like Cinderella and not really disagreeable at all, or need not have been were it not for the hairbrush. The old woman floundered about, and abused her shrilly a few times, but Rachel had learned not to be too alarmed at this, and that the yelling was not totally strange to a sort of rough kindness. And everyone else was away. Even the old man had set out early with a scythe, to cut the tall grass and make hay of it. And when he came back she brought him a jug of wine, which she had learned how to do properly, from the barrel in the cellar, and afterward she went with him while he did the animals in the strange conglomeration of sheds and shacks at the back, cunningly built with the weirdest odds and ends: a true "bidonville." Already she had learned not to mind the hot jungly animaly smell. It was only the enclosure where the dogs were kept that frightened her: nasty beasts, leaping and slavering and throwing themselves against the wire and barking hysterically every time they saw her. But it was not really because of the dogs that she had so terrible a fright.

They were going to look at the baby ducks when her eye was caught by another enclosure of wire—wedged between the dogs and the house of the rabbits, with a wall built of old boards, and a lean-to sort of roof of pine poles supporting old tiles— which was empty. The pig had been kept there, Christine had told her, but the pig had been killed for bacon, with a very sharp knife and a great pot of boiling water. . . . Rachel had not wanted to listen to that bit, but she had listened. The old man had cleared it out since last night, and there was a bundle of fresh hay there.

"Are you going to get another pig?" Rachel asked.

The old man grinned his toothless grin.

"That's for you," he said.

Rachel shrank away, frozen, feeling herself go quite white and bloodless.

She had heard of people fainting, but had never understood how it was done, and now she realized, because she felt her legs would refuse to hold her up. They were witches. Now she knew why Marie-Thérèse was like Dracula. They were going to keep her like the pig, and make her fat, and then one morning they would come with the very sharp knife and the great pot of boiling water. . . . She had wondered and wondered why they had stolen her. She knew now. It was to eat her. Like cannibals, but there were not cannibals here. There were witches, though.

Jackie had told her that people used to believe this about Jews, and this was why some people still didn't like Jews. It didn't sound very likely—in fact, a typical Jackie fantasy—but Papa, when she asked him, said it was true, that at one time the peasants used to believe this. She could see now: the witches were cunning, and when a little girl vanished they blamed it on the Jews. The horrible old man cackled at her terror.

"Joke," he said with his piggy little eyes all shiny. Rachel knew it wasn't a joke. She crept into the kitchen and sat on her chair, not daring to move at all. The old woman said nothing. Perhaps despite everything the old woman would save her. But Marie-Thérèse was stronger, as well as being a witch. When Marie-Thérèse came back . . .

But when she came back (Rachel had prayed against all hope that the car would break down, that something, anything would happen; and when she heard, as she had known she would, the noise of the motor outside, she thought she would faint again; she prayed she would, so that she would be unconscious and not know when the terrible fierce hands reached out to take hold of her), nothing happened. The witch just looked at her with dull bored eyes, and said irritably, "Go play with Christine. I'm tired; I don't want to look at yer."

Only too thankful, Rachel crept out. But she could not play; she felt so listless and tired, and her legs would not carry her. She sat down in the angle of the wall and the floor, outside in the passage, and Christine, nothing loath, sat down alongside, smelling as usual of pipi, but Rachel was too numb to object. As long as nobody came out . . . And nobody came out. The old woman was making the supper, and the old man was tired now, and the young man, who had been busy all afternoon in the side cellar, which was like a junkyard full of rusty iron and bits of old motors, seemed tired, too; he had got his own beer, and had been sitting for nearly an hour, dully staring and smoking and biting his nails, and seemed uninterested in her.

She didn't want to know, and at the same time she did want dreadfully to know. She wanted to listen. She knew that listening at doors was bad manners and she didn't care. What manners had these people? She wanted to know because there was a corner of her mind that still refused to believe in the knife and the witches, and she had to know, and in there they were talking about her; she knew that because Papa, too, said "Go out and play" when he was going to talk about her. And Christine wouldn't give her away, because she wanted to listen, too. Rachel hated that but somehow accepted it.

It was easy to listen because they shouted. They always did shout. Every conversation was like an argument. But they were arguing, too. They also mumbled, and when they all shouted together it was difficult to disentangle. But she could get the drift. And the drift was at least partly reassuring. They were frightened. They wanted to get rid of her. But it was not at all reassuring as it developed, because they were frightened, and they might kill her: that much she knew from Mama.

"Why do people kill people?"

"Nearly always because they are frightened."

"But why are they frightened?"

"Sometimes because they are ill and suffer pain, or imagine they do. And sometimes for no reason. Why are you frightened? No reason at all, generally. It happens to us, and then we have to try and reason our way out of it."

"I'm sicka the sight of her."

"Easy for you. You're away all day. What did you want her for, then?"

"We got what we wanted. Made them shit. They're frightened, all right."

"You can't just bring her back."

"Too true. Place'll be crawling with cops. Just take her away 'n' let her loose someplace."

"She'll tell."

"What can she tell? We've been over all that. I told ya and I'll

197

tell ya again, they'll never catch on. Not in a million years."

"Dopy just to let her go now we got her. Screw 'em a bit first."

"How?"

"Telephone."

"You think that's clever? Be listening. I know how they work. Yer voice'll give ya away."

"I'm not going to let her go just like that. Where's the satisfaction? I want to hear 'em squeak. What else was it good for? You're not going to phone, anyway. You're such a fool, you'd give it away."

"Fool is it? Who got her? Who thought how to get her? Not you. And you keep your mouth shut; where I am, see, the whores keep still and let the men talk."

"You hearing that, Carney? You going to stand for that?"

"You shut up. Carney can shut up, too, or I'll belt him. I never married no prostitute."

The voice of the witch would have gone through all the walls in the house.

"You shut up and you hear me, Pierrot, stupid cretin. What are you but a pig peasant? Where I come from, the girls keep quiet for their men and not for no yobbo out in the cowshed, with the shit sticking the straw in his hair. You just try me, monkey, and you'll find I don't need no Carney to help handle you. When the cops got you, you sung real small."

"Shut up, the both of you," said the old woman's voice. "You, Pierrot, don't use that talk about your brother's woman, and you, girl, mind that evil mouth of yours and let the men speak."

"I was always against."

"You're against anything might threaten your belly. All you think of. Think y'selves all smart for getting her. Any kid with half a ballock could do as much, but how to handle it then takes brains, and who got brains? Me."

"And me."

"Y' got a few dots 'n' you too scared to use 'em. S'now I'll tell you, 'n' belt up 'n' listen. Phone, you say. Right, I'm all for it.

Make them shit and hear them at it, I ask nothing better. Tell 'em we got her, now come 'n' find her. Or what's left of her." And the witch broke into a squawk of laughter so horrible that Rachel could not bear to hear any further. She crawled away along the passage and up the stairs, the harsh voice pursuing.

"Not from no phone box, because that they can trace. Y'got to have an automatic phone, because that they can't, and we know that back where I come from, which isn't the sticks, and you just leave this to me. You can listen if you like—get a kick out of it."

Rachel heard no more. She dragged herself up to the attic, lay down on her bed, and thought she was going to cry, but somehow she was too numb for that. She fell asleep. She hadn't paid any attention to Christine. The little slop would run and tell, no doubt. She just didn't care. Nobody could help her now. The witch was too strong.

When the phone rang, they were none of them alert for it: even Bernard's fibers had been sufficiently undone that he only rolled himself along the sofa toward the stupid thing. Jérôme, probably, fussing about tomorrow's "board meeting," as he called the weekly sit-in with the accountant and the sales head.

"Delavigne," he said in a voice which was not slurred; he had not had all that much to drink, just enough to be comfortable.

"That you, Delavigne?" said a woman's voice, sharp and suspicious.

"In person," said Bernard, bored. Sounded like a long-distance operator. Probably be Martial—ridiculous name for a salesman—from Barcelona: they were making inroads on the holiday-camp circuit, and he would be fussing again about supplies.

"You lost anything, Delavigne?" said the sharp grating

woman's voice, instead of the expected "Hold the line, please."

Bernard sat up abruptly. Colette was already snatching the spare earpiece. Castang's hand came down gently on hers, and held the microphone between their two ears.

"Who is calling, please?" said Bernard in a neutral voice.

"Ha." Screech of laughter, jangling the mike. "Like to know that, I bet. This is confidential. A friend, say, who wishes you well."

"What is it, then? Get on with it, whatever it is." Good, thought Castang. You're not stupid, whatever else. That's the way; irritate her, make her clack.

"You'd love to know, eh? Just love it."

"You've got a wrong number," said Bernard, and hung up.

"Bloody good," said Castang, delighted.

"But . . . why did you cut off? It's news—news of whatever kind, we must hear it," Colette said, innocently bewildered.

"Have no fear," said Castang. "She'll ring back. Hasn't sung her song. Don't worry. This is it. Let it ring three or four times, Bernard, get her stretched." When the phone rang again, they all four sat as though paralyzed, glaring at it greedily, as though it were a chilled bottle of Roederer, beautifully sweating with condensation, appeared by magic down in the obscure rock-face chamber, in the deep places of the salt mine. The sweat was standing on Bernard's forehead.

"Patience," said Castang gently, bringing his voice up over the jarring ring of the phone. "For-ti-tude."

"You being funny, Delavigne? I'm the one who's laughing."

"Let me in on the joke. What is all this?"

"You'd like to find what you lost, wouldn't you?"

"What do I have to do—offer a reward?"

"You think everything's for sale, don't you, because you never

200

had any dealings with honest people, ever. You got a lot to learn. You need to start getting a bit grateful and learn to be less proud-stomach. How did your first day go? You know what I reckon? That in a few more days you won't be sounding so cocky."

"You rang up just for a nice chat, is that it?" Bernard was keeping his voice even, but his free hand was making nervous circling gestures, asking for something. Colette and Castang stared at him, puzzled. It was Vera who looked in her handbag, hitched herself off the edge of her chair, and handed him a paper tissue. Bernard gave her a grateful look and mopped at his face and neck. The voice was coming faster as it gained in confidence.

"A nice chat, a nice chat," mimicking his voice sarcastically. "Yes, that's what it|is for me, because this time it's us that's on top. We can take things easy, we don't have to come and go when you blow the whistle. I got news for your wife, too, if she is your wife. She's the judge, huh, sits there without a worry in the world giving orders. Saying," mock pinched accent, " 'Oh, pleeceman, take these ruffians away and lock them up.' But this time I'm giving the orders and you're there sweating."

Bernard's hand with the tissue in it stopped abruptly and he gave a startled glance at the telephone—a thing to make one laugh, ordinarily.

"If you have a proposition, make it." His fist with the balled-up tissue made a jagged jab at his glass; Castang picked it up and put it carefully in his hand. He tucked the receiver into his neck while he swallowed and fumbled angrily for a cigarette he couldn't find; he was sitting on the packet.

"Oh, a proposition?" The voice was secure now: it had him reined in. "You mean like some sort of contract where you give us something and we give you what you want, is that it? Let me tell you, I wouldn't make any agreement with you, not over as much as a pound of tomatoes. I wouldn't trust you not to break it, because I know your lot, nothing but a pack of twisters."

"Since you've just rung up to call me names," said Bernard calmly, "consider it done and go on back to bed."

"Not so fast, big shot; just remember we're on top now and we tell you what can be done and what can't be done. You want her back, don't you?"

"Naturally."

"Nat-u-rally," mimicking. "All cold, like you couldn't care one way or another, trying to jew the price down."

Bernard took the phone away from his ear, put it down on his lap, closed his eyes, and breathed very slowly, deep in, deep out, then wiped his face again, and picked the thing up afresh.

"What use is this? Suggest something concrete, straightforward, and I'll give you a straightforward answer. As far as I have understood, you're not looking for money. Apparently you feel some sense of grievance against me—or is it against my wife?"

A chuckle came over the line, rich and juicy.

"Sure. You'd like me to tell you. And my name and address while I'm at it."

"I don't care what you tell me. Stay as anonymous as you please. Just tell me what you want in exchange for bringing the child back."

"Don't want anything. There you are. That surprised you, eh? With you it's always nothing for nothing and not much for a sou. Looking to make deals, trying to get bargains. And we're not bargaining. We got you where we want you. We got your kid, and maybe we let it go and maybe we don't, and maybe we just drop it on a roadside on its bare ass like any stinking vagabond tinker, because that's all you are. And maybe we do that tomorrow or some other day or whenever we think we got time to spare. And take that to wipe your ass on, because you won't get better."

"If you want nothing from me"—Bernard was trying to keep his voice down, and not get shrill—"I can't see what use it was to ring me up."

"I wanted to make you shit, you bastard. And, no mistake

about it, I have, and I will, and I'm laughing." And with an abrupt clank the phone rang off.

Colette let herself slide onto her knees on the floor and buried her face on her elbows in the seat of the chair. Bernard went on wiping his face automatically, his jaw muscles twitching, staring straight in front of him. Vera had turned herself sidewise and was studying a picture on the wall in intense concentration, horribly ashamed at being a helpless bystander to suffering.

Castang looked at the three of them and for a moment did nothing at all. Then he leaned over and picked the phone up.

He clicked the receiver, waited a second, and then said, "Johnny? You got it all? . . . No, I think bring it up. Just reverse it to your mark, snip it off, and come up with it; we'll get a better result up here. . . . Yes, just rethread and set it on automatic record: I want you here, too; your opinion's going to be vital." He put the phone down, considered for a second, leaned over, smacked Colette lightly on the bottom, and said, "Oops-a-daisy, girl: half time. Our turn to play with the wind. I've never had the chance to do that to a judge before. Organize your face; the police will be here in a moment. Efface the traces of the orgy; this is your lover speaking. God's teeth, Vera, stop letting your imagination run riot. Bernard, tell me I'm not mistaken, and that the fancy high-fidelity set has a tape recorder incorporated."

"What was it again? 'Bare-assed stinking vagabond tinker'?"

"You'll hear it again. In fact, you'll hear it enough times that anesthesia will have set in, worn off, and been replaced by common or garden nausea. Open the door, would you? That's Johnny. Hallo, Johnny, didn't I tell you this would pay off sooner or later? Can you make this machine go? It's got more switches and little red lights than the cockpit of a jet. Well, snip a bit off this and splice it up or something. Come on, Bernard, show us how to switch this damn thing on." There was a soft heavy amplifier hum, a loud scratching noise, and a voice suddenly boomed out, "Delavigne," sounding like Adolf Hitler in the

Nuremberg stadium. "Jesus, turn it down. No, stop it. Get a good balance first, the woofers and the tweeters and all the rest. Pity we've a double distortion, first from the crappy phone mike and then from the lousy black box amplifier. Try your best, Johnny." The loudspeakers in the corner of the room boomed and whispered and spoke: "Delavigne, Delavigne, Delavigne. That you, Delavigne, that you, that you, that you, that you—"

"For God's sake, Johnny."

"Won't do better than that."

"Ladies and gentlemen, take your seats. *Gone With the Wind* is about to begin. Just an easy conversational volume, Johnny, no need to take the neighbors into our confidence. Look, the two of you. We've crossed over. The wind is now blowing down our side of the pitch. We've been knocked about a bit, but we're very lucky. Unless I'm much mistaken, there's jam enough in this to catch any number of wasps with. Concentrate all you can. Have you heard the voice before? Can you place it in any context? Does it carry any association? Never mind any associations of words for the present, just concentrate on the voice; sorry, I'm repeating myself."

"You seem excited," said Colette sourly.

"You bet your ass, Shah, as Lauren Bacall said to the Peacock Throne when told she was a good dancer."

"Damn it, he's happy," said Bernard sarcastically.

"The voice; just listen to the voice."

The recording was played through.

"No," said Colette.

"Zero, I'm afraid," said Bernard.

"What sort of accent would you call that, Johnny?"

"Overlaid," said the technician stolidly. "Predominance parigot."

"Parigot, hell, that's peasant. Jump to the bit in the middle where she got excited. Now give me a rallentando. Stop. Now get that. 'Cassé' and 'causé.' That's peasant. 'Ca-ah-ssé.' 'Cau-u-sé.' "

"What I meant by overlaid. Underneath I think it's parigot."

"I'm not sure but that it isn't the other way round. Peasant who went up to Ivry and acquired the rhythms. We'll get a language expert. This is going to be easy."

"I thought a recording wasn't evidence of anything."

"Can't one have the call traced?" The two sentences were spoken together.

"Mixing it up," said Castang, "both remarks are bullshit. Tracing a call is a thing only done in detective stories. Could be anything—La Rochelle, Valenciennes, for all we know. And a recording isn't evidence, but what it leads to is."

"Easy," said Johnny. "Can't count the relays this end, but the way it comes through, the quality of the tone. There's not that much amplification added—in fact, it's relatively faint. If you want a quick guess, the way I originally heard it, I'd say inside the département—not much over fifty kilometers either way. Need a phone engineer for an informed guess. Playing it off my box will give us the original power, and at least a notion of the relay used."

"Get Richard on to that first thing. Now the words. The words are full of clues like a stuffed tomato."

"Aren't you reading too much into this?" asked Colette in a voice made dispassionate.

"I'm not talking about the tone," said Castang. "Like your tone, and with knowledge of the facts, we would say you were trying not to set your hopes too high. We're looking at the choice of words; expressions."

They played it again twice.

"Now," said Castang, "it's a party game. Whose little notebook has the most annotations?"

He had had a couple of glasses of red plonk, at home. And one glass of champagne. Just enough to set the motor going.

Vera had found something to look at and feel satisfaction. Almost happiness. The man had been utterly miserable with helpless frustration. Nothing but double handfuls of air to show for all his work. And a bit of rabbit shit, which he'd been too discouraged even to laugh about. He'd been brought so low that he'd even dallied with the notion of something totally reckless and irresponsible like bedding poor Colette (who'd have loved that, and been childishly comforted at somebody else being as deep in the shit as she was herself, poor wretch). But now he could move again, and show everyone he was a cop, after all.

"There's a whole heap," he was saying with pleasure, "of interesting characteristics, which we ought to be able to straighten out into guidelines. You've all three got good analytical minds.

"The voice: you say you don't recognize it, but since she knows you it's a fair bet you know her. You may never have heard her speak much. A woman who has lived some time or been brought up in Paris, but is probably of peasant origin, and we can say—linking this to the rabbits—lives, in all likelihood, in a country district, perhaps isolated but in this region, judging by the accent. Does that mean anything to either of you? Some disgruntled ex-employee, Bernard? Recall that Jérôme is proud of knowing anyone who works for him, and at a pinch we can get him to listen to this recording. A witness of some kind, Colette, in a case you instructed or judged? Think.

"Second point: pure malice. No ransom involved. This hasn't been done cold-bloodedly for money, but in hot blood and poisoned with hatred and unbalanced envy. Makes it all miles easier. There's a tremendous grievance against either of you, or both. In fact, one could go as far as to say that the grievance is against you as a family rather than as individuals. They attack you through your family. Isn't it a good bet to suggest that the grievance they imagine is something they—because there's obviously a clan—felt as an attack upon their family? Now—we ought to be able to do something with all that."

"My mind's a perfect blank," said Bernard, puzzled. "I've never sacked anyone. It's a thing I'm so bad at that Jérôme always does it. I'm generally regarded as a soft touch for the hard-luck tales."

"They seem confident of being safe from discovery," said Colette, who had pulled herself together and was ready to discuss things calmly. "I don't quite see, Henri, if it's as easy as you seem to suppose, how they would not realize that it would point to them. I mean a peasant may be ignorant and uneducated by our standards of looking at things, but they're notoriously cunning. It's almost impossible, as any judge knows, to bring a successful charge against a peasant. You know—sly. Wriggling out of things. The witnesses are all perjured."

"Sure. But I'm hoping that sheer rancor—and everything in that voice stank of sheer rancor—will be blinding them somewhat."

"Lord God," said Bernard. "Sheer rancor. You can't surely just accept that as a sufficient motive for the cold-blooded kidnapping of a helpless small child."

Castang made an irritable gesture. "I see that, and there's probably some ulterior motive we don't know about, some morsel of self-interest; they are probably going to try to turn this to their advantage somehow even without money. As Richard suggested, the dropping of a charge or the liberation of a prisoner. Rachel must be a hostage for something or someone. But I'd like to say that this must be a great relief to you. You can be sure henceforward of one very important thing: that Rachel is not only alive and uninjured but safe and even relatively well cared for. She's a valuable hostage and they'll look after her."

"That woman sounded so cruel," said Colette bleakly.

"Brutal, maybe. But I think the threats are mostly just bigmouth."

"I don't think I agree with you, Bernard," said Vera suddenly. "I think it might, yes, be sheer rancor. You're neither of you peasants. Henri is a little Parisian stump-in-the-gutter. But I'm a peasant: I was born in a shack with an earth floor, and got my first shoes when I was ten. I know of dreadful things done out of sheer rancor. I remember a man's legs being cut with a scythe, so badly that he never walked again—the tendons were severed—on account of a cat that he'd killed several years before."

"There's generally money involved," said Castang, with his police experience.

"An ancient lawsuit," said Colette, looking at Vera lovingly, "or a disputed heritage. A girl jilted or a boy betrayed."

"You none of you know me," said Vera. "I'm a very rancorous, unforgiving person."

They all stared at her aghast. Vera! The gentlest of souls.

"But then it's insanity," said Bernard, troubled. "If it's blind unreasoning rancor on such slight grounds, then such people are out of their minds. They may do the most dreadful things to Rachel."

"Not legal insanity," said Colette.

"Not insane from a peasant point of view," said Vera. "To us it would be all quite consequent and comprehensible. And I don't think you need worry. They—we—wouldn't avenge ourselves upon a child. Animals—yes. Poison all the chickens. Even hamstring a horse. It would be like putting weed killer on the neighbors' dahlias. But the innocence of a child would be respected."

"I hope you're right," said Bernard, looking at her with the uncomprehending eyes of a hamstrung horse.

"We're sitting here getting morbid," said Castang. "A while back, I was accused, with some justice, of excessive priggery. This isn't doing us any good. What we need is a change of scenery. Let's go out and have a few drinks."

"Huh?" said Bernard drearily.

"We can't go out, surely," from Colette.

"Why not? She won't ring again. Her idea is that we should stew now in our juice and suffer grinding torments. Why play it her way? We leave Johnny here to finish the bottle"—Johnny had been, as was his habit, sitting silent and immobile, waiting to be spoken to. He grinned at this—"and bugger off to a bordel. I'm in the mood for doing something illegal."

"It's all right, Madame," said Johnny to Colette, comfortingly. "You don't do any good now. She'll know that from now on the police will be listening. If she rings again, it'll be an effort to cover her tracks. I'll stall her with some talk. The recorder in the basement is on automatic. If you care to go out, as M. Castang suggests, I'll be here. You've got a wonderful high-fidelity; if you'd allow me, I'd play myself some music," humbly.

"Of course I'll 'allow you,'" said Colette, touched.

"Settled," said Castang. "Let's go to some dirty scruffy night-club and look at the striptease, and drink homemade champagne, and be obscene. That's where we'll get ideas. Here we're gone stale."

"Madame la Juge in a dirty cabaret," Colette said, tickled.

"Nobody will recognize you. We'll take Bernard's car. Nobody will recognize me, either, with all these bourgeois women out on a dirty-minded slumming trip."

"The idea is good," said Bernard.

"Nearly as good as sleeping with one another's wives," said Vera with an irony so gentle that it scarcely touched the others.

"Let's go and have a pee," said Colette to her. "Nightclub johns . . ."

"Know any good addresses?" asked Bernard.

"I know a really filthy dump full of Spaniards," said Castang happily, "where the pubic hair gets shoved practically in your face."

"Lead me to it," said Bernard, delighted.

"Don't forget it's to stimulate your memory," with one of those gross laughs that men exchange while the women are safely in the bathroom.

There was no light at all except a flickering candle here or there. Candles were the general theme: a naked girl on the tiny dance floor was doing suggestive things with a lighted candle, covering herself with grease.

"Like a dirty picture painted by Georges de la Tour," said Bernard, interested.

The champagne was so nasty that Castang poured his surreptitiously in the bucket. The girls were delighted, as only really virtuous women are when dipped agreeably into an atmosphere of vice. The stools at the unlit bar were full of boneless whores slumped dully on the bar top waiting for business to perk up. They would not be too dreadfully disappointed, thought Castang, even in the pitch dark, because the customers are either German politicians come over to see what money can be made out of our shaky aircraft industry, or English Members of Parliament studying European notions of democratic rule. Plus Spaniards, of course, being happily filthy-minded because of censorship at home. Pass the butter, as Brando said to Schneider.

"Damn it," said Bernard. "Can anybody read the label on this bottle? My mind's still a blank."

"Never mind about the label," prompted Castang gently. "Just find something you have done, maybe deep in the past, as Vera said, which might have split family solidarity in a peasant community."

As usual in nightclubs, the sexes had split up. The men sat there with their legs stretched out in a superior manner "looking the whores over" (except that it was too dark to see), while the girls were giggling together in a corner at private female jokes. The stripper writhed and illuminated her pubic hair with candlelight, and gave a loud yell in an effort to wake up the stunned parliamentarians with constituencies in Somerset. Who had been looking forward all day, poor dears, to luscious French food and French whore-by-nights to follow. What they got was steak and chips, and a very wearied stripper from Yugoslavia. The package trip to Lloret would have been cheaper. Luckily they were euphoric from a plethora of champagne made in large stainless-steel vats in the Rhineland.

"How long have you had that country cottage?" asked Castang suddenly. "Do you always spend your holidays there?"

"I spend mine there—I hate the seaside in summer. Colette mostly goes for an extra month to Arcachon, sitting in a black bikini under a parasol, getting all bronzed and sexy, and yelling at the child. 'Rachel darling,' " in a high soprano that made two whores look round. " 'Don't go near the dirty water, darling.' "

"What's wrong with Arcachon?" asked Castang, interested.

"My belly hangs out over my bikini," said Bernard gloomily.

"So does everybody else's."

"Yes, but instead of bronzing, I just go red, and scratch all night, because there's nothing to eat but polluted shellfish tasting of diesel oil."

"So you'd rather have a mountain holiday? Where d'you go?"

"Just to the country, but when we were poor and didn't have the shack we used to go to my parents' house. Colette of course didn't care for that much. Once we borrowed a cottage belonging to my Aunt Joséphine."

"Tante Joséphine," Colette struck in as her ear caught the word, "I was just thinking about her. Do you remember the row?"

"Oh, good God, you mean when I gave the boy a smack. That was utterly trivial, though."

"Tell about Tante Joséphine," said Castang persuasively. "Nothing's too trivial."

"Oh, it was silly," said Colette, laughing. "Bernard's Tante Joséphine is a terrible old biddy who reads the financial pages and rings up her stockbroker every five minutes. She's a compulsive gambler, only she plays the bourse instead of the casino because the odds are better."

"She has a cottage over in the valley of the Aube—heaven

knows why, except there's a vineyard goes with it and she thinks it is smart to be a landowner," said Bernard, laughing. "And if you've carrots you're a backwoodsman, but if you've vines, even when they're no good at all, you're gentlefolk. She's a horror."

"And she lent you her cottage?"

"Oh, it was one year ages ago; Colette was still a student, and I wasn't making anything, and it was all the holiday we had. Rachel was tiny, still getting pushed about in a wagon. There was a squabble with the farmer across the valley who claimed it was his right to pick the fruit trees, which was all lies, of course. That's all—as trivial as it sounds."

"Go into more detail. What boy? What smack?"

"Oh, well; it was just nerve. I mean we couldn't care less about the fruit: there was loads, but he was taking advantage of us. You know—Joséphine watches every penny, and would have driven a bargain, and after all I felt I had to watch her interest, and he was barefaced. He sent the boy to strip a tree, so I went down to shoo him out of that, and the boy—he was about fifteen—was rather insolent and I gave him a clip around the ear. This is really too absurd."

"Maybe," said Castang.

"And did the farmer across the valley keep rabbits?" asked Vera softly.

"As I recall, a whole zoo. I never noticed rabbits in particular but it's possible. He wasn't a real farmer: one of those peasants who do a little bit of everything—bit of wine, a few chickens, a pig. The fruit trees, I suppose, made an attractive profit. Joséphine said afterward he was always trying to diddle her over them, and he must have thought us green young ducks after that tough old turkey."

"That's quite clear," said Castang. "Where is this place?"

"Bellac-sur-Aube—up at the top of the valley that goes down to Lotte. Good step from hereabouts—it must be over a hundred kilometers; it's the next département."

"Not that far. Up to Lotte is within our region, inside our competence. Is there a tribunal in Lotte?"

"Canton tribunal," said Colette. "Correctionelle would come to us, and assize, of course."

"That's what I thought."

"You're not seriously thinking—?" said Bernard.

"Don't know whether I am or not. Good grief, look at this one; is it a man or a woman?"

It occupied their curiosity for nearly ten minutes, slinking about in a tight sequined gown and pretending to beat up a very obviously female young thing in pathetic rags which tore off, as Vera remarked, rather too easily and who, as Colette remarked, was rather old for a schoolgirl. Her habiliments were removed with much prancing and whipcracking amid a variety of conventionally lesbian offers, after which the sequined gown got skinned off, displaying odiously frilly undies, which gave the game away to Castang; he was, after all, a detective. A smart tussle ensued with the by now naked nubile one, as a climax to which the frilly undies and the blond wig shot off in a heap to disclose a rather poorly equipped male, who was greeted with jeers as well as cheers, and some catcalling from the Spaniards, who plainly had no very high opinion of his slightly limp attributes.

"What on earth are we doing here?" asked Colette crossly.

"Quite right," said Castang. "I've been thinking of a verification we could make."

"What of?" asked Vera, which provoked a laugh. Despite protestation, Bernard was judged incompetent to drive further and it was Castang who wheeled the Citroën out of the parking lot.

"Where are we going? A better bordel?"

"The best of bordels," he promised, "and which I can drive to blind, drunk, or asleep." Nobody was surprised when this turned out to be the courtyard of the Cité Administrative, where the Regional Service of the P.J. has its offices. Vera stayed in the car: the P.J. offices were even less treat than a bordel.

The P.J.'s night shift was still, this early in the evening—for it was only midnight—occupied in catching up on its paper work. Adjunct Commissaire Sallebert, the commander of this lethargic platoon, was himself a lethargic person, inclined to be fat and greasy-haired. They had some slight difficulty with him, because he didn't like Castang, and Castang didn't like him.

"You're up late."

"We got a bit of an alert."

"Yes, so Johnny tells me. Doesn't sound very helpful."

"There may be a bit of a lead somewhere in Richard's papers."

"Come, now, Castang, I can't allow you to frig about with Richard's desk unless he authorizes it."

"What do you want me to do, phone him at this hour? He'll be delighted."

"What is it you want, anyhow?"

"He has a list that was made today of all the cases judged by Mme. Delavigne in the last couple of years."

"Are you crazy? That's a confidential document belonging to the Palais, and it's restricted. Not for just everyone's eyes. Commissaire or over."

"That being so, I'll ring the Proc and ask for a ruling, since Mme. Delavigne would like to refresh her memory."

Colette was not insensitive to this appeal for support.

"Really, M. Sallebert, I think you could stretch the point, since you're aware, of course, what has been happening."

"That's all very well, Madame, but you realize that I am only responsible to M. Richard without a direct intervention from the Parquet."

"In my capacity as judge, however . . ."

"With all respect, Madame, the judge in charge of the dossier hasn't left me instructions covering the eventuality, and while of course I'd be delighted to do anything I possibly could as a person, my official responsibility is engaged."

"Yes, M. Sallebert, of course. Would you like me to give you an official service note absolving you from all responsibility, which I take entirely upon myself? It could be added to the dossier. You see, that way nobody could accuse M. Castang of overstepping the regulations."

"I hardly see, Madame, what justifies me in going rummaging among M. Richard's private papers in his desk when, after all, he will be here tomorrow morning, and at that moment I feel sure you'd have only to ask him unofficially. . . ."

"Yes, M. Sallebert, but in the meantime there is a bewildered and unhappy child somewhere in the night. With your permission, I will ring M. Besson and ask for his authorization for access to my own files."

"Come, Madame, please don't let's allow this to slip onto an emotional level. I know they're your files, and there's no necessity for us to disturb M. Besson. I'm simply obliged to point out that this extract from the Palais archive is an official document belonging to this office for which in M. Richard's absence I am answerable, but in the circumstances I am happy to bend a regulation and allow you to see it. M. Castang, on the other hand—"

"Please put an end to this," said Colette in her magistrate's tone. "You know perfectly well that M. Besson gave full powers to M. Castang to conduct this investigation, and that in consequence he is clearly entitled to access to any relevant documents concerning it, no matter what their origin, and since as you remark I am not the judge charged with the dossier I think it best that you should get that confirmed by M. Besson personally."

"I beg your pardon, Madame, but the moment you see in me an agent in any way prejudiced I retire. You must believe that I am only carrying out the orders of my superiors, and you know that Commissaire Richard is extremely punctilious about departmental discipline, and since I am directly answerable to him for everything during the hours of nighttime—"

"M. Sallebert, your scruples do you credit, and count upon me, I shall not fail to establish your credit, insofar as the warm recommendation of a magistrate can carry weight with your superiors, the very next occasion that I find myself in M. Besson's office."

"Je vous en prie, Madame."

Colette and Castang went together into Richard's office.

"Now the bastard's certain you're my mistress. Or I'm your lover, if we're to follow departmental procedure."

"Hush."

"That's all right, now he's gone off in a huff. Here it is, on his desk, in full view, as that bastard knew perfectly well; not locked up in the drawer or anything. Confidential document my ass-hole."

"Henri, je t'en supplie."

"Come over this side of the desk where I can get a good grip of your bottom."

"Now, look!"

"Sorry, it's the effect that greasy cringer has upon me. Now, here—Lord, what a lot there are. I'd no idea there was so much juvenile crime. Still, in nearly a thousand square kilometers . . ."

"It's just names and addresses. Here," ripping off the paper clip, "you take this half." There was a silence.

"I hope Bernard's not seducing my wife in the Cité Administrative courtyard."

"He's more likely to be asleep. Heavens, yes, what a lot there are."

"How big a place is Bellac? It would be a postal address?"

"Yes, just about."

It was Castang who found it, which was fair.

"What was the name of the farmer over the valley from Tante Joséphine?"

"I've no idea," said Colette. "I never had anything to do with them. I remember that Bernard came back and said there was

216

warfare over the fruit trees. The orchard was down at the bottom of the valley, the far side of the vine slopes. Almost out of sight of the house. You know how Bernard is—a man takes a certain relish in defending the property. I suppose they thought we wouldn't notice a few miserable baskets of cherries. I'm sure I never did. We used to picnic down there, with Rachel in a basket. I do recall vaguely there was a scruffy boy. When Bernard said he'd given him a slap, I thought nothing of it."

"So the name Pierre Gaboriau means nothing to you."

"No—wait, now. Wasn't it dangerous driving?"

"Quite right, Madame la Juge. And unintentional homicide."

"It's over a year ago," murmured Colette. "Are you thinking—"

"I'm thinking it's a cross-reference," said Castang calmly. "That's all until we link it up."

"Gaboriau. I remember it now quite well. Rather a nasty boy, sullen, with all sorts of grievances. Not a speck of remorse, naturally; that's always what's so discouraging. It's everybody's fault but theirs. Terribly commonplace, alas. The boy was still under eighteen and officially a juvenile. They went to a Saturday night ball and got drunk and crashed on the way back and the other boy was killed, and this one got scarcely a scratch; the ways of God are inscrutable."

"But surely the insurance refused to pay, then?" said the policeman.

"There was a complex legal argument, and the ramifications now escape me. But briefly there was a clever defense, to the effect that the other boy knew perfectly that the first was a juvenile, had no license and no insurance, and was drunk and incompetent to drive anyway. There was no way out on the civil side: the responsibility was divided. It went to appeal but was thrown out. On the criminal side, which was where I judged it, it is always difficult to know how much to assign to the parents. He was about six months in jail pending, and I think I decided that that was quite enough. Banned from driving for ten years and some supervisory measures, but I forget what. Out there in the country it doesn't go for much anyway, with the shortage of personnel there is—absolutely chronic in these scattered outlying districts. It worried me at the time: I can't recall much more than that offhand."

"Let's jump before Sallebert catches us having a kiss-up."

"Really, Henri, you are impossible sometimes."

Bernard, shaken into wakefulness and jogged, was unhelpful. "M. Mouton, or something like that. I don't remember any Gaboriau. You're barking up the wrong tree. As I always said, it was something utterly trivial. Can't possibly be this."

From the dark at the back of the car, where she had been knitting, or telling her beads, or heaven knew what—one never did quite know what Vera was up to—a placid voice said, "Was there a Mme. Mouton?"

"Not Mouton, but something like that. Heavens, yes, frightful old cow, came storming out yelling when the boy ran home crying after I'd slapped him. We had a real battle there in the orchard," recalled Bernard with relish. "Said the boy had bad ears, mastoid, and I don't know what, and I'd slapped him and this would be a drama, et cetera. I told the old bitch that was just too bad, and they should have thought of that before sending their brat climbing up robbing other people's cherry trees. Defeat of angry stout party. End of story. Flea in ear. General withdrawal breathing fire and threats of chopping down cherry tree. Disregarded same. Retired with honors of war. You're just not telling me this is serious."

"Had Mme. Mouton been married before?" asked Vera implacably.

"No idea."

"I think we check," Castang said, unrelenting.

"How, in God's name," sleepily.

"Palace of Justice archives."

"How the hell you do that this hour of night?"

"We get the concierge out of bed," said Castang ruthlessly.

This was optimistic. Nobody had ever tried to get into the Palais de Justice at night before: nobody had ever wanted to. There were enough massive bolts and bars and heavy wrought-iron trelliswork to contain King Kong; in fact, one would not be surprised to find a live dinosaur plodding pathetically about those gloomy corridors, sadly searching for something to eat. But what do they protect, these bars? To be sure, Degradation of a Public Monument is an article in the Penal Code. Perhaps somewhere there is an uneasy realization that a few people are scattered about who really care about justice, and who might be tempted to start their reforms by knocking the whole frightful pile down.

Some detective work was needed to find out where the concierge lodged, and much further physical effort to get him out of the arms of Morpheus, and much tact to soothe his savage breast. When at last a Newgate-like series of bolts had been undone, with a steady undercurrent of grumbling, Colette made haste to neutralize any latent anti-feminist feeling with a large tip. Castang didn't have to work in the place: she did. Like all public buildings in France, the Palais de Justice is ruled entirely by the concierge. They get very arbitrary and incline strongly to megalomania. Even the Proc listened humbly with downcast eyes when—as frequently happened—he got button-holed and made to listen to a tirade about cigarette butts on the barristers' robing-room floor.

"And if there's ashtrays provided, they get stole. Advocates! I know a few what should be in jail," darkly. M. Besson was tempted to say that he did, too.

"I'm afraid we're going to find an awful mess," said Colette apologetically. They did. Her secretary ("a nice, bright young girl") and she had had many a brilliant idea for simplifying and modernizing the magisterial filing systems, all frustrated by her greffier, a gentleman of the old school given to scathing remarks about bright young men from business-administration schools "whatever those are" and with a dislike of metal office furniture ("where's my can opener?"). Aphorisms abounded. "Wood is noble." "Dust is honorable," and of course the classic "I can lay my hand on anything blindfold." What was so infuriating was that he could. He'd had to, this day, with the instructing judge and the Proc and the P.J. (a disgrace, that) calling for the most unlikely things. He'd gone off late in a notable huff, leaving everything nicely arranged on the floor, the way he knew how it should all go back.

It took Colette, as a consequence, nearly half an hour to find Gaboriau, Pierre. She had spent this time on her knees on the floor.

"Very good, and suitable for magistrates," said Castang, sitting all male and lordly at her desk in her chair. She looked at her grimy hands with distaste and went off to wash them, cross and edgy, and just too tired to give vent to it.

When she toiled back into the office, Castang was sitting smoking and thought-collecting with his face so blank that she knew he had been disappointed and told herself calmly that she wasn't going to cry or anything; there wasn't a tear left in her.

"I'm sorry, Henri," she managed to say.

"Sorry, my dear girl? What for? Everything is done. Except the hardest part. Which is going to be waking up a judge at this hour."

"Oh, Henri, don't torture me."

"Torturing you, now; I could rape you in the middle of your own files if it wasn't for that pig of a concierge. Be rather piquant."

She realized dimly that this was only an expression of tension relieved; a very great tension—indeed perhaps a breaking strain.

"Tell me what you have found," she said softly.

He held up a file and patted it. "Mme. Mouton—whose name, I may say, is Moustier, because, as Vera acutely suggested, she's been married before—is formerly Gaboriau. It's all in the file. Every damn thing is in the file. Very thorough, our legal system.

It's all there. Every scrap of it. A complete case. All we need now is to go and get Rachel."

"Then why is the hard part to come?" she said, uncomprehending and unable to believe this.

"Because I can't move without a warrant, and we want to move fast."

"But surely that can be managed." Signing a warrant was something Colette did every day: they got handed out like theatre tickets.

"Not quite so easy, I'm afraid. You saw the way Sallebert was. I agree; he's a lazy fat greasy bugger. He's also my hierarchical superior. Even if I get a warrant, it would be putting myself hopelessly in the wrong to try and bypass him by getting Richard out of bed. Whether it's arrest or even just search, it's in a country district and only the gendarmerie can execute it. We'll have to wait till morning."

"I can't. I won't." Threatening hysteria. "If you are really serious—Henri, have you a certainty?"

"Yes."

"Then, oh, I don't care—let's go and see M. Besson. No—it's old Jérémie. God help me, he doesn't like me much. Whether I appeal to him as a woman or as a colleague, I can't see him . . . No, I won't give up. I'll come with you; I'll cover you. I'll take the entire responsibility. You're not just cuddling me? You are sure?"

"Sure as that the earth goes round the sun—no, I'm not in the least sure of that. Never mind: I'm sure. I won't waste time; I'll give my argument to the judge."

The concierge was glowering at being kept so long. His glance would have accused them of making love on the floor of Colette's office, but luckily such enormities had not entered his head.

"I'm so sorry, M. Mangin. But it really was important. I can't tell you how important. Something absolutely vital to me or I'd never have disturbed you."

M. Mangin looked at her with sympathy. He knows, Colette thought wildly. Better not ask how. Concierges always know everything.

"That's all right, Mme. Delavigne. Happy to be of service to you."

For the rest of her life, Colette would never know whether this was just an assumed air of importance, or whether he really had known.

Bernard and Vera were both asleep in the car. Or asleep ... well, the way one might sleep on a station platform at three in the morning, sitting on a suitcase.

"My God. At this hour."

It was another thing she would never know. Was it just because it was the police at two in the morning? Was it because she was a young woman as well as a colleague? The judge did not come down in any orange striped pajamas. No. He was dressed, down to his tie, and brought such a chill with him into the dark little study that it was no warm June night with the big clattering bugs wheeling round the lime trees outside. Office hours in November in Goose Bay, Labrador.

But he showed no impatience, no irritability. In a way, one would have preferred that. That dry businesslike tone: that way of looking at the two of them as though they were just two more unshaved and sweaty ruffians clattering in with the handcuffs still on.

"Spare me the details, please. I feel sure, M. Castang, that you would like to give a multiplicity of details to palliate the impression of haste and confusion. But no details, please."

Colette's mouth was full of her tongue: she could feel it right down into her throat muscles. She kept her lips shut.

"Yes, sir," said Castang respectfully. "M. Delavigne, while defending the interests of a relation who has a country property in this village, was forced into a hostile attitude some years ago, and was sufficiently irritated to slap a teen-age boy caught flagrantly stealing fruit. We have identified the same boy as one who, while still a minor, was brought before Madame here on a homicide-by-imprudence following a dangerous-driving charge. It escaped everyone. A dissimilarity in names; a woman twice married. The juxtaposition is casual and trivial, but the psychiatrist's report on this boy is cogent. And cumulative. I don't want to say it is conclusive until you have read it, sir."

The judge read it, took off his glasses, and said, "At two in the morning, one is naturally eager to take things as conclusive."

"The one item of physical evidence left upon the putative scene of the kidnapping was a scatter of rabbit droppings. It points strongly to a pattern of this nature."

"It pointed, with equal force, to the decidedly unbalanced man on whose terrain this hypothetical rabbit had been exercising itself," said the judge levelly, holding the earpieces of his glasses by the fingertips, dancing them gently up and down. "You went, then, in a high state of enthusiastic excitement to M. Richard and convinced him that a search warrant should be forthcoming. If I'm not mistaken, Castang—"

"No, sir," cursing that old Léon from the bottom of his heart.

"He has placed a verbal complaint before the Parquet for wrongful search and seizure. He promises a written complaint. He was sent to me—he gave me an exceedingly tiresome quarter of an hour. He talked a great deal about abuse of powers. That was this evening. Now, a few hours later, you come to me with another tale of unbalanced peasants nurturing grievances. Two tales: two too many, M. Castang."

"With respect, Monsieur le Juge, Commissaire Richard agreed that it was indispensable to eliminate that old man from the inquiry. I don't think it quite fair to blame the P.J. for his being a monomaniac with a grievance against the courts of justice."

"And what proves to me, M. Castang, that this is not another instance of uneducated persons with an imaginary grievance?"

"With respect, sir, the existence of one old man who is notoriously a troublemaker in legal circles—one could call him a professional lover of litigation—cannot excuse me from pursuing another line of inquiry because of the similarity. Could that similarity not be superficial?"

"And could it not be said, M. Castang, that, seeing you at this hour, in Mme. Delavigne's company—and, be it said only in the privacy of this room, smelling of alcohol—that it would be a natural conclusion to imagine you emotionally involved in this affair, to a degree that I would prefer to think does not concern me?"

"Sir," said Castang slowly, "even if you think it unforgivable, I have to say one thing. I think that M. Richard knows me sufficiently well not to take such a suggestion seriously."

The judge did not show, by as much as a twitch in his expression, that he had heard this. He tapped his glasses slowly on the dossier Castang had brought.

"This file, Mme. Delavigne, which belongs, I think, in your archive—you have taken this from the Palais? Just now? As a result of this idea you had late at night?"

"That is quite correct, Monsieur le Juge."

There was a short silence. "Castang, I am going to ask you to be good enough to wait for a moment in my hall. I wish to speak to Mme. Delavigne in private." Castang got up wordlessly and left.

"Mme. Delavigne . . . Colette, my child, I must speak to you bluntly. You are a magistrate. Are you thoroughly aware of what you are doing and what you may be risking?"

"Yes," said Colette flatly. "Have you another question, Monsieur le Juge? I will answer it with scrupulous truth. Knowing what it may mean."

"En connaissance de cause," repeated the judge reflectively. He raised his eyes suddenly. "Are you prepared to give me a word of honor? Even though that term has become meaningless?"

"I give you my word of honor as a woman and as a magistrate, and believe me I know that my career and my life are in balance. I am no man's mistress." He looked at her for some time, nodded, put his glasses on, went back to a second reading of the dossier.

"When you judged this boy—with considerable leniency as it appears to me—you were utterly unaware of his identity as a youth your husband had punished upon another occasion with a slap?"

"Totally. I do not rely upon the discrepancy in names. I had no idea of these people's name. Even the slap was reported to me later at a remove, and I did not attach importance to it, then or at any time."

"Was any complaint made to authority, as a result of the slap?"

"I have absolute trust in my husband when he tells me not, and even if there had been, that it would have been thrown out. Flagrant provocation. There was never doubt, as he tells me, as to the ownership of the fruit trees."

"It is alarmingly tenuous," said the judge slowly. "I can of course see that there is a cumulative effect. . . . I am an old man, Colette. You are a young woman at the threshold of your career. I have made judicial mistakes. Some of them have had grave consequences. I believe—I can do no more than believe, but as to my belief you have my word of honor as I have yours—I believe, as God sees and will judge me, that I have never instructed a case, and forwarded the papers to the Chamber of Accusation containing my intimate conviction that a crime has been committed, without the certainty that I held that criminal. Forgive me—you are a young girl. Have you measured your responsibility, my child?"

"Yes," whispered Colette. "Not here. This is my child. I am only its mother."

"Quite so. The more responsibility for me. Suppose I said to you—we have had a variety of scandals lately. Where, conceivably, a Judge of Instruction might be thought to have acted impetuously—giving way, shall I say, to the pressures of publicity. Maybe—even without feeling the absolute certainty that the police investigation had been properly carried out."

Colette said nothing to that, having nothing to say.

"You come to me with a heart-rending situation. The police come with a line of facile patter." He had got up and was walking jerkily up and down, stopping to twitch the curtains straight with an automatic gesture. "I should tell you to drink a tisane and go to bed. And send that young man home to compose a report for his superiors. I'm not suggesting that the elements collected here are worthless. They can be verified. But you have shown me nothing that explains, for example, this telephone call you have received."

She felt that all her energy had dribbled away. She did not know what to answer. In other circumstances, she would be saying these things herself. She had said them, frequently.

"Monsieur le Juge . . ." she said feebly.

"Yes?"

"Do what you can for me."

He walked to the door, opened it, called, "Castang, come in, would you," and went to sit down at his desk.

"Castang, this telephone call—there was no specific menace?"

"To abandon the child somewhere. What alarms one most and convinces me that we should not lose time is the mixture of violent impulse in these people with the realization of possible consequences. I'm afraid . . ." He hesitated; he hadn't wished to say this in front of Colette. "They were able to make a careful, calculated plan to possess themselves of the child. Now that they've got her, they don't know what to do with her. No long-term thought. They've achieved their main point, presumably, of acquiring a sadistic satisfaction in giving pain and anxiety. They say they'll let her go. It must surely occur to them that she knows enough to identify them—to recognize them, at least. They feel safe from discovery. But will they—by daylight —still feel as safe?"

The judge glanced sidewise at Colette. She was sitting dully staring in front of her, too tired even to move her eyes. She gave no sign of having heard. His fingertips fidgeted as though he wished to drum them on the desk. He reached for his pocket, produced a silver fountain pen, uncapped it, opened the drawer of his desk.

"I'll give you a warrant for arrest," abruptly. "Search and seizure won't help you at this hour of the night. You realize what that means?" Castang nodded. ("You," blunt.) "I had no very great difficulty this afternoon. An old man who is a public nuisance in more ways than one. But this . . . You know what it smells of, Castang? An operation arbitrarily decided and enforced in the middle of the night, an inquiry where the press has been stifled, an affair which any advocate would draw as a private war between individuals, where a magistrate was using police force to a private end? It smells of the Gestapo, Castang. Have you thought of that? You know what it will mean to you? Have you seen yourself in a court, an officer of Police Judiciaire openly accused of abusing your powers out of private interest and corrupt friendship? You'd destroy her, too, you know that? The entire public would conclude you were her lover. And your wife . . . Before I give you this warrant—have you thought of all that? Resolute? Very well." The magistrate made the quick automatic gesture with which one signs one's name on the piece of paper that is a check or a rental agreement. He held it out.

"There is your warrant. The rest concerns you. I'll telephone Sallebert—make your own arrangements with the local gendarmerie. Before you put it in your pocket . . ." He glanced at his watch. "Two-thirty. In less than six hours, Commissaire Richard will be at his desk and you will have opportunity to place the responsibility where it belongs. No? Good." He got up. He stared at Colette, who got up automatically and smoothed her skirt. He smiled suddenly, and turned back to Castang with a completely unexpected sprightliness.

"You've read *The Three Musketeers?*"

"Yes," flabbergasted.

"Recall the passage in which Richelieu says, 'Young man, I promise you that if I can again say what I have just said, I will say it.' " Castang sketched a sort of bow and went out. The judge put his hands on Colette's shoulders.

"I've done what you asked. What I could," he said gently.

Bernard was not asleep this time. He was walking up and down the pavement beside the car, with the mechanical jerkiness of a sentry outside the palace.

"Drop me back at the P.J. office," said Castang tonelessly. "I've got to get a car."

"And us?" asked Bernard, aghast. "What are we to do?"

"Nothing at all, I'm afraid. Tisane and bed, as the judge has sensibly suggested."

"You come back with me," said Vera. "My turn for hospitality."

"And it's one telephone number I don't have to look up in the book," said Castang.

"I'd like some coffee, I think," said Colette in a perfectly relaxed tone. "And some bacon and eggs, or onion soup or something."

"I'll peel onions," said Vera. "I'd rather enjoy the activity."

"You got him to give you that?" said Sallebert with a kind of admiration.

"Oh, he didn't lose the opportunity of telling me I'd get busted like a burned match."

"Well, pal. It's your funeral."

"You don't sound as happy as you might."

"Look, cock," said Sallebert, unforced. "I don't give a damn whether you're sleeping with her or not. Because if you do that, all I can say is you've earned her."

"I'll remember you in my will," said Castang, not nastily.

"You're not mad at me?"

"Not a bit. I'd have done the same."

"I wish you joy. No, hell, I wish you success. Really. Straight up."

"Thanks," said Castang, starting the motor.

"Jesus, it's heavy. Be a storm in the hills. Well, we could do with the rain."

"A good hailstorm. I'll stand out in it, in the middle of the field. Bloody scarecrow."

"You said it." The car drove off out of the courtyard.

"Richard will guillotine you, pal," said M. Sallebert out loud. "And I suppose you'll imagine that it will make me dead happy. Which isn't necessarily so." He looked up at the dark clouded sky, and wished it would break. He could do with a shower.

Castang drove. From here it was about a hundred kilometers. Be lucky to do it in under two hours. Thunder out there in the hills, that was a certainty. Knock the dust off the car. He shifted into top gear.

Three robbers sat in a cave.

One of them said to the other, "Tell me a story, Antonio."

And so the story began.

"Three robbers sat in a cave. One of them said to the other, 'Tell me a story, Antonio.' And so the story began.' "Three robbers sat in a cave. . . ." ' " Third gear. Second gear. Fourth gear.

"You gave it away," said the young man furiously. "Thought you were so smart."

"Shut up," said the young woman fiercely. "Know all, know nothing."

"I don't think there's any sense in keeping her," said the old woman.

"Never did," said the old man.

"Shut up, you. We're free to do as we please."

"They could be listening. They do that. Tap the lines, like."

"Shut up."

"Nothing to do with it. They can't find us; there's nothing whatever to give us away. No need for you to start getting scared."

"They could recognize your voice."

"Who could? Who's heard my voice? Who knows me?"

"Not that we're thinking of. What good is she to us, now?"

"Get rid of her."

"What could she say?"

"Describe us. Give names. That's what."

"Describe us! Give names! You think a kid that age is able to? What you got inside that head of yours?"

"She's asleep. Take her, put her in the car, drive her out a good way. Dump her on the road. She'll come to no harm."

"Get wet, maybe."

"She'll wander about. She hasn't got a clue."

"Clue enough to say 'Marie-Thérèse'! I told you you shouldn't mention any names."

"Look—don't be so goddamned dumb. How many are there in France?"

"I told you, I always told you, she'd blab."

"Shut up. What d'you want, then? You think we should knock her on the head or something? You know what that'd be? Murder, that's what."

"I'm not having any of that talk. That's not for us. We're not like that. She's just a kid. I'm not having her injured."

"Nobody says injured. Blindfold her like, turn her round a few times."

"And do it now."

"Going to be a storm."

"So she gets wet. Do we never get wet? Don't be such a bloody drip. Now it's dark. You want to do it by daylight?"

"Suppose she sees the car number?"

"Oh, yeah, and suppose she sees the color of your eyes. You can turn the lights out, can't you? What could she ever tell? I ask you, what could she ever tell? Doesn't amount to a row of beans."

"Enough to put us in jail, maybe. They'd say it was kidnapping."

"Nix, unless you ask for money, it isn't kidnapping. We just took her for a ride."

"Well, I say it's kidnapping." It was Carney. "I think it is even when you don't ask for money. And I say it's bloody risky. Who knows what she can tell?"

"You out of your bleeding mind or something?"

"I don't see what you're all on about. Look at all those Vietnamese kids. Napalm and stuff. Doesn't have to hurt. Back of the neck, like a rabbit. Then you know you're safe. I mean you're certain."

"I'm not having any of that talk."

"Look, just shut up. Or I knock *you* on the back of the neck."

"You and who else?"

"Shut up. Stuff it. Too much talk."

"Too much beer talking."

"We're agreed, right?"

"We're agreed, right."

It was one of the scattered, straggling villages, strung out along a main road, commonplace all over France. Hilaire Belloc, in *The Path to Rome*, says they are a sign of Roman civilization. Villages huddled together in a heap for protection are a sign of barbarianism. There is truth in this. But there are different sorts of barbarianism. Village like any other, thought Castang, sliding down the main street, which was the only street: shuttered café, deserted gasoline pump; usual village mairie, half school and half fire station: not a soul awake. Houses sealed, shutters blind, chickens all locked up behind high walls: fox trots down the center of the street, 100 percent frustrated. Right down the other end of the village, a house with a sort of little barrack built on behind it. A milky illuminated sign saying "Gendarmerie." Castang parked his car. Nobody was astir. The duty officer was sleeping on a camp bed. He rang the night bell. A light went on. A sort of uncombed orangutan in boots opened the door.

The folklore of the country gendarme, or of any village cop, as rustic but shrewd, all boots and heavy breathing, licking the stub of his pencil in a laborious transference of semiliteracy into adminstrative jargon, is one of the clichés dear to clued-puzzle detective stories, but has no more than a few superficial shreds of truth. The gendarmerie is one of the most disciplined bodies in France. So it should be: it is a military body organized in a military hierarchy. It is also extremely sophisticated, for as a relatively small body, thinly spread over a large and amazingly varied terrain, it is hard worked and has learned to apply a great deal of ingenuity to combating the chronic shortage of men and material, for a parsimonious government keeps it extremely short of money. It sees, daily, a cross-section of the follies and futilities of mankind that would stagger any urban police force. But what perhaps gives it an exceptional quality more than all else is the power it possesses and uses so sparingly. The gendarme is pretty well everything his municipal colleague is, as well as handyman in the fire and ambulance services, public works and rural engineering, but he is also an officer of judicial police. Out in the wilds, where the twentieth century sometimes knocks its nose upon the seventeenth, commissaires and magistrates and procs are far-off and seldom seen. The extremely elaborate separation of powers and the subtle distinctions between legislative and executive, which prevail in the city, and insure that no Gestapos arise upon the territory of the Republic, are in the country fused. A country gendarme is in title an "officer of Police Judiciaire," and compared to him Castang is very small fry.

It wasn't an orangutan at all: this was no more than a trick of the light behind the glass door. Crumpled slacks and sweaty shirt sleeves—the thunder kept muttering in the hills, and the atmosphere was close and oppressive—did not prevent him from looking trim and alert. He gave a massive yawn, but it was nearly four in the morning.

"Come on in." Lightning flickered over the hills, looking pale and ineffectual. "I wish it'd make up its mind." The two men stood on the doorstep together, looking up at the unseen charged clouds. A few scattered drops of warm heavy rain sploshed on the dusty leaves.

"When it does come," gloomily, "probably be hail and rip all the vines to bits. Or create a flash flood. I'll probably be out bridge-building before morning." The gloom had no self-pity in it. He didn't sound as though it would be a treat, but he wasn't complaining.

"Where's the patrol?"

"Out looking after some Dutch tourists," without even a grin, "who brought their own grub with them and got food poisoning as a consequence." He flipped the switch on the shortwave transmitter and said, "All right, Sam, pick up thy musket, lad; how goes it?"

"Ya, boy, I hear you" came the voice, horribly distorted by thunder and static. "Going down the valley, the three of them in the back. Ten minutes from the clinic: no real worry, not in coma, just galloping dysentery. Deliver them, right, and then back to pick up all their camping stuff or some bugger'll pinch it. Thirty—no, say forty minutes."

"Okay. Logged. Out. Right, sir, what's on your mind?"

"I'll give you a quick breakdown," said Castang, "so you can see whether we have to call the brigadier, because I've a notion we'll need him."

"Ho," said the gendarme. He listened in silent patience, and said "Ho" again at the end.

"Yes, I better call the brig. You want some coffee? Nescafé, I should say. I leave you alone a moment."

When the brigadier appeared, he was in pajamas, with the rumpled-schoolboy look of a man just waked up, the placid manner of a man used to it, and a considerable five-o'clock shadow. He sat down at the desk, spooned Nescafé into a cup, said "See that the water's boiling," and looked at Castang with mild expectancy.

"I gather you want me to execute a mandate," he said, putting his reading glasses on. "Yes . . . Well . . . We can't go doing that in the middle of the night, can we, now? Right, well, it's only two hours to sunrise. Let's see what we know. We don't keep files on every rabbit in the neighborhood, you know. Gilbert, look in that cabinet there, the 'Things Judged' one, and find me Gaboriau."

"I daresay," said Castang, "that what isn't in the file might be as interesting as what is." The brigadier looked at him impassively.

"Don't get me wrong—no offense meant," the brigadier said. "But you're none too sure of yourself, are you? All right, all right; a nod's as good as a wink. You have a mandate signed by the Judge of Instruction. There's no name on it, but you've got these people in mind. And it's sort of collective, huh?"

"There's a whole clan of these people—as far as I know. I'm hoping you'll know more."

"Easy does it. Mine's a large district. Bellac is ten kilometers up the road. Orders are orders. You've a mandate for me; I'll execute it. But we'd better not have any excesses of zeal, because I'd be answerable for them. You come out here hotfoot

234

in the middle of the night and wake me up—no, no, I'm not criticizing. But there's no name on this mandate. That's fair enough; you know about this young man, and an old couple, and there's a young woman been on the telephone, and taking it all round we'd like to know a bit more, you and me both—that's reasonable, isn't it? So we look at this dossier first. Gaboriau—yes, now I remember him, nervy young sod. Still, not a very helpful observation, that. Now let's see who signed this original report on that road accident. Sauvage. Well, now, Gilbert, seems to me you might get Sauvage out of bed. Not getting impatient, are you?" to Castang.

"No. I'm not going to go about telling you how to do your job."

"Then we're happy. I was wondering—or let's say the thought crossed my mind—that you might be a bit hipped at what seems an absence of zeal, like, which a judge might think was as bad as too much. But I don't mind telling you," mildly, "I like to look before I leap."

"I don't mind telling you," said Castang, slipping without trouble into this habit of deliberation, "that it's all right by me. I suppose I seem about as welcome as the dysentery charging in like this, twitching and biting my nails, but I've been on the go since this time yesterday."

"Man," said the brigadier, "don't think it. A kidnap case—yes, I know; we had it on our telex last night. And a judge behind it. And a P.J. officer with a mandate. You're going to get everything we can give you. Including, I hope, a bit of thought. Talking of dysentery, where's the patrol, Gilbert?"

"Be back any minute."

"Then you might make us some real coffee. And be ready to nip out, like, for when Arthur gets his first batch of bread out of the oven. Now this is Sauvage. Jesus, man, where'd you get those pajamas? This is M. Castang from the P.J. and he wants to know something about the family Moustier in Bellac."

"They got a grievance," said M. Sauvage, sitting down and

scratching with a hand like the blade of a Caterpillar backhoe. "I don't know what it's about, but whatever it is they got a grievance." The resemblance was increased by his pajamas, which were Caterpillar yellow.

"I've only got one question, really," said Castang. "In this clan, is there by any chance a young or youngish woman who speaks with something of a parigot accent?"

"I'm not quite sure how that goes. There's a lot of screaming fishwives there."

"Got a tape recorder around here?" asked Castang.

Time passed easily, out here in the country. The car patrol rolled in, encumbered with much camping material and an amazing number of opened cans, most of which seemed to contain apple sauce, and some sordid remnants of cooked chicken to be sent to the lab for analysis. This took everyone's appetite away, until Officer Triboulet finally arrived with fresh bread, and invited Castang to breakfast. Officer Triboulet got into trouble for having left the milk out. The thunder had turned it sour. But the storm had passed over without breaking, which everyone agreed was just as well, since the grapes were at a vulnerable stage. They always are, thought Castang, but kept his mouth shut. Breakfast finished, with a good deal of jam dropped on the table, the maréchaussée departed for a wash and reappeared unrecognizable, not just with gleaming jowls but in freshly pressed khaki gabardines. ·

"We won't take the jeep," said the brigadier. "The van's more discreet, like, in case we have some arresting to do."

Castang had had time to ring Vera.

"I was asleep." Her voice came thick and clogged. "Sorry, darling—I didn't drink much, but it was still too much. They've gone home, at last. End of the tether. And you?"

Yes. The last twenty-four hours were now earning compound interest. "Going up against this place now. Virtually certain. But . . . no, skip it. Just keep hoping for the best. Stay in bed. I've no idea when I'll be back, but if you want me, or if you hear from Richard before I get the chance to phone in, ring the gendarmerie here."

He didn't phone Commissaire Sallebert. He had nothing to say.

"Can I borrow your razor?" he asked the brigadier.

Rachel was within grasp. A quarter of an hour's drive. It didn't somehow sound like a trumpet call. He was very tired, and he didn't feel there were any reserves left.

Oh, well. Even in that ghastly shit-hole of Dien Bien Phu, Bigeard had kept his paratroops shaved. They hadn't had any reserves, either. Why did he feel so depressed? Rachel was within grasp.

Sauvage drove. Up the valley, around a big bare hump or "piton" of limestone, and suddenly a beautiful, gentle, irrigated vista. And the high hills as backdrop.

"Up at the top," said Sauvage briefly, changing gear: the tires scrabbled on the stony track.

The Volkswagen minibus slammed to a stop noisily, and several dogs began a hysterical barking. A big slab-faced, slab-sided oldish woman peered out with a mask of black blank hostile suspicion. The brigadier jumped out like a boy of twenty and sketched a dazzling salute.

"Bonjour, Madame," bearing in at the door like a woodpecker.

"What's this then? What you want? Hey, you go easy there. Private property." The brigadier took his képi off politely, laid it on the kitchen table, and said, "This gentleman is an officer of the Police Judiciaire from the city." The old woman showed no sign of being impressed at all.

"What's that, then? Looks like an insurance salesman."

"No need to be impolite," said the brigadier crisply. "Now,

then. M. Castang here is the bearer of authorization signed by the Judge of Instruction to search these premises. So I'd be obliged, Madame, if you would ask everybody present in this house to gather here in this room. All right? Right, Sauvage, just take a look out the back, would you?"

"Hey, hey. Not so free, there, you. What is this?"

"Here is the authority to search, Madame. I must ask you not to cause obstruction."

"You can't go pulling women out of bed. Here, you, where d'you think you're going?"

"Just seeing where the door leads to," said M. Sauvage comfortably.

"Nobody's pulling women out of bed. Just call them, would you."

"My son Pierrot's day off; he needs his sleep."

"Yes, sure. We have our beauty sleep broken, too. And you've a daughter, I believe."

"No, I haven't, Mr. Clever. You're barking up the wrong tree."

"That will be quite simple for you to demonstrate, then," said the brigadier. "Stepdaughter or daughter-in-law or whatever she is, we'd be glad of the opportunity of seeing her."

"Well," said a ferocious voice. "You see her. And so what?"

Handsome, thought Castang with spontaneous admiration. That may not be quite altogether the word, in view of handsome-is-as-handsome-does, but pretty is altogether too faded a word. A woman like wood charcoal. Just blow on her, quite gently, and the sullen red will glow bright, and the concentration of heat will astonish you.

A mass of blond hair round a keen, aquiline, slightly gypsy face snapping with vitality. Some body, too. She was wearing nothing but a short salmon-pink nylon nightdress and faded baby-blue mules with pompons on them. Splendid legs were naked to mid-thighs. Splendid breasts were pushed out aggressively, the ferocious nipples dark as the barrel of a gun showing up through the semitransparent material.

"What the hell are you? What the hell you want? What d'you think you're doing here? Now or any other time?"

"Here," said the old woman, not very shocked or embarrassed, but just sufficiently both to have her style cramped, "you better put something on."

Castang had heard from the first syllable that this was his quarry. Despite himself, he was impressed.

"So what?" said the vision. "Show them my ass they wouldn't dare hiccup. What d'you mean by this, hey? Out of here, this is private property. Lady here in her nightdress, you buzz off, understand? And make it quick."

The brigadier had put on an utterly wooden face. His voice stalked stiffly over regulation phrases.

"Being present in virtue of a mandate duly signed by a judge of the requisite tribunal, I'm under no obligation to withdraw and you'd better go and put some clothes on."

"Want to get an eyeful, do you, dirty-minded prat that you are. Well, you won't get it."

The brigadier called forth all Castang's admiration at that moment.

He didn't budge at all. "My dear, you could show me your beautiful curls all the way up to your navel and it would just be dandelion salad to me: I'm a married man. And *now go dress,*" in a ferocious bark that stopped the dogs in the yard, rendered insane by Officer Sauvage stumping about at the back door. He came in to see what all the row was about, and stood transfixed at the pink nylon bottom. The young woman didn't budge any more than the brigadier did.

"I'll put my clothes on in my good time and in my orders, not yours, hick." Her eyes came round to Castang. "Who're you? A bailiff?"

He leaned his bottom peacefully against the table. "My name

is Castang. I'm an officer of judicial police. We've met. Which is to say I had the pleasure of listening to you on the telephone last night."

The green eyes under their finely arched eyebrows snapped at him.

She whisked round abruptly to the door. "Get out of my way, you," she said to Sauvage. He did, politely. The whole body arched indomitably at them. For a moment, he really thought she was going to hitch up the nightdress and say "Kiss it." He could see the buttocks clench. She hesitated, and then whisked out, slamming the door. The brigadier said nothing. Castang admired this disciplined silence.

"Careful," he muttered. "Create a short circuit."

"Ask the men—and the women, too," woodenly, "to get dressed."

The old woman stood her ground. "They'll get dressed when they want. When it's time to go to work. I stay here. Keep my eye on you. No knowing what you might not try to pinch."

"All right," said the brigadier. "All the jokes are over now. Up the stairs, Sauvage: too much obstruction. You, too, Castang; you know what you're looking for. You'd better keep quiet, Madame. Politeness is one thing, respect is another. And law is something else. You choose to play it the hard way."

"Robbers!" screamed the old woman. Sauvage was mounting the stairs placidly, in an armor of indifference that Castang— with a fine view of his backside—regarded with respect.

His technique, too, left nothing to be desired. Without once losing a polite stolidity, he routed through the whole house, as unimpressed by the young woman's fervent access of modesty —"You can't come in here: I'm dressing"—as he had been by the opposite. Getting spat on, getting her nightdress flung in his face—it all bothered him about as much as a fly.

From the attic to the cellar, and they paid particular attention to both, there was no sign whatever of Rachel. In the one there was a little girl, who screamed with quite unfeigned fear, and in the other there was exactly what you might expect. Nothing anywhere showed the slightest sign of any departure from the normal. Castang avoided looking at Sauvage, but saw enough of him to realize that Sauvage was taking pains not to catch his eye. No reproach. But, brother, where do we go from here?

They finally got the whole band assembled in the kitchen, muttering and mouthing threats. They were going to go straight down to the town to lay a complaint. They would get lawyers, they would tell the press, there was justice in this country, they would soon show that the poor were not to be trodden upon, and exploited, and abused, and fucked about by a pack of stinking fuzz that was nothing but a Gestapo under the thumb of the rich and paid—and bribed—to abuse the poor. Castang put on the same impassive front as his allies, who were showing a remarkable solidarity. His courage, though, was not high: it was always notoriously difficult to prove anything in the face of a clan of peasants, even if everybody knew they were guilty as hell. God knew what breath of suspicious mistrust had alerted them. They *were* guilty as hell. He knew it. But what did he have? A slightly drunken, disjointed, inconclusive, trivial tale of a rustic squabble involving Bernard. The completely irrelevant fact that this sullen young ruffian had been judged once— a year ago—for drunken driving and manslaughter by Colette. And a tape recording of a phone call, which was not evidence of anything: no court would touch it with a ten-foot pole. No court would want anything to do with a circumstantial suspicion case against a peasant family. Various unpleasant, inconclusive, and thoroughly depressing landmarks in the history of criminal trials were at the forefront of his mind. Gaston Dominici . . . Marie Besnard . . . that nest of maddened hornets in Bruay-en-Artois . . . For a small-time P.J. cop, even backed up by his Commissaire, even backed up by the whole family of Judges of Instruction, to be sure of their guilt was not enough. Not nearly enough . . .

The brigadier, appearing completely unfazed, was address-
ing the assembled populace.

"According to information received, you fall, the lot of you,
under a grave imputation of a very serious crime. The instructing judge delivers me in consequence this mandate for inquiry,
search and examination, and, if necessary, arrest. You had better be very careful. You'd better forget all that nonsense pretty
quick about running to complain to the canton tribunal and all
the rest of it, because that stuff could have a nasty backfire. You
can go to work: yes, yes, stop fussing. You others can go about
your normal business. I leave you free for the moment, with the
warning that you are all bound to hold yourselves at the disposition of justice at any moment and without notice. And you'd
better be very careful."

"Bullshit," said the old woman.

"You can't hold what's in the past against me. That's already
judged. Victimization, that is," said the young man.

"You've kept me late for work," said the other young man,
the one called Carney. "I lose by that and I'll bleeding well sue
for compensation."

"I'll have you filthy fuckers," said the young woman. "Oh,
yes, I know how to go about that. I come from Paris, I know a
trick or two for you. Bursting into my bedroom when I got no
clothes on—I'll sue you for rape. And abuse of power. And
wrongful arrest. Illegal force and constraint. Oh, yes—and I'll
go to the office of *France-Dimanche*, too. We'll see to knock you
off your perch. I know a few what's going to lose their jobs."

"You'd better stop quacking—or else you really will be late
for work," said the brigadier, unmoved.

In a dignified and menacing manner, the forces of the law
withdrew to previously prepared positions.

"Not very clever" was all the brigadier said on the way back.
Sauvage said nothing at all.

"Well?" said the brigadier back in his office, alone with Castang.

"Got a black eye there."

"Yes," in an elaborately not-blaming-you tone.

"You could hear for yourself. That screaming cow's the one who made the phone call. There's no mistake."

"No."

"The child has to be found."

"Yes."

"And even if we do find the child . . ."

"Yes. And how. And when. And where."

"I haven't wanted to think about it."

"I can understand that," said the brigadier shortly. "I've got plenty of work. And I'll have to make a report on this to the lieutenant. You see, I don't know what you're aiming to do, right now."

"I'm going to go and give that some serious thought," said Castang.

"You heading back to town?" not without a certain sympathy, because that fellow there was buggered, if ever he saw a fellow buggered, and the ground under his shoes was getting kind of hot. Whereas he himself was covered completely, from start to finish. And it wasn't a lot of chat from that trouble-brewing shit-stirring crowd of peasants that would worry him. He felt quite sorry for Castang. Still, for an experienced man, he'd stuck his neck out rather far.

There was a new gendarme on the desk, one he hadn't seen.

"I'm going down the village," said Castang.

"Okay," indifferently.

"What's the pub like?"

"Nothing much. Their white wine's honest. Reasonably." Both were words one could stretch.

It was the old man from Hanoi who came into his mind. At that little old café back in the village there . . . where the white wine was honest, even if nothing else was. The old man who had laughed at him, who'd seen too many dead children, too many good soldiers thrown away in futile operations, too many bright young officers left to fertilize fields. Who had remarked that even a senior civil servant would never have a secure retirement just on his lousy pension. What did taking a few bribes matter one way or another? The district still got peaceably and even surprisingly efficiently administered.

He, Castang, didn't have any children. He ought to be grateful for that, instead of letting it chew at him. Hell, he'd got that chewed at, between Vera and Colette—a tiresome bitch, that one—he'd got all nibbled away on one side and had lost his balance.

Well, he had his law degree, anyway. And a certain amount of experience. There would be a job somewhere. They wouldn't starve to death or anything. They might even do a sight better than they were doing right now, because this was a thankless job if ever he saw one. Bernard and Colette had loyalty, and would do what they could, and that could be quite a lot. Richard had loyalty, too, and would give him the fairest deal possible. It wasn't disgrace. Everyone would give him a good recommendation.

The kind of good recommendation you give a fellow when you want to see his back limping offstage fast.

Whoever let him down, gently or not, with or without a lot of lip service, Vera would not. It might have been said—it had been said—that he'd made an imprudent marriage and it hadn't done him any good. But he had, by God, a woman who would stick with him no matter how sodomized he got.

Was there anything he could do? Ring the office? Ring Colette and Bernard? Ring Vera?

What could he say to any of them? What interest would it have to anyone? Unless he got Rachel back, he wasn't worth a licked postage stamp to man or beast. He ordered another glass of white wine, drearily. Sitting here in this dimwit dump getting sozzled. Go home to bed, fool. Get some sleep. That at least will knit up a few of the raveled sleaves of care.

He didn't even notice the phone ringing. Ten veal cutlets

today, butcher, six entrecôtes. Oh, and a bit of calves' liver if you've got any. Day like this, we could easy do twenty chance lunches with the tourists.

"Your name Castang? Phone for you." He lurched over.

"Gendarmerie here. The city's on the phone for you. Your Commissaire. I told him you'd ring back."

"Thanks." It had caught up with him sooner than he'd expected. But why try to put it off? He might as well have driven back right away, taken his castor oil, and gone to sit patiently on the pot till the effect appeared.

Hell, he might as well ring and get it over. And ring from here: what good would discretion do him now?

"Hallo. Give me the boss. Of course it's me; who the hell did you think it was?" Even his voice had apparently gone unrecognizable. Or had the word got around so fast on the grapevine that Castang had slipped on a banana skin and busted his stupid tail?

"Castang here."

"Where the hell are you?" Richard's voice, cool and drawling, clear as though he were in the same room. Sounding utterly unworried. Fair enough. He didn't have any worries. He hadn't gone and got himself amorously mixed up with any pretty young women who happened to be magistrates.

"Village pub."

"I see," said Richard much too brightly. Sounding, if possible, amused. Castang the Entertainer. We've had the performing seals; now bring on the clowns. "Good. Now, listen carefully." Oh, yes. He knew it all by heart. But he'd listen real carefully.

"You pissed or something?"

"No. My voice might be funny. I've been up all night."

"Serve you right." Oh, all right, all right, don't rub it in.

"But foaming," said Richard frivolously. "Red-eyed. Mad. Sinking your teeth in the wallpaper."

"Look, spare me the wit."

"I'll spare you the wit, buster. Running round the countryside without telling me. With a negligent roll of those big muscular shoulders, put on to impress lover-girl. All done by little me. Me big chief Hollywood Indian, me solve crime without any bleeding commissaires. Me act big hero. Me get bullet in belly last reel, but me make heroic deathbed, tell girl me love her truly with last gasp. Is that what you're up to?"

"All right!" yelled Castang. "Skip that, and I'll spare you my withdrawal symptoms."

"Christ, boy, how much trouble can you make me! Proc's been taking my skin off."

"Tell him I shit on him, pending the moment I tell him myself. If he's hiding behind the administrative channels, I'm not."

"Look, are you drunk?"

"Not yet."

"Well, shut up, will you?"

"Yes, sir. Yes, sir."

"I've had a series of complicated telephone calls."

"Who'd have thought it?"

"Fabre's rung me. Raynal rang Fabre. Gendarmerie headquarters rang Raynal. Some bright eager lad—like you—out in the sticks has shown zeal."

"Yes, I know, I was there."

"Look, keep your mouth shut. The child is found."

"What?"

"The child, Rachel Delavigne, is found."

"Hold the line."

He just didn't care any more. As long as she hadn't seen it coming. As long as they hadn't made her suffer. A chop in the back of the neck, the way they did the rabbits, which at least was no worse than a guillotine. The body might twitch. So did a rabbit's. But the mouth wouldn't talk, any more than the rabbit's would.

"Give me another glass of that stuff." And drank it. And went back.

"Sorry, but you do realize. Something of a shock."

"You're not paid to be in shock." Joke. "So's she in shock."

"That's one way of putting it."

"Look, Castang, straighten yourself out, even if you have been up all night. I said the child's in shock, and mildly hysterical."

"You mean she's alive?" said Castang stupidly.

"Are you? Get your goddam ass over there. Vicq: it's about thirty kilometers from you, over the line. And take a tubeful of Alka-Seltzer. And stop mucking about. I send you because you're nearest. And get yourself waked up, because this child's parents are in a flaming uproar, and I've got to handle them. All right, boy? Move."

He did his best. Fastened his safety belt, and drove carefully, under sixty miles an hour, and everything.

Rachel was alive. Very much alive. The storm had broken where she'd been. She'd been absolutely drenched. There'd been hail, too. She hadn't sheltered under a tree, because she knew that was a dangerous thing to do. She'd gone on walking. A farmer who'd been trying to keep the hail off his vines, and who'd got up early to know the worst, had found her in his field. Lying under the vines, like a dead bird. His wife had undressed her and wrapped her in a blanket and given her hot milk. And called the doctor.

"Well, there's a considerable degree of shock. What d'you think—dark, thunder, lightning, rain, hail, and some enormous fear behind. If she could speak at all, she'd be gibbering. We can stave off the pneumonia. Of course you can't question her; don't be ridiculous, man. Even if you could, she'd say nothing coherent. She talks all the time about her bag."

"Her bag?"

"Don't ask me. I'd like to have her mother here. You've identified her, as I understand it."

"Her mother, I think I'm safe in saying, will be here very shortly." There was a loud squawk of brakes on the gravel outside the clinic. Castang, knowing that little yellow Alfa Romeo, said, "On cue," in a cute voice that made the doctor glance at him with an awful look: about five cubic centimeters of paraldehyde is what this one needs.

"All right, Colette. The fleet's in at Mobile."

"Henri." She rushed into his arms, and fought her way out of them instantly. "Where's my child?"

"Right here. Sleepy—easy, she's pretty dopey."

"Mama," said Rachel. "I've lost my bag." And relapsed into sleep.

"Her bag?" said Castang stupidly.

"She must mean her schoolbag. She didn't have any other bag."

"What on earth should she be worried about that for?"

The gendarmerie of Vicq didn't want to know anything about anything. Since they knew nothing, but had got the child back —and that was the important thing, wasn't it?—they continued to know nothing. It was the brigadier, from Bellac, who drove over in the jeep and did the detective work.

"Hallo, Castang. My respects, Madame: my felicitations, if you'll allow me. Well . . . it looked like a shot in the water. If we look again, might be in the gold for all that. But they'll deny everything, you know. And we didn't find as much as hair ribbon."

"Good heavens, man," said Colette hotly, "she'll recognize them. She'll be able to tell when she comes out of shock."

"Madame, forgive me. You're a judge. And even a Children's Judge. How much credit do you give to eight-year-old witnesses? You must know that she'll say—it will be suggested— anything that is put in her mind to say. Her word, supported by some very circumstantial evidence. Telephone calls! Rabbits!

Doesn't mean much. Against theirs. A united front. Not difficult for them. All they've got to do is stick to the same lie—that they don't know nothing, and they're being put upon. Now, in the circumstances, Madame"—no, not a rustic dogberry, this chap —"there's going to be a lot saying it's a put-up job. Bourgeoisie against country people. Not my pigeon, Madame. But if you'll forgive my saying so we'd be well advised to steer clear of that sort of trap until, or unless, we can find something that can't be accused of any class prejudice, like."

"She keeps talking about her bag." Colette's mind was quicker than Castang's.

"Bag?"

"When she was pinched," said Castang, "she had her school-bag with her."

"And they had got rid of it." The brigadier's mind was quicker than either. "They'll have ditched it. Literally. In the ditch."

The thing was, it was not at all easy to discover where exactly Rachel had been pushed out of a car in the middle of the night with a storm coming on. There were a lot of country roads. And a lot of grass—and weed-grown ditches. Miles and miles of them. A case of dogged does it. But that afternoon—Bernard was there by then, and Richard was there by then, and even Castang had had time for long, gabbling, confused telephone calls to Vera—the gendarmerie waded step by step through sodden ditches with the weeds waist high, starting from the spot where the farmer found Rachel lying under his vines, and they found her schoolbag. By that time, M. Besson, the Procureur de la République, in person, had arrived. With him there, not to speak of laboratory technicians from the P.J., fingerprints were found on the outside—or the underside, if you prefer—of the schoolbag. Perfectly good fingerprints. Incomplete, being smeared on grained leather, but as damning as anything Poirot ever found.

"My dear man," said M. Besson to the lieutenant of gendarmerie, "I've no doubt but that your brigadier—a most able and skillful officer, if you will allow me to say so—will take a certain personal satisfaction in arresting this woman. In fact, the whole boiling lot."

"The boy, too?"

"The boy, too." M. Besson, along with Colette and a somewhat incoherent Bernard, had spent an hour by Rachel's bed. "She says quite clearly that a young man with the aid of rabbits entrapped her into entering the car. There is not the slightest doubt, and I am going to prosecute this in person."

The moment certainty begins, frustration sets in. Colette felt nothing but lassitude. Our troubles are only just starting, she thought.

Why did I ever begin? These things have roots in a tiny moment of irresponsibility.

Why was I so frightened? I reacted frenziedly because I felt under attack.

And presumably the same thing applies to these people. That woman, whom I have only heard but whom Henri has seen—he tells me that she has a small child. A bit smaller than Rachel . . .

Look at Besson. He's thinking hard, planning ahead. Says he's going to prosecute himself, and to look at him you'd think he was possessed by righteous indignation. Not a bit of it. He'll know how to handle old Jérémie so that no inconvenient facts come out. Because he knows—or at least he has an informed guess, since Richard has talked to him.

Bernard's thoughts were parallel.

I started this, he told himself gloomily. Come to that, I suppose I started the whole thing off with that idiotic and gratuitous squabble over the fruit trees. Which was only showing off, throwing my weight about, trying to impress Colette with Joséphine's being the bourgeois landed proprietor. She never gave a damn about those lousy cherries. In fact, she was happy to let the fellow have them, because he let her have manure for the vines.

But if I hadn't insisted on making a criminal complaint, and dragging the P.J. into it . . . I thought I was being clever, getting the two of them tied together and stuck with it, so that they would realize their responsibility. The result would have been the same, I suppose. The gendarmerie would have found the child, and made the complaint themselves, and there would be a criminal instruction just the same. But there wouldn't be a huddle of magistrates determined to cover up a small disgraceful fact. They can just go blithely ahead ordering psychiatric examinations of this woman and this boy. They won't order any for us. Besson can be relied upon. There are moments of temptation in his own past.

Who knows, anyhow, what little irresponsibilities with other people's wives he may have. . . .

Castang drove home. He didn't have to arrest anybody. The gendarmerie would do all that. The Judge of Instruction would go into all the whys and wherefores.

What little grain of torment prompted that woman? Pretty woman, too. Could that be something, back in the past, that Bernard . . . He likes—was it Colette said that, in a snappish moment, or was it that old priss at the office who told me he "liked kitchenmaids"?

No. Shut your eyes, boy. You're responsible for your own actions, not for those of others.

Your own are quite enough to be going on with.

Rachel had to be found. That was your job, not just your responsibility. I don't think that Richard will say anything. I have a kind of notion that he and Monsieur le Procureur have had their heads together about the whys and the hows.

It was perfectly accurate. M. Richard received him with no sign of fluster. I'm glad to hear it, he said with objective calm. It could have been very nasty. You've been rather lucky, haven't you? You can go home now. Give me a written report tomorrow.

"And by the way, Castang . . . In the future, you'll be a little more careful about your friendships."

He went home. Vera was asleep, having been up all night, too. She woke, of course, and asked whether he wanted anything.

"Well, perhaps there are a couple of things to get straight."

"Never explain."

"No, but I think you might have a few false ideas."

"They're better left untouched, you know, however false they are."

That's it.

Draw a veil over the whole thing.

74 75 10 9 8 7 6 5 4 3 2 1

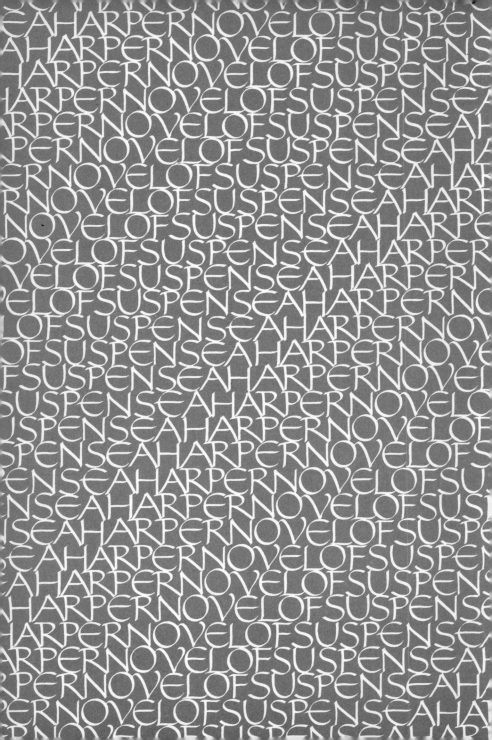